02/19
£1.00

Brian Thomps... *Jackson's Story* ... anthologies and collections. ... him many awards. He has writt... ...d documentary films, including episodes for the BBC's *Great Railway Journeys* and *Great River Journeys*, as well as popular television series such as *Crown Court* and *Rockliffe's Babies*. His plays for the stage include *Tishoo*, which ran at Wyndham's Theatre in the West End, and the highly regarded *Turning Over*, at the Bush. He lives in Yorkshire.

Brian Thompson

CHELWORTH

PENGUIN BOOKS

PENGUIN BOOKS

Published by the Penguin Group
27 Wrights Lane, London w 8 5 tz, England
Viking Penguin Inc., 40 West 23rd Street, New York, New York 10010, USA
Penguin Books Australia Ltd, Ringwood, Victoria, Australia
Penguin Books Canada Ltd, 2801 John Street, Markham, Ontario, Canada L3R 1B4
Penguin Books (NZ) Ltd, 182-190 Wairau Road, Auckland 10, New Zealand

Penguin Books Ltd, Registered Offices: Harmondsworth, Middlesex, England

First published 1989
10 9 8 7 6 5 4 3 2 1

Filmset in Goudy (Linotron 202) by
Rowland Phototypesetting Ltd, Bury St Edmunds, Suffolk

Printed and bound in Great Britain by
Cox and Wyman Ltd, Reading, Berks.

In the county of WILTSHIRE, close to the village of Hincham, near Salisbury, a house now building, the seat of the Anstey family. Sir Geo. Anstey, for the merit shewed to His Majesty in the late wars, wherein he played a Diplomat's part, was made Earl in 1775. The family having prospered here since 1608, whence they came from Northumberland, the new-created Earl of Hincham commissioned Mr Tressell of Bristol to build on the site of the old Manor, for long the home of his most perspicacious and dutifull forebears. Here is being raised a fine brick edifice, of noble proportions, and having two most generous Wings to't, commanding views over the hills round about, and of the Avon river, that runs close by.

Beckwith, A Concise Gazetteer of the Counties of Wiltshire, Dorset and Somerset, London, 1791

One

The new Düsseldorf Airport has the reassuring hush that goes with great enterprises and international glamour. The restaurant and coffee terrace are on the first floor, and overlook a German bomber of the Second World War, whimsically parked on a nearby roof. Many Germans taking coffee find this a jovial sight; and there is something touching and pathetic about such a tiny warplane, now no more than a toy, commemorated in a great international airport where the 747s touch down from North America. Well, the Junkers 52 seems to be saying, times change.

One June, on a sultry and overcast day, the kind of day when the trees seem heavy with water, passengers looking out from the terrace noticed a bright blip, a flash of light, away to the horizon. Many put it down to the approach of thunder. After all, the sky was that curious greengage colour that is often the backdrop to an electrical storm. Several glanced at their watches in a sort of nervous reflex, and then shrugged.

Wesling Charter Golf Tango 542 crashed shortly after three o'clock, fifty seconds from take-off. The Lear executive jet was on its initial climb when it suddenly stood on one wing and sliced sideways through the outskirts of the city. There would be witnesses who saw it with an engine clearly on fire. It slewed, screaming, through the heavy sky and levelled up just beyond the great Nord-Westphalen Chemicals plant. A wooded hill no more than eighty metres high stood in its path. It was probably the last thing the pilot saw. The little silver jet, with its green and blue markings, hit the stand of trees and disappeared over the immediate horizon. A blinding flash of light followed, after which came a huge crump of sound. Before the eardrums could clear from

7

that, there came the sound of fire appliances racing to the scene.

There was very little anyone could do. The wreckage was spread throughout a field of cabbages, over several hectares. Police and firemen in bright yellow slickers ran through the mud and acrid smoke, trying to identify enough of the wreckage to pinpoint survivors. Helmut Meineke, the principal police officer on the scene of the crash, leaned against the wing of his car and lit a Dutch cheroot. It needed no great experience to see that no one could outlive the last terrible seconds of Golf Tango 542.

It was beginning to rain in earnest. Meineke retreated to the passenger seat of his car and began unlacing his shoes. He reached behind the seat for a pair of short rubber boots, thinking about his daughter, who was in training to be a stewardess.

Half an hour after the disaster a police officer found a passport on the ground, over three hundred metres from the epicentre of the crash. It was in the name of Richard Ewart Stanley Anstey. For a while there was a little mystery about this passport until it was realized, after consultation with the airport authorities and the air charter company, that Richard Anstey was one and the same person as the Earl of Hincham, the plane's only passenger.

There is a ten-hour time difference between Europe and Hong Kong. Michael Anstey was given the news of his brother's death in his penthouse overlooking the lights of Kowloon Harbour. He and his partner, Huan, had been working late when the first wire service report reached them. Huan, grave and polite, accepted the drink that Michael poured, but held it in his hand without sipping it.

'You are now seventh Earl of Hincham, Michael.'

'It would seem so. Yes. Very unexpectedly.'

Huan studied his friend. Michael was in his early fifties, tall and fit, but with a habitually forbidding expression. There was, in Huan's opinion, a boy locked up inside this man, a sad and lonely boy. But he dealt mostly with the man, whose business acumen and ruthlessness was a byword, even among the Chinese. Huan smiled gently.

'This is a very ancient title?'

'No.'

8

'To lose a brother is a cause of great grief.'

'My brother and I were not close.'

Michael peered a last time at the computer screen they had been studying, and then switched it off. He pushed back his chair and swung around in it.

'I am sorry, Huan. I appreciate your sympathy. Our lands and title have been held for two hundred and fifty years, but I hardly ever think of all that. I know nothing about England any longer. I suppose I will have to go there and . . . I don't know . . .'

'You prefer to be left alone,' Huan suggested, setting down his drink untouched.

After he had gone, Michael walked through to the bedroom. Rosie lay naked on her stomach, one knee bent, her arms above her head. It was as though a camera had frozen her in the action of swimming through the satin ripples of the sheets. Her body was lit from the sky outside, where a huge moon had risen. He studied his mistress fondly. It was in a way like having a great child for a plaything. She was hardly older than a child. The genes that gave her a darker than usual Chinese skin had also bequeathed her a long back and short, strong legs. Her hair lay tangled on the pillow.

'I'm not asleep,' she said.

Michael smiled and went to sit by her on the bed. Rosie rolled on to one hip.

'I've been crying.'

'What nonsense.'

'Now you will leave me.'

Michael stroked away a strand of hair that had caught in her lips.

'Who has said so?'

'You will go home.'

'I have no home.'

'You have a castle.'

'Those are just stories I made up to amuse you. There is a house, and some land. I don't know how much. I was younger than you when I saw it last.'

He laid his broad hand on her ribs and rocked her gently.

'Come on, buck up. It's not the end of the world.'

'It is,' Rosie wailed.

Once, he had been at a drinks party on a yacht moored out in the bay. While the guests were talking and flirting, the body of a young boy, a refugee, had floated past the boat, swept out to sea by the strong current. Although everyone had noticed the naked corpse, no one made the slightest effort to do anything about it. Conversation continued, more drinks were served. It was the day he met Rosie, sitting under an awning, anxious and knock-kneed, her breasts exposed through a transparent mauve blouse.

'Listen to me,' Michael said. 'Something has happened, that's all. Something that I had put to the back of my mind. You know I am happy here. You know we are happy. I am very fond of you, Rosie. Nothing is going to change.'

'You'll go home and I'll never see you again.'

He withdrew his hand from her moist skin and walked to the door.

'Will you please stop using the word "home"?'

In his time, he had said that he loved her. Like the story about the house in England being a castle, it was something he had made up to please her. She was lovely and he liked to see her in his home, but that was all. She lay on her back staring at him, the way cats do, her eyes unblinking and serious. Michael frowned and went to make himself another drink.

There was a pool in the basement of the building, and Rosie demanded to be taken swimming. He sat on the edge, dangling his legs into the water, while she swam naked, her glossy black hair clinging to her neck and shoulders.

'What is England like?'

'You've been there,' Michael protested. 'I took you there last year.'

'To London. Only to London.'

Where she had spent four days in relentless shopping.

'England is part of a little green island that believes in ghosts, and the past, and the care of lawns, cricket, and cream teas.'

'You like cricket,' Rosie objected. 'You went to Australia to watch cricket.'

'England is a mystery, wrapped up in layers of mysteries.'

Rosie dog-paddled, her breasts floating free of her ribs.

'Tell me about your part of England.'

'I used to think it very fine once, when I was a boy. You could ride . . .'

'Yes, go on.'

'You could ride for fifteen miles on land that was ours, across fields that had not changed their shape for a century or more. I liked it. But then, when I was a boy, I would have exchanged my whole life for the idea of a beautiful girl like you in a pool like this, and black satin sheets on the bed.'

'I don't believe you,' Rosie said.

'Well,' Michael smiled. 'There are mysteries and mysteries, Rosie.'

She duck-dived expertly. When she had been very young, before she became a rich man's plaything, she had swum for the Colony, had even gone to Perth for the Commonwealth Games. She loved the freedom of swimming naked.

There were more tears. They made love, and she slept, with that faint snore that he would always remember her by, her thumbs tucked inside her closed fists, her body sticky with heat.

When the phone rang, he was half expecting the caller. He confirmed that he would fly home for the funeral the next day or the day after, made a few polite remarks, and rang off. Though his arm ached from cradling Rosie, he tried not to budge but lay staring at the ceiling, where a bay breeze tinkled the little chandelier she thought so cute and had made him buy. Its crystals jigged in what he had always thought – even before tonight – a mournful dance.

In Paris, it was the dead hour of the afternoon. After speaking to her husband, Virginia Anstey walked through her apartment and stood on the absurd little balcony, toasting the roofs of the district. Despite herself, her heart was pounding.

'Here's to the new Countess of Hincham,' she said, over the rim of a Pouilly Fuissé. Her hand shook very slightly, and she was surprised to find the air cooling a faint damp between her shoulder blades.

Keith sat on a couch, his chin in his hands, and did not respond to her toast.

Virginia was in her late forties. She had lived in Paris since the final separation from Michael, and though her clothes came from

London, she might easily be mistaken for a Frenchwoman of the kind that many of her age and class try to emulate. She was, and she knew it, famous for her containment. That particular cool, mixed with a sardonic turn of mind, made her very chic.

She looked back from the balcony and burst out laughing at Keith, all tousled and woebegone.

'Cheer up,' she said.

'I'll try to look on the bright side,' Keith muttered.

'Oh come on,' Virginia said. 'I had to ring him, after all.'

'Of course you did.'

He took her hand, and kissed her on the wrist.

'A matter of form,' he said.

He was an economic historian, a working-class boy from Cambridge, from the wrong side of the tracks, risen to be a Fellow of New College, Oxford, whose books were the subject of study in schools and colleges throughout the English-speaking world. Nothing in his life quite matched the *affaire* that had developed in the past two and a half years with this elegant, nervy woman, whom he had been consternated to find was the daughter of an earl: and was now the wife of another.

'I suppose you've moved up a few places in the line of succession. There's that to celebrate.'

'Dear Keith! The Hinchams are descended from eighteenth-century nobodies, not Plantagenets. Bit easier to get tickets to the Royal Weddings, there's that I grant you.'

'What will he do?'

'That's a question I asked all the time when we lived together. I don't know. According to the best gossip, he's nicely placed in Hong Kong, with all those people who are ready to shift their money into China.'

'He's rich.'

'Yes, but we're not going to start that, are we? I'm rich. I'm bloody rich. I know it infuriates you, but what does rich mean?'

'I sometimes think you people never really grew up. It's all a game, isn't it? Wendy houses in the nursery, with somebody else to do the dirty work.'

'We *are* in a bad mood,' Virginia scoffed. 'What are you complaining about? You're here. He's not. *You* screw me, don't you?'

'Oh, we're going to say screw now, are we?'

'What do you want? You speak French at least as well as I do, you know things I will never learn. You jog, for God's sake. And I love you. Yes, let's do say screw. Let's do it too. Now, if you like.'

Keith rose from the leather couch and walked to the long windows that opened on to the balcony. Earlier in the day he had given a tutorial to a very bright girl, from an England, a particular England, Virginia had never once visited. This girl, with her terrible clothes and combative manners, had said to him, 'You know what's wrong with you? It's the company you keep.' She meant Oxford, and New College, and privilege (although sharing in all these things herself). But Keith had taken the remark in a different sense.

'The thing is, Virginia,' he said, 'I don't want him to have you. I don't want what he represents to have you either. I want *me* to have you.'

'Cuddly Keith.'

'Don't mock me. I love you.'

'Of course.'

'Perhaps he'll fly home with his Chinese tart, do the stuff at the funeral and shove off out of it.'

'A pound to a penny,' Virginia agreed, thinking of Michael, and how utterly unlike rumpled, dreamy Keith he was.

They went out to eat with friends of hers, and Keith was witty and grave, absurd and passionate in turn. He made people laugh, and yet he could also make them attend to the last intricate detail of a historical anecdote in attentive silence. He brushed back his hair with his hand in a way she loved, and (to the consternation of the Basonpiers) rolled cigarettes with enormous incompetence. She added to the mild scandal of Keith's sparks and ash by taking his free hand and laying it in her lap. Madame de Basonpier noted the gesture, and approved it with a certain sly smile she reserved for lovers.

'*Mon cher professeur!*' her husband cried in alarm. The faint scent of burning wool came not from the carpet, but from Keith's jacket.

In London, Holland Park had been bathed in wonderful watery sunshine all day long. It was the magic hour of cities, when everything is an exhausted sigh – it is not yet dark, but the traffic and business of day have gone, leaving those who live there the chance to relax. Lord Esholt was at his wine merchants, which was to say a small shop close by Holland Park Tube Station.

Ronnie Esholt was the acme of old-fashionedness. His Rifle Brigade blazer (which nowadays he lovingly brushed himself), his grey flannel bags and his brogues from Went and Wilson were a kind of Ruritanian uniform, into which was poured this erect, supercilious and – as many people never found out – shy man. His hair was smoothed with a preparation he had come across in Cambridge thirty years ago – not as a student, but on his way back from a disastrous Newmarket. He swore by it, as he swore by hats from Lock, Gieves suits and holidays in the Bahamas.

'I think,' he said in his rich, plummy voice, 'I'll have another dozen of the Beaune. And give me some of that cheap gin.'

The young man behind the counter nodded. Invariably Ronnie inspected the full stock before (invariably) giving the same order. Ronnie looked round the place with a hearty sniff.

'Do you ever get dogs in here?'

'With their owners, sometimes, yes.'

'Do you know, I hate dogs. What a bloody country. I used to like dogs, but even the dogs have gone to the dogs these days.'

'I believe so,' the young man said.

Ronnie looked at him sharply.

'You've heard it too, have you? And then on the news tonight we hear that the bloody man Tunstall has been suspended for fourteen days, and won't be riding Epharisto next week as a consequence. Another fiasco!'

'How does that affect your plans?'

'Well,' Ronnie said loudly, appalled at the impudence of this stranger he had met at least once a week for the past three years, 'I really don't think that's any concern of yours.'

And he walked the three hundred yards to his house in a perfectly foul mood. Though his wife Olivia had warned him it was dangerous to say so these days, the fellow in the wine merchants struck him as a raging nancy. This short journey to the wine store round the corner was as far as Ronnie ever walked, in London or anywhere else. And were he to be asked, he would claim a perverse pleasure in ignorance. Though the huge white stucco houses rose like cliffs all around him, the street itself was a tideless estuary of the petty, the ugly and the mediocre. That was his firm conviction. Americans Ronnie had met stood in profound awe of him for the honesty with which he lived his life. He actually knew very little of things – and knew that it was so – but he spoke as he felt. He was profoundly honest.

He turned in at the stairs to his mansion and paused to fish a lager can from the Japanese maple Olivia cherished in a huge white urn. Still erect, still moving with rigid control, all the same he expertly drop-kicked the can over the cars parked outside his house. It landed with a satisfying crash.

And there was another blind impertinence: the freedom with which oiks with names like Barry and Kevin put their motor cars bang outside one's front door. As happened with Ronnie's bad moods, they grew into mighty fretwork palaces of exasperation.

Olivia was on the telephone to the vicarage at Hincham.

'Look, it really is rather important that I speak to your husband. You may know – oh you do know, good – yes, thank you so much – we do rather need the services of the church and its parson at this sad time.'

She rolled her eyes at Ronnie, who went to make himself a gin and tonic.

'Yes, well perhaps you could go round the village and find him. Yes, of course. Oh, is he really?'

She cupped her hand over the receiver.

'Isn't it priceless? We – the family that is – own the entire place with the exception of the church and vicarage, and you would think –'

Ronnie tugged the telephone from Olivia's hand.

'This is Lord Esholt,' he said in his loud, uninflected voice. 'My wife's brother, Lord Hincham, died today in a tragic accident. Now what we want from your better half is a simple service and an interment in the family vault, as early as possible next week, but not Gold Cup day, is that clear? Then buzz off round the village and find him. He shouldn't be too difficult to spot. Find him, give him the news, including the point about the Gold Cup, and have him ring us back before −?'

'Ten,' Olivia supplied.

'Before ten this evening. Thank you for all your help.'

He banged down the receiver.

'What these fellows do with themselves in the week is a complete mystery to me.'

Olivia regarded her husband with her habitual expression of half-disbelief. She took the gin and tonic he had mixed for her.

'Not a word from Michael, of course. Fast asleep in Hong Kong, I dare say.'

'Ring him up and get him out of bed.'

'I wouldn't give him the satisfaction.'

'I can't imagine what satisfaction there is in being got out of bed.'

Olivia sighed. She picked up the telephone again, and looked up the number of a friend who had no connection whatever with the Earls of Hincham, but could be depended upon to see the awful side of things. By which, as it soon turned out, Olivia meant the business of organizing the funeral. Although she was older than her brother Richard, he was spoken of as though he had died in his sleep at a hundred and five.

Ronnie crept from the room, and went upstairs to watch television.

Two

Michael flew from Hong Kong on Sunday. Before he left for the airport he went downtown to a seedy business and warehousing quarter, to the displeasure and amazement of the cab driver.

'Hey, listen,' the cabbie said in film American, 'you gotta have some good reason to be down here, man. I'm tellin' ya.'

Michael turned his glance from the raucous streets to the driver, who was primped up in a spotless white tee-shirt with the logo of the Los Angeles Police Department.

'We're going to see the man who owns your cab,' he murmured.

The driver spat out of the window and went into an intense sulk.

They were going to see Huan's father, who owned the China Sea Cab Company and much else besides.

'It is thirty years since I first came to Hong Kong,' he reminded the old man after they had exchanged elaborate greetings.

'I remember the occasion with pleasure,' Old Huan whispered. 'You came from Saigon for some small business, and stayed for three years.'

'You have an enviable memory.'

The old man smiled.

'You left with honour.'

'You predicted I would return again with honour.'

'That too happened. You have shown honour in your partnership with my son. We have been fortunate to know you.'

Michael glanced round him. Every day, Old Huan came to sit in the office of the original wholesalers, from which his wealth had grown up. It was a very unprepossessing place. The founder of the family fortune sat at a rickety desk strewn with papers, took tea and read the newspapers, waited on by a great-niece. On the other side of the glass partition, the wholesaling business continued unaltered since the time when he had given twenty hours a day to it. There was a muffled babble of voices. Dust hung in the air, and the uncarpeted floor of the go-down sprang underfoot as clerks and porters hurried this way and that. Old Huan owned two apartment blocks, including the one in which Michael had his home. He owned a cab company and a tuna cannery where the catch from his fishing fleet was processed.

'You have heard I must return to England.'

'Your loss is a heavy one.'

'It is a matter of business, Huan.'

The Chinese broke into a gold-toothed cackle of embarrassment.

'Michael, my friend, if you have come to tell me merely that you must go to England on business for a few days, then I am flattered. I will not contradict you. But you may permit me some surprise.'

Michael hesitated, then smiled ruefully himself.

'Very well. I don't know why I have come to see you.'

'Your heart is full,' Old Huan said.

'Yes,' Michael said, startled.

'Of course. And yet you cannot say why. Some piece of the world that before you considered small, and of no significance, has suddenly become the centre of things.'

'My brother.'

'It is possible,' Old Huan allowed. 'We shall see.'

It was he who turned the conversation to pleasantries thereafter. When they parted, Michael was surprised at how dry and papery the old man's hand had become. He rose from his desk only for a few moments, and when Michael glanced back through the dusty glass, the great-niece was bending over him like a nurse in her white blouse and blue skirt.

He thought of this on the plane, dozing and reading, 33,000 feet above places he would never visit, whose existence he could only guess at. The monotone hum of the cabin, that normally he could so easily tune out, was annoying. He felt decidedly edgy.

Not until they were an hour from Heathrow did he speak to his neighbour, a tall, rangy American woman his own age, her skin drawn tight over her cheeks and temples.

'Is your visit a holiday, or are you going home?' he asked politely.

'My God,' she drawled. 'It speaks! I'm going home to Philadelphia. And not a moment too soon. I never want to see another temple for as long as I live. You're British, of course.'

'Affable and talkative,' Michael affirmed.

'For sure.'

The American pointed to a doodle Michael had made next to his crossword.

'Who is Rosie?'

'She lives in Hong Kong. Just before I left, she bought herself a fur coat. A sable.'

'She's young,' the American decided. 'I'd have stung you for gold.'

'I'm seeing her again in a fortnight,' Michael protested.

'Uhuh. And I'm the Director of the FBI.'

He glanced at her. The Philadelphian had unbuttoned the first three buttons to her blouse, and the gap revealed some surprisingly soft flesh. She smiled.

'When a kid goes out to buy a fur coat in a snowy climate like Hong Kong, something's cooking. I've been married three times. I have wardrobes that are like trophy rooms. I take it you're married to someone else.'

Michael laughed.

'Perhaps you really are the Director of the FBI!'

The American scowled humorously. She laid a thin, freckled hand over his.

'You're a very sexy guy. I've been making up stories about you since we left the East. And whatever's happened to you in reality, you still wear your wedding ring.'

'Have a large whisky,' Michael proposed.

'Now you're behaving like a stand-up Britisher.'

'You approve.'

'Make mine vodka,' she said.

Later, as they came in to join the stack over London, he pointed out the landmarks, etched by strong shadows under a bright sun. It was disconcerting to be so excited. He knew that from below they were just another silent jumbo drifting across the otherwise cloudless sky. All the same he caught himself urging the plane to its destination. It was something he hadn't done for a long time.

'Nice to have met you,' his companion said in her snappy way. 'And thanks for looking down my blouse. It felt good.'

She walked ahead of him into passport control with a swinging showgirl gait. And without looking back. Michael stood in the queue to enter England behind three Chinese businessmen arguing ferociously about tickets for Wimbledon.

Virginia's Air France flight had landed twenty minutes earlier. She caught a cab to her sister-in-law's house in Holland Park, and found Olivia fuming with rage. Baines, the Esholt chauffeur, had rung from Heathrow to say that Michael had refused the offer of a car, and said merely that he would be in touch. Then he had disappeared.

'Absolutely typical. Now we don't know where he is. I wouldn't put it past him to turn up with some woman. Not that Chinese girl he brought home last year, I hope. My dear, the clothes! One really didn't know where to look.'

Virginia smiled.

'It's good to see you again, Ollie.'

'I keep forgetting you are still married to him. But he is such a cad. You're going to tell me no one says cad any more, I know. I could kill him. Muggins here has had to organize the funeral – it's the day after tomorrow, by the way, if the idiot parson can remember. We're not going to have any trouble with you, I hope.'

'Of what sort?'

'You know perfectly well what I mean.'

'Oh, Keith. He sends his apologies and won't be turning up.'

'There isn't another family like it anywhere,' Olivia decided forcefully.

'Are we so very different?'

'Well, I think we are. Ronnie's round at the flat Richard had, in Ladbroke Grove, if you please. With just scraps of carpet and so on, but a Canaletto on the wall.'

'What about Chelworth?'

'Chelworth?' Olivia shrugged. 'Who could live there? That's been out of the question for years. Anyway, he was selling it, I think. Chelworth doesn't come into it. Except that we all have to traipse down there. I can tell you this: I am *not* opening the house. We'll have the funeral and people can buzz off and do as they please after. It's not my house to open.'

She glanced at her sister-in-law without warmth.

'Would you have any idea at all where the man has got to?'

'None,' Virginia replied.

'He doesn't even know anybody in England. He has no friends, nobody remembers him. What am I supposed to do, ring round the hotels?'

'You'll just have to wait,' Virginia suggested.

'I really don't have your saintly patience, my dear.'

Seeing the sudden angry red spot appear on Virginia's neck was really the only pleasure Olivia got from the afternoon. And to ram the point home, she did in fact ring round a few of the London hotels.

Hincham is a large village. Its exceptionally long main street boasts a couple of coaching inns, and is divided by a bridge over the Avon, against which stands an ivy-clad paint and varnish works. Though Salisbury is no more than a few miles away, the spire of the Cathedral cannot be seen, although to the east it beckons travellers off the rolling uplands. In Hincham you look out upon a folded and more secretive landscape, dense with trees near the river, and criss-crossed by lanes running between high hedges. In early summer there is a breathtaking sense of plenty, although the fields, when you examine them carefully, are no more than banks of pebbles. The feminine roundness of the landscape is made almost entirely of gravel.

Just as in Salisbury you cannot go far without noting, in shop windows and pinned up in tobacconists, a flyer which reads SAVE OUR SPIRE, so in Hincham there is a vigorous campaign to save the village. This means, practically, that the people who have houses of character there wish no more new houses to be built. But, like anywhere else within an hour or so of London, new and hideous houses *are* going up. They are dull imitations of lodges and villas, on plots too small to contain them, the meagre gardens tricked out with willows, or anything to create an illusion of a better, more pastoral past. The smart money got in first: the chapel, the railway station and the workhouse have all been tastefully converted. Cottages that once housed agricultural labourers are now the cherished homes of retired colonels, headmasters, bank officials and their ilk.

There is something missing in Hincham that the English are beginning to miss with increasing dismay. There is very little sense of continuity. What is happening now, today, has no roots in what happened before: the history of this little town has been written, to be sure, and is sold in the bookshop and post office. But to read about Hincham in the past, as it was, is to sense an utter dislocation. There is an underground stream of disappointment that sometimes bursts out above ground in unexpected ways. Some people point out that the town used to make things – agricultural machinery, butter and cream, furniture. Now it makes nothing, and is at the same time richer than it has ever been before. This is a puzzle only to the poor. Once or twice a year, for the past three years, there has been a flare-up of violence. Gangs of youths attack each other in the main street, wreck pubs, vandalize and loot. The rich call for more discipline, more police, stiffer sentences. The young, if they could frame the thought, might consider most people in the town already half-dead. Hincham was national news in 1987. Youths climbed the portico of the White Hart Hotel and tore down the Hart itself, weighing half a ton. A girl was crushed to death, and in fighting between the police and the mob, a second youngster drowned in the river. The television pictures showed what many people would consider a model English village, the very stuff of dreams.

Commander Firbank, RN (Ret.), agent to the Chelworth estate, was, as he always told people, not so green as he was cabbage-looking. This humorous warning he claimed to have learned from his Dorset nanny, but like a lot of things to do with Firbank, the nanny was an invention of his. He was indeed a retired naval commander, but anyone looking him up under the appropriate list would have discovered that the years of his service were spent principally at the Pay Branch, in Wetherby. People are often ineffably stupid about class; and it took very little to fool them. Firbank (who had the prime characteristic necessary for deception, which is an overwhelming self-regard) had found a late vocation. He had only to meet Richard Anstey a couple of times to convince him that what the place needed was a touch on the rudder from someone of a no-nonsense disposition.

It was consequently very vexing to have his employer (whom Firbank delighted in calling Mother Goose to his drinking cronies) turn himself into a log of charcoal in a corner of some foreign field.

The Commander affected such bluff sentiments nowadays as a habit of mind. He had, so to speak, grown into the part. The house had not been lived in by Richard since Jubilee Year, and Lord Hincham was seldom seen. Firbank *was* Chelworth to the tenants of the estate, and to the minor gentry round about. He did not know that several aristocratic neighbours had written warning Richard that his agent was a lazy and incompetent fool; but even if he had known, it would hardly have troubled him.

'The one thing one does acquire,' the Commander was fond of saying, 'is complete mastery of a lee shore.'

Or, to vary the nautical metaphor, Firbank had his employer squared away. Chelworth, it had to be admitted, was a job a little beyond him. On the other hand, its owner showed not the slightest interest in the place, apart from wishing to sell it. And there Firbank had expended most of his fitful energies. For several years, since the first approaches of a union pension fund, Firbank had reduced the house and estate in his mind to a negotiable transaction, rather than bricks and mortar, or fields with actual crops in them. He had stopped seeing trees, or grass, or roofs rising above woods. Instead he saw money. Properly handled, a great deal of money.

So it was with a mild irritation that, driving back from a prolonged pub lunch, he saw a stranger standing in what he had grown to think of as one of his own top fields. He drew up beside the fellow's car and jumped out.

'Oi! You there! Yes, you! Get out of that field if you will.'

When the man turned, there was a faint flutter of apprehension in Firbank. He looked a pretty flame-proof cove, as a matter of fact. His dark eyes took their time about examining the Commander.

'Whose horses are those?' Michael asked, pointing to a couple of thoroughbreds.

23

'They're mine as it happens, squire. Now shove off. We don't tolerate trespass on this estate.'

'What happened to Hodnett, who used to have that farm?'

'Oh bloody hell,' Firbank groaned, feeling suddenly relieved, and putting two and two together. 'You're not one of that insufferable local history lot from Swindon, are you? Never you mind about what happened to Hodnett, you get your arse off my land.'

Michael studied him without moving, and Firbank wondered what the hell he would do if this chap turned nasty. He blew the gas from his lunchtime beer with blue lips and cuffed his nose.

'You are standing on land where we prosecute for trespass.'

Michael hesitated, and then moved back towards the gate.

Thank Christ, Firbank thought, with Sunday fervour.

'This is a working estate, chum. Haven't got time for local history. You bugger off back from whence you came.'

It sounded good, this mishmash of the hearty and the peremptory. It seldom failed, Firbank had realized. What people needed from the ruling class was a bloody convincing performance. Even tarts liked it. He drove up to Oxford from time to time to diddle a girl in a godawful flat on the Cowley Road; and she loved it. He played the silly old buffer who got a bit excited and pinched and paddled a bit too hard, and though it probably hurt like hell, she absolutely loved it.

Daisy Hodnett poured tea from a huge brown betty. Her husband watched with a faintly mocking fondness. Michael sensed they were uneasy to meet him on such terms – Jim Hodnett had switched off the television and taken off his spectacles with a curious long-sufferingness.

'I perhaps shouldn't have called.'

'Nonsense,' Daisy said.

'Fancy you thinking old Dad might still be alive. He'd be as tickled as hell to think it.'

'Your father-in-law was very good to me,' Michael explained to Mrs Hodnett.

'Heard all those stories. Know all about you and Jim when you were boys. They say you live in Hong Kong now.'

'Read that in the paper,' Jim smiled. 'Sort of James Bond sort of thing.'

'Don't be so daft,' Daisy said. 'Don't you listen to him.'

'He used to make these wonderful ship models,' Michael said. Jim Hodnett beamed.

'Fancy you remembering that. We was going to sail 'em down the Avon, weren't we? Remember when we took up archery along the Robin Hood lines? Was out in the stock-yard, old Dad came out and shouted, if you want to kill somebody with that bow 'n' arrer, you bugger off up to the house and kill one of your own family.'

'I remember very well,' Michael said. 'What happened to your father's lease? I mean why aren't you working the farm?'

'Ah well,' Jim said. 'We was the victims of rationalization, I think they call it. Your brother had an agent, Firbank, the Commander. He was for amalgamating the tenancies, going with bigger farms, clearing out the hedges and coverts.'

'Does he farm himself, this Firbank?'

'Him?' Daisy scoffed. 'He couldn't raise a packet of nasturtiums.'

The remark amused her husband, but Daisy found an opportunity to recant her opinion when she and Michael had a look round the garden. It was surprisingly dense with herbaceous plants in vigorous health.

'Jim relinquished his lease to the estate and was paid good money for the balance. I maybe spoke out of turn about the Commander.'

Michael shrugged. He flicked an old tennis shoe with the toe of his brogue and sent the Hodnett dog loping.

'Who does the garden? D'you do it?'

'He used to be interested. Had a shrub nursery for twelve years out on the Cotley road. Got a good reputation in the end. But he's a lazy beggar, is Jim.'

She glanced at Michael.

'He often talks about you, wonders what you're about. He can remember every day of those years, when you were children.'

'What little I know about the country comes from Jim and old man Hodnett.'

'So he always says,' Daisy agreed in her dry, intelligent way.

'This Firbank character . . .'

'That's really for you to find out for yourself. They say the estate's being sold.'

'I'd heard that vaguely. I don't know any details.'

'I feel sorry for the house. Lovely old house like that. It's a crying shame, milord.'

Michael looked at her, startled. She was the first to address him by his title. Daisy lifted and let drop her shoulders in a little gesture.

'No use pretending you're not who you are,' she said shyly.

'I hadn't even thought of things like that. Tell me about the house.'

'We're not supposed to see it, even. Keeps those front gates locked. He says the police insist.'

'Firbank again?'

'We go in from time to time – trespassing I grant you – just to say hello to the Murdochs. Your butler, I suppose Harold would be. Poor dab.'

'Come and show me,' Michael commanded. 'We can meet Jim for a pint afterwards.'

'Good God!' Daisy whooped. 'Jim couldn't take the likes of *you* for a pint! He'd never live it down!'

'I know what you mean,' Michael murmured.

In the end he went by himself, walking across the fields, as he had done once as a child, in all seasons and at all hours of the day. In Leck's Wood he had waded naked in the stony stream, playing at being the first man on earth, in search of a wife in the form of Rachel Tubbs, an adventurous nine-year-old Eve, whose father was a coachman. On Barrow Hill, one midnight, he had seen a fox dragged down by cold and hunger, the ice clinging to his coat, the moon as bright as day in the frozen landscape. The fox had limped across the snow, paused for a glance about him and then fallen, like an exhausted dog.

For most of the journey there were memories; and always there some snip or detail of Chelworth itself in the trees, as if beckoning. Invisible from the road, it seemed to float over the fields and woods. In the days of Michael's childhood, when his grandfather still held the title, no matter what the month there would be smoke rising from the chimneys, and sometimes even the sound of a Mahler symphony, played on a wind-up gramophone with thorn needles – an eccentric musical taste of his father's that infuriated the fourth Earl.

He broke out of the trees opposite the gates to the house and brushed the burrs from his slacks. It was one of those moist, still evenings when the smells of the country and the light from the sky seem to conspire to produce a dramatic effect. Michael found that, against his will, he was trembling. It was all so green, and signed by water and earth: not for a very long time had he experienced such a cathedral quiet.

And, he thought wonderingly, it was his: he owned the constituent parts of this great mystery, or at any rate it was occasioned on his land. He crossed the road to the gates of Chelworth, rusted into their hinges and locked with a chain and padlock. The drive curved away in a crescent, overgrown and tussocky with grass. The last time he had seen all this was when driving Virginia away after a disastrous interview with his father, thirty-three years ago. Then, the journey to London had taken over three hours, all of it made (on that occasion) in tense silence.

There was a toot, and a Range Rover drew up. Commander Firbank, RN (Ret.), lumbered out and walked towards Michael.

'Right ho, squire. We'll have your name, I think.'

'I am the Earl of Hincham,' Michael said. 'And this is my house.'

Three

After some confusion with cars, Virginia travelled to the funeral with Michael's lawyer, Alan Rawtenstall. He turned out to be a breezy and irreverent thirty-eight-year-old, to whom Michael was of course a complete stranger. Nor had he met Richard more than a few times.

'David Rowe, our senior partner, thought it might be time for a change. He looked after the late Lord Hincham but now he's passed things to me.'

'Was that a mark of confidence?'

'Well, I married his daughter eight years ago,' Rawtenstall confessed. 'That might have something to do with it.'

He drove his Citroën GTI very fast and chatted amiably about London and Paris. He was even mildly, though cautiously, flirtatious. Virginia decided that she liked him.

'The thing about all this,' he said, 'is that I have only a very vague idea of the exact nature of your husband's inheritance. The will is perfectly sound, of course, no problems there. But I have to admit I have never clapped eyes on the place. Our dealings with the sixth Earl were on the sketchy side.'

'Things will be very different now,' Virginia promised. His laugh was a hearty and unfrightened one.

'I can imagine! Your husband's reputation goes before him.'

'And is?'

'It's said in the office by someone who knows him that he is not in the habit of suffering fools gladly. He lives in Hong Kong, I believe.'

'Have you ever been there?'

'Ah. No.'

'You may get to know it well before long.'

'Gosh! Do you think so?'

'I should look out for a good lightweight suit.'

Alan laughed. He glanced at his watch.

'Should I take you to the hotel?'

It was a question she had been asking herself.

'What do you think I ought to do?'

'We're in good time. You might perhaps welcome a coffee. I'll drop you off. I'm afraid I had better scoot on to the church, though. It's entirely up to you.'

Neat, Virginia thought. Neat, and done with a light touch. Alan's father-in-law had obviously briefed him well about these new Hinchams.

'Let's go to the hotel,' she said, 'and I'll see if I recognize anybody.'

She was amused to see from his glance that he was embarrassed.

She gave her name to the receptionist and went to wait for Michael in a little stone garden formed from a courtyard of the hotel. A convention of business men was in residence. Young men in the image of Rawtenstall marched about with name-tags pinned to their suits, carrying the first freebies of the day, which were bright yellow document cases with a company logo printed on them. The more senior managers sat about in senatorial poses, drinking coffee. The oldest, and most vulnerable to a sudden golden handshake, had already started on the Scotch.

Michael saw her before she saw him. She wore a black wool suit and a white blouse, and her light hair was cut in the French fashion. A broadbrimmed black hat lay on the stone bench beside her. She had her chin in her hand. He recognized that alert, quizzical look, which carried with it a very faint reprehension. 'Why does she walk about looking as if she smells a rat everywhere?' his father had demanded, exasperated by her on first sight. But seeing her sitting in the little hotel garden, her legs crossed, her head cocked to one side, Michael felt an enormous and sudden affection for her.

'Hullo, Ginny,' he said.

'What an amazing place to meet.'

They were the first words they had exchanged face to face for three and a half years. He kissed her lightly on the cheek.

'Gunbridge Wood and Partners are the market leaders in creative design. I have it on the authority of Rex Somebody or Other, who has bored me to tears at breakfast. The hotel is infested with creative designers, all of them exceptionally urgent about it. How are you?'

'Your sister is absolutely furious with you. I suppose you realize that?'

'Did you travel down with her?'

'No. With your lawyer, who's merry enough. You look thin.'

'I'm sorry if upsetting Olivia has caused problems for you. Are you well?'

Virginia smiled.

'Very well.'

'You look –'

He hesitated, and brushed back his hair, a gesture he made when he was tense. He glanced round him.

'We could order coffee, perhaps.'

'If you think there's time.'

'You look beautiful, is what I was going to say.'

She smiled with a prepared vagueness, as if he had said something of no importance.

'You really have been pretty awful, you know. By staying out of touch. Ollie has been going flat out at things for days. She is most fantastically angry.'

'The funeral people have ordered me a limo. Can I give you a lift?'

'Perhaps not,' Virginia said carefully.

'Then take my car. It's from Avis. After the service, I'll drive you back to London.'

She looked alarmed.

'Won't you need to stay on?'

'We can talk. I take it you're going back to Paris?'

'Tomorrow.'

'There we are then. I'm driving back tonight, or later this afternoon.'

He fished out the keys to the rental car before she could say anything. Walking her to where it was parked, he took her arm just above the elbow. He could sense her stiffen at his touch. When he too casually withdrew his hand, she glanced sideways with her fine grey eyes. The funeral limousine was turning in at the carpark to the hotel.

'Good luck,' she said, lightly.

The funeral service was conducted with that new informality that in a sense Michael's generation had pioneered. It was unstuffy, but it lacked grandeur. The Minister, Mr Davenport, whom Ollie had hounded up hill and down dale all weekend, was a pleasant, unflappable and goodlooking man in his thirties, who seemed to borrow some of his engaging qualities from television: it was a style Michael had not seen grow up in England and which he found faintly dismaying. This sense of disappointment was confirmed in him by Ronnie Esholt, after Richard had been interred. They wandered back through the graveyard together.

'Rum sort of parson. Hearty stuff, but I wonder if he's sound. He has some quite wonderful theories about all-round cricket he wanted to talk to me about. Then, what can you expect? Minor Counties. They feel horribly out of it, I shouldn't wonder.'

'How are you, Ronnie?'

'Oh, much the same,' Ronnie mumbled. He had seen Olivia approaching. Michael kissed his sister lightly on the cheek she presented to him. Olivia grimaced.

'I suppose we should be grateful to you for turning up at all. Ronnie, go and talk to someone.'

'Certainly. Absolutely. Who, exactly?'

Olivia simply waited. Ronnie nodded and ambled off.

'You realize everybody is talking about you.'

'Who is everybody?'

'I've let it be thought there will be some sort of memorial service in town, later. Daddy's was at Hanover Square, but that's up to you. I wash my hands of it. The agent, the naval officer, seems a good sort. He's asked us back to Pear Tree House, or what used to be Pear Tree. *He* owns it now, for some reason. I suppose we should put in an appearance. Chelworth itself was always out of the question. You've seen it?'

Michael studied his sister, who was still very attractive, all the more so for some men because of her wonderful disdain.

'Are you very angry?'

'That would be rather a pallid way of putting it. Are you coming to Pear Tree, or what?'

'I'll talk to you tomorrow, Ollie. About the legal side of things.'

'Tomorrow is Gold Cup at Ascot,' she snapped. 'I am trying to find out what it is that you intend to do *now*.'

'Doesn't it strike you as odd,' Michael asked, feeling suddenly irritated for the first time that day, 'that we are all being terribly laid back about owning just about everything as far as the eye can see?'

Olivia laughed without mirth.

'Laid back! What an enchanting expression. What would you have liked – peasants kneeling in the roadway with lighted candles? A junk regatta?' She turned and walked off, passing Alan Rawten-stall making his way across the tussocky grass of the graveyard.

'Lord Hincham, we haven't met –'

'I know who you are, Mr Rawtenstall,' Michael said crisply. 'And thank you for coming. My agent, Commander Firbank, has invited people back to what used to be an estate house. I'd like you to go along, if you will.'

Alan's glance was sharp.

'Certainly,' he said. 'I, um – perhaps this isn't the time to mention it – but I think you should know your late brother was some way down the road to selling the estate.'

'I knew that.'

'You're saying you won't be at this thing the Commander's putting on?'

Michael examined his hands in a thoughtful gesture, the fingers of one in the palm of the other. The sun was coming out again, and there was a smell of newly turned earth to remind them where they were. The mourners were beginning to congregate on the path to the lych-gate, most of them looking in their direction.

'I shan't be coming to Pear Tree House, no. I want you to keep your eyes open. We might meet tomorrow in London, you and I, say seven-thirty in the morning? We'll talk about things then.'

'Seven-thirty in the morning,' Alan agreed, with just the faintest of smiles.

'We'll go for a walk. I'll meet you up at the Flask in Hampstead.'

'Are you going back to London now?'

'In a little while, yes. I'm going to say a few words to the vicar. See if you can find my wife. She has the keys to the hire car.'

It was of course the unspoken agenda of the drinks party Commander Firbank had put on at Pear Tree. The tenants of the estate, and a very few friends of the late Earl, stood about on the terrace of the house, admiring the view, commiserating with each other about the loss of someone they hardly knew, and wondering where in heavens Michael was. Ronnie Esholt found Alan nursing a glass of wine. He nodded at the glass.

'Good wine. Have a look at the label when you go inside. A hundred and forty a case, anywhere in London. What do you make of that?'

'Living like a lord,' Alan suggested.

Ronnie stared.

'Very good,' he said at last. 'But at least the fellow's made an effort. You're the lawyer, are you?'

'Gillis and Rowe.'

'Well, I think your client has behaved like a shit. You can tell him so from me, when you see him next. He should be here! God knows who all these people are, but he should be knocking about. Common courtesy. Talked to the parson?'

'Yes, briefly.'

'Has he told you about his all-rounders theory? Suspect, I'd say.'

'He played for Shropshire as a young man, apparently.'

'There you are!' Ronnie said, triumphant. 'I knew he was suspect.'

The Commander himself had something to say about Michael. He buttonholed Alan in a rather richly appointed sitting room, closing the door on the rest of the gathering and talking almost in a whisper.

'You might make clear to his lordship that I am only trying to do my job.'

'I'm sure he understands and appreciates that,' Alan murmured.

'Well, it's damn bad form.'

'Would you like me to tell him that, too?'

Firbank rubbed his lips with the back of his hand.

'Most of his tenants are here. His agent is here – *I* am here – and available for instruction. There are some locals whom he will need to meet.'

'The estate is being sold, I believe?'

'Well,' Firbank said, nettled. 'You are the bloody lawyers, you must at least know that.'

'Is the house closed up?'

'Christ,' Firbank said in alarm. 'He hasn't gone to the house, has he?'

Michael and Virginia made their way to Chelworth down the farm road. The blackthorns on either side had lurched towards each other, and the stone and brick track was overgrown with grass and thistles. They passed the Home Farm.

'There used to be a man living there called Buller that my father drove mad, I mean actual barking mad.'

'What else can you remember?'

'Bringing you here for the first time, of course.'

She said nothing to that.

'Whose cows in the fields? Yours?'

'I've no idea,' Michael said. 'I just don't know.'

'It's all a bit Sleepy Hollow.'

It was in fact intensely dismaying. They were startled to see an elderly man running up the path towards them, dragging on a black jacket.

'My Lord,' he gasped. 'Yes, and milady also! Oh dear! We had no idea. We just happened to see the car from the house.'

'Are you Murdoch?' Michael asked.

'Murdoch, sir, yes. Oh dear! You couldn't have come the drive way because the gates are locked, I expect. We did not know exactly whether to attend his late lordship's – oh my word!'

'Murdoch,' Michael said gently. 'Would you be kind enough to make some tea for my wife and me?'

'Tea?' Murdoch muttered, amazed. 'Tea? Yes, we have tea. If you will excuse me –'

He turned and ran ahead of them down the path.

'Annie,' he shouted, 'it's tea they want!'

Virginia stared after him.

'Who is he?'

'The butler.'

Michael's memory of the house was thirty-five years old. Nothing could have prepared him for what he saw when they came into full view of Chelworth for the first time.

It was the lawns that gave a surreal touch. For some inexplicable reason the grass of Chelworth was newly mown and the lawns well kept, perhaps because a contract entered into long ago was still honoured. Across those neat and trim lawns, the house sat in suffering silence. Some windows were boarded up, all were curtainless. The long facade was blank and sightless. Agricultural machinery was scattered in the courtyard and there were bales of hay stacked in the portico entrance. The very first impression was of an immense barn, forlorn and irrecoverable. Impulsively, Virginia took Michael's hand.

'Michael, I had no idea. This is just awful.'

For she remembered it as he did, in the fifties, when his father presided over Chelworth with stiff-necked reserve. Then, the house had fifteen servants, and Lord Hincham's Rolls was brought to the door each morning in case he might happen to want it. Then, four gardeners toiled in the grounds. The Hinchams gave and received hospitality from all over the county, and while the political connections of the earldom were non-existent, Geoffrey Hincham had a crony or two in the Cabinet who came to shoot or fish.

And now, here it was, this same place, reminding Michael of nothing so much as a blind beggar.

'Let's go inside,' he said.

Chelworth was begun in 1785, ten years after the title had been created. The old manor house was pulled down, and in its place was erected a brick edifice of a scale that might have astonished the gentry, had not the whole county been building in the same grandiloquent idiom. Chelworth money came in those days from Bristol, which was a handy euphemism for slaves and sugar. The first Earl, cautious and niggardly though he was, produced in the end a house of great beauty. For two generations the family's connection with the West Indies was maintained, until at last, with the product of their infamous wealth, the Earls of Hincham settled down to be old-fashioned and incurious country people, with a slight taste for study and scholarship. The third Earl began this trend by amassing an important and much prized library of scientific texts. Branches of the family provided bishops and generals, travellers and recluses, in what was then the ordinary way of things – but the title was held by a succession of shy and unambitious men.

Michael led Virginia from room to room of this house where he had been born, his sense of disquiet growing as each door was flung open. The place stank of mould. Sheets covered the furniture, and the carpets were rolled. He drew back a sheet from a sofa and touched the velvet. It was damp to his hand.

Murdoch appeared, flustered.

'We are in the Blue Room, milord. Would you take tea here?'

'When was the house last lived in?'

'We do have industrial cleaners in once a month. But I have mentioned to the Commander, I have indeed, several times –'

'Just answer my question, Murdoch.'

The old man squeezed up his eyes.

'There was a small dinner given here at the time of the Queen's Jubilee, and that would be in – oh dear –'

'Do you live here entirely alone?' Virginia asked.

'With Mrs Murdoch, milady. We have excellent references –'

'Do you have a flat?'

'Rooms, yes.'

'May we have tea with you?'

He blinked furiously.

'With us? Of course.'

He scuttered away, calling to his wife down the corridors.

'It has died, Michael. How terrible. You must believe me, I had no idea.'

'Why should you?' Michael asked, with that dangerous calm she remembered from the days of their marriage. 'It was in this room that I told my father we wished to be married. Do you remember?'

'Yes,' she said.

He touched a burlap sack with his foot, and inside it the crystals of a chandelier jangled. It reminded him of something; something disagreeable in the present circumstances.

The Murdochs lived like gulls on a cliff, in a little sitting room that caught no light from outside. It was furnished like the seaside bungalow to which they might otherwise have retired several years ago. Her knitting sat on a paraffin stove. The parts to a vacuum cleaner were spread on a newspaper.

'We could – indeed we did – provide excellent references, milord. I was for many years butler to Sir Joseph Coultard, and we came here when the old Earl – that is to say your brother –'

'How old are you?'

'There's no point in concealing it,' Murdoch said with a sudden flash of pure ordinariness. 'I'm seventy-six. We have tried, sir. We see no one, month to month, except the police and the cleaners. Your brother has not been here since, well, I can't remember when we last saw him. He was, I understand, the director of several companies in the City.'

'What have you been told about the sale of the estate?'

'Oh, there have been rumours! What have we been *told*? Nothing!'

'But you have made some plans along those lines.'

'We expect to be sacked at a moment's notice, any day now,' Murdoch said simply.

'How much are you paid?'

'Six hundred and eighty-five a month, sir.'

'And your wife?'

'That's the two of us.'

Michael rose, and looked out on to a bright and blustery sunny day that might as well have been happening on television, so remote was it from the little room with its cooking smells and faded fabrics. He turned back, unsmiling.

'I'm going to terminate your employment now.'

Murdoch flinched, but then nodded.

'As I say, we've expected that.'

'I want you to take your time in looking about for what you will do, but I'll pay you two years' salary and a terminal bonus – say twenty thousand pounds. Does that sound fair?'

Murdoch stared at him, his watery eyes filled with tears.

'Twenty thousand, when last winter we had no electricity for a fortnight?'

'Does that mean yes you agree, or no you don't?'

Murdoch burst into tears.

The air outside the house seemed several degrees warmer. Virginia studied Michael with care.

'Your first decision as Earl of Hincham.'

'Not my first,' he said, dark and exceedingly angry.

'Those poor people.'

'Who?'

'The Murdochs.'

'Yes,' he said. 'I promised to take you back to town.'

'Michael, I am so terribly sorry you should have seen it all like this.'

'I am glad we came,' he said.

They drove back in almost total silence. Michael drove much, much faster than she had grown accustomed to in recent years. She found it a little disturbing, however, to recognize in herself an ancient trust: she was comfortable with him, at least as a passenger. He was one of those drivers who never talk about the road, never exclaim aloud or shake their fist.

Virginia asked to be let off in Chelsea, where her father had a flat near the Hospital.

'Of course,' Michael said.

'I am glad we saw the Hall, despite the shock. I wouldn't have liked to cherish dreams, when the truth is so awful.'

'Do you still have dreams that you cherish?'

'Everyone does,' Virginia muttered, cursing herself for blushing.

'I am glad we saw it together,' Michael said. 'Are you still at the same address in Paris?'

'Yes, of course. Drop me off here, if you will. I'd like to walk for a few minutes.' She hesitated. 'I forgot. You said you wanted to see Bill.'

'Now's not the right time. Are you sure about the walking?'

'Yes,' she said.

He drew up at the curb and held out his hand. Virginia took it.

'What wonderful manners we have,' she observed drily.

'Take care of yourself, Virginia.'

'Yes. Thank you.'

He drove away smoothly, pulling out to overtake a bus and disappearing momentarily from her view. She found she was looking to follow the progress of the blue car, and she checked herself with a shrug of annoyance.

The wind that had seemed so apt at the funeral, tossing the branches of the chestnuts and whispering in the grass, was here whipping up dust and grit. Her eyes stung.

Four

Alan Rawtenstall decided to walk to his early morning rendezvous at Hampstead. His wife Frankie thought it was a hoot, seeing him trying to decide what to wear.

'Agricultural gaiters and a brown bowler, surely.'

'Very funny. Your father got me into this, remember. No wonder he made the bloody man my client.'

'Is he a bloody man?'

'He's a bit barmy,' Alan said.

'Probably wants to get back to the fleshpots of Hong Kong. Ask him if you can take me when you fix up to see him there.'

He was very careful not to be late for the seven-thirty appointment, but all the same found Michael already there, sitting in the pub garden, reading the *Financial Times*. Alan's client threw down the paper and rose with no more than a nod of greeting.

'Shall we go?' he asked, calm and neutral.

They strolled in the pale sunshine, hands in pockets. It was already apparent to his lawyer that Michael greatly preferred the company of men. They chatted for a few moments about cricket. Alan found his client relaxed, but wide awake and alert. Even in generalities, he pushed for the most concise expression. There was a bottom line to every remark. It made him peremptory: Alan could see that some people would find him a truculent bastard.

'What did you really want to talk about?'

Michael smiled and lit a cigarette.

'I came home to bury my brother, you understand. Just that. I had no clear thoughts about the house and estate, but finding it was up for sale was no great shock.'

'I imagine you didn't expect to inherit quite so young.'

'That's irrelevant. There's something not quite right, however. I can't say what, but something smells. Tell me about Chelworth.'

Alan considered his reply carefully.

'About three years ago, your brother told us he was contemplating selling all his properties except an apartment in Ladbroke Grove. The interested party was a union pension fund and there were some preliminary negotiations. There was no particular hurry and I'm afraid I know nothing of your brother's actual motives. Then – I've scribbled this all out for you with dates and so on – his lordship instructed us to look into a counter-bid from another source. It was made from the City, but with some local involvement. That much we knew.'

'Who?'

'They played their cards very close to their chest. But a name that cropped up in every conversation yesterday was that of Ewan Chivers. A former county councillor, with interests in property, road haulage, and gravel. The local headman, as it were. A close neighbour of yours. The counter-bid is a consortium of interests, and of course since your brother wanted to sell on the best terms, it hasn't been our business to look too deeply into the local connections. I'm afraid I can't take you much further down that road without a lot more enquiry.'

'Why would there be a local connection at all? Does this Chivers want to live there?'

'He may do. But I doubt it.'

Alan hesitated.

'Look, there are several possibilities. That whole area is a rich bed of gravel. That's one. The other – and I'm guessing – is that sooner or later, with or without gravel, the land use of estates like yours, close to London and with a good motorway, must change.'

'To what?'

'Well, if I were a local millionaire – as Chivers is – I would find more value in building houses on the land than keeping cows. The MP is someone I know slightly – he's a Conservative, of course, and very often on television – talk shows and so on. He's called Russell Fairless. He and Chivers are chums, it seems. That could have resonance.'

'And Firbank?'

'May fit into it somehow. I don't see how. A lot that was sacred about agricultural land, and farmers, just isn't any longer. Fairless may have a stake in the consortium. He may have an interest at any rate. He would be a very useful ally, because of his connections to the relevant Ministers. He may know what's out there on the horizon, as it were. As to the Commander, all we can say at present is that he might have been more forthcoming about all these matters. But, strictly, if you intend to sell in any case . . .'

He waited, but the opening he had given Michael was ignored. He glanced at his client. Michael's general manners were impeccable, but he could not help sometimes seeming arrogant. As if to disarm that criticism, he suddenly smiled broadly.

'What are you doing today?'

'I need an hour in the office, then I'm at your disposal.'

'Good. Do you have morning dress?'

'Er, no. Where are we going?'

'We're going racing.'

The odds-on favourite for the Ascot Gold Cup was beaten into second place by a twelve-to-one outsider, to the intense displeasure of Ronnie Esholt. He was further incensed to find that his brother-in-law had wagered a monkey on the winner. It confirmed all that was wrong with the world. Ronnie's party had taken a house for the day, near the course, and everyone had gone there to drown their sorrows and talk about something else.

'I think it's Charlie Prendergast's place,' Ronnie grumbled, not bothering to look around him. 'Someone like that, anyway. We take it most years. You can't move on the roads, of course. It helps to have a drink and wind down. And anyway it's the thing to do.'

He regarded Michael with a mixture of distaste and fear. Olivia had more or less ordered him to put a flea in Michael's ear. Ronnie was not all that good at facing down someone of his own class, which he supposed Michael was, in a funny sort of way.

'Look here,' he said. 'We're all most frightfully angry with you, I suppose you realize. There is such a thing as good form. I mean I do believe there's a certain code.'

Michael laughed.

'I never thought I would hear that phrase again.'

'Oh really? Well, it does rather sum things up. You leaving *us* to look after the bloody parson and so on yesterday, and you flitting about like a bat in a belfry. Pitching up here without an invitation and so forth. Ollie is in a foul temper. I understand you have a different way of looking at things out there in Hong Kong, and I quite understand you aren't exactly bosom pals with your family, but all the same . . .'

Michael poured him another glass of champagne.

'I'd forgotten what a bloody fool you are, Ronnie,' he said with smiling good humour.

The people at Charlie Prendergast's house roamed this way and that, drinking and eating from a buffet set up in a striped marquee on the lawns. Conversation was conducted in loud, clear tones, like the chiming of handbells. The topics were the Royal Family and its clothes; other people's babies, or dogs; the condition of houses and gardens, some of them far from England; and travel. Nobody worried about the content of what they were saying, the meaning was all in the layers beneath. So it was that guests learned indirectly that Trudi Bassett-Ligon was almost certainly alcoholic; that Rupert Phipps *had* run off with the Beaumont girl; that Lady Westingham had been declared senile, and so on. And though breeding forbade too close an inspection of Michael, it was in the air that the new Earl of Hincham was present, and that he was, as had always been said, a shit.

'You have made yourself a laughing stock,' Olivia told him. 'Most people think you are behaving like an Argentinian or something.'

'Most people? You mean this lot?'

'How very wonderful to be Michael Anstey. Well, it does so happen that the country *is* people like this. People who have some sense of decency. And who resent you coming here as if you're merely making a decision to sell up a factory in Kowloon or somewhere.'

'I thought it was Richard who was selling up.'

'You know damn well what I'm talking about,' Olivia snapped. 'You know nothing about England, about us, about manners – nothing!'

'I make my point again, Ollie. Have I said that I was selling?'

Olivia stared, then laughed.

'Oh my God,' she said, 'you're not going to play the noble earl down there, I hope. That would be rich. With your little Chinese tart to pour the tea, no doubt.'

'Make your mind up. Either I'm a fool for selling, or a fool for not selling. Which will it be?'

'It's a question of values, I'd have thought. We seem absurd and irrelevant to you, I am quite sure; but this country is not some grocer's dream of power and wealth. We are not all of us tarred with that brush.'

'Or sliced from that side of bacon,' Michael suggested.

'I loved Chelworth,' Olivia shouted.

'When were you last there?'

'You are such an arrogant man.'

'I was there yesterday afternoon. I see that Firbank has been invited today. Why is that?'

'It's not your party and it's none of your damn business.'

'The house has died, Olivia. Or almost died. I don't want a lecture from you as to my duties, or my fitness to be friends with this rabble. I shall want to speak to Firbank.'

Olivia glittered at him with her icy blue eyes.

'Rabble, is it?'

'On first acquaintance, yes.'

She turned and walked away, her high heels digging into the lawns.

There *was* someone there he knew rather better, and that was Bill Toller, Virginia's father. Lord Toller was one of the few hereditary peers to speak regularly in the televised proceedings of the House of Lords, and so (to his secret pleasure) a minor political celebrity. He sat on the cross benches. Michael found him at peace in a corner of the garden, watching finches dart and flutter.

'Hullo, Bill.'

'What a delightful surprise,' Toller murmured with his famous slow delivery that gave a faintly mocking tone to what he had to say. But the handshake was firm. Michael sat beside him.

'I'm afraid I've just upset Ollie by calling her friends a rabble.'

'Are they? I don't notice these things nowadays. I only come to events like this as a spy, you know. Since we met last, I have taken up the plight of the London homeless. Some of my baglady friends want to believe the worst of the rich, and I bring them the evidence. I would say we are among the no more than averagely stupid today. You look troubled. Tell me what it is.'

'I went to Chelworth yesterday.'

Bill laid a hand on Michael's sleeve.

'That I knew. Virginia stayed last night. You had a nasty shock.'

'Bill . . .'

'Let me say first, Ginny was just as upset. I can well imagine. It happened to me, I believe you know, when I inherited. It was 1947, that terrible winter. I never wished to become a landowner, much less a peer of the realm, and the winter and coal rationing did for me. I sold. But I often think about the place.'

'Has Virginia gone back to Paris?'

'She has,' Bill said calmly.

'I would like to see her there.'

The old man spread his hands gently.

'You surely don't need my encouragement.'

'I was prepared to face your discouragement, perhaps.'

'Oh, Michael. I have known many couples a lot less happy than you and Ginny who have stayed together for fifty years. Paris is still quite a pleasant city at this time of the year. Go, by all means. Go with my blessing, indeed, if that is what you wish.'

He glanced up and his face broke into a grin of pleasure. He held out his arms to a tall and gently plump girl in her early twenties who advanced across the lawn. She leaned over and kissed him on his forehead, her blonde hair falling on to his cheeks.

'Hullo, Grandpa.'

She turned and faced Michael without speaking.

'Hullo, Tish,' Michael said to his daughter.

'When did you get in?'

'I flew from Lisbon this morning. Did Jamie make it to the funeral?'

'No. Do you see each other, these days?'

Tish wrinkled her nose.

'As little as possible. He's in Colorado, apparently. Backpacking. How childish. What a son you have. What a brother I've got.'

'How is the villa business?'

'Oh,' Tish said, offhand, 'thriving. Terrific. Is your Chinese girl with you?'

'No.'

'She's supposed to be very beautiful.'

Michael laughed.

'She is. I think I have offered you the fare to Hong Kong more than once, Tish. Not to meet her, but to come and see me.'

Tish shrugged. She had, for all her bounce and preoccupation with her own good looks, an unfortunate way of distancing herself from people with a tiny and wholly unconscious smirk. To someone her father's age, what shrieked in Tish was uncertainty, a sense of insecurity. The villa company Michael had mentioned employed her in the most menial tasks. It was run for a rich and loud-mouthed Kent builder–speculator by upper-class youngsters Tish's age; from the first day it was clear she would sleep with the manager and at the same time be given the worst jobs. When she complained to the company's owner, Terry, he had simply laughed in her face. Sharon, Terry's formidable wife, told her that girls like her were ten a penny, and if she didn't like it she could sod off.

'You know of course that Mummy has a lover.'

'I believe so,' Michael said gravely.

'It's disgusting.'

'Ah. That I didn't know.'

'He's called Keith. He's really wet.'

Michael smiled and took up her hand. He could feel the resistance to this gesture as something electric produced throughout her whole body.

'Isn't she free to do as she wishes?'

'I think it's foul. God, I hate England. All these terrible people, with awful clothes, saying the same thing over and over.'

'Portugal is a bit different, is it?'

'It's wonderful,' Tish said. 'I don't want to belong to any of this. The country's completely finished, in any case. You were very clever to get out when you did. Everybody knows it's hopeless to try and live here.'

'Tish, I have a small piece of business to transact today. But now

46

that you're back, I want you to stay on for a day or two. There's something I want to talk to you about.'

She shrugged.

'I'm really not at anybody's beck and call.'

'I'll reach you through Grandpa. You can reach me through my club. Or through the lawyers.'

'Aunt Ollie says you're behaving like a yob.'

'I want you to stay,' Michael persisted gently, 'at least until the middle of next week.'

Tish shook her hand free of his.

'I do as I please these days.'

He watched her walk away. The form of her body was shown as a dark shadow under the thin white cotton clothes she wore. She looked fit, and sunburned, and she walked jauntily enough – but all the same she looked lost. Alan Rawtenstall joined Michael, his glance on Tish.

'Pretty girl.'

'My daughter,' Michael murmured.

Firbank was drunk. He wasn't falling about drunk by any means, but he had taken enough to feel that with luck he could bluff his way through the rest of the afternoon. It had been a shock to see Michael and what turned out to be his lawyer pitch up at Ascot: Firbank was panicked for a few moments, not knowing whether or not to cross and speak to his new employer. But Michael cut him dead. Thus, when they came back to Charlie Prendergast's Firbank deemed it sage to hang about in the background. He talked for a while to some dreadful old hag from Northamptonshire and discussed the girl in see-through white with Rory McLeish, who had a taste for girls with, as he put it, plenty behind the saddle. But all the time his radar was tuned to Michael's presence.

The Commander had drunk enough to begin to feel aggrieved. This bloody Hincham was spoiling an otherwise good day's racing. Firbank was in his element at occasions like this: there was always an attentive woman or two wishing to be flattered by him, and the men indulged him as a sort of unofficial Foreign Secretary. The Commander was especially hot on the Arab–Israeli conflict, where he thought the whole bloody lot could be wiped out without loss to anyone. He watched Tish approvingly. With the sun back-lighting those silly trousers of hers she was the stuff of daydreams, no doubt about that. One of those big healthy blondes who knew what it was all about. And mad enough to try anything.

Then the fellow's lawyer came to him over the lawns.

'Lord Hincham would like to see you in the house for a moment, Commander.'

'Oh he would, would he?'

Firbank set down his champagne glass with elaborate care and ditched his cheroot into a border. As he passed the girl with the splendid body he was chilled to learn, from what was being said to her by the old duck from Northants, that she was Patricia, his employer's daughter. He cursed under his breath and tugged at his tie, feeling that the bounce had gone out of things somewhat.

Michael quite deliberately chose a position by the mantelpiece from which to address his agent. The room, the light outside, the noise of people chattering to each other, reminded him of school. It gave him a perverse pleasure to make this interview a carpeting. Firbank stood in front of him, his chin jutted. Michael stood in silence for a moment or two, savouring the atmosphere in the room. There was more than an air of the headmaster's study, even, in the furnishings of the room, down to a First and Third oar and a few silver-plated pots. He looked hard into Firbank's watery blue eyes. Firbank cocked his head with a little show of bravado.

'You wanted to say?'

'First of all, any sale contemplated by my brother, to any party, is off. There will be no sale in the immediate future, is that clear?'

Firbank looked astonished.

'My lord –'

'Have I made myself understood?'

'Yes, of course, but –'

'Secondly, if, as I am led to believe, the counter-bid for the estate included representation from the locality, I wonder why you have not yet advised the lawyers of this.'

'Do your lawyers want to hear every piece of pub gossip?'

Michael's glance was cold enough to freeze this remark on Firbank's lips.

'Do you know a man called Minton?'

Alan Rawtenstall glanced up sharply, perplexed.

'Minton is your neighbour,' Firbank said.

'He is,' Michael agreed. 'His land shares two boundaries with mine. Is it true that Minton's land was put up for sale this week?'

Michael waved down Alan's interruption.

'I am asking the Commander.'

'You are remarkably well informed.'

'I asked you: is it true?'

'I couldn't say,' Firbank muttered.

'Is it true that this land will be bid for by Mr Ewan Chivers?'

Firbank felt his heart lurch. Michael's face was as if carved from wood.

'I wonder why you can't comment, Firbank. I have been in the country only a few days, and I seem to know more about the valley than you.'

'I was intending to make a proper report of the estate and property at some more appropriate time.'

'And who was to be the judge of that?'

'I find this animosity difficult to understand, milord. We seem to have got off on quite the wrong foot. I'm not a fool. There are local issues that affect the estate. I'm not sure how you know about Stan Minton's place but the bones of it are as you describe; and I was, as I say, going to put them in context for you. At a better time.'

'You say you're not a fool. I'm pleased to hear it. You may reflect, however, that what I need are facts. I do not need context. I can derive that from the facts myself. Who is Ewan Chivers?'

'A neighbour.'

'You know him personally?'

'I know most people in the valley.'

'I saw Chelworth yesterday. You were meanwhile kind enough to entertain the funeral guests at Pear Tree. Do you own that property?'

'Your brother sold it to me in 1980.'

'I see. At full valuation?'

Michael watched him drop his chin. He could sense Alan Rawtenstall holding his breath. But Michael was a veteran of such confrontations. He shrugged, and immediately asked another killing question.

'At Pear Tree, my lawyer Mr Rawtenstall noticed two paintings, a portrait by Hoppner of the third Earl, and another by Beechey of Captain Greville Anstey, R N. Whose are these?'

'They came from the house.'

'And whose are they?'

'They are yours, of course!'

'Then, what are they doing in your house?'

'Lord Hincham, you will permit me to say that you have been in this country only three days, and in that time it has not been I who has evaded you.'

'What else that is mine is lodged with you?'

There was sweat gathering in the hairline on Firbank's brow. He cuffed his nose with the back of his hand. Michael ignored the gesture.

'There is a battle, Firbank, between the accountants and the insurers, is there not? To save you the trouble of evading the question, I have spoken to the insurers before coming here today. There are questions they wish to raise about the inventory. Is that so?'

'This is all in my report to you,' Firbank whispered.

Michael studied him without expression. Outside in the gardens, there was laughter at some pleasantry or other. The agent was fumbling for another sentence.

'There may have been some slight irregularities, and some differences of interpretation, some . . .'

'Very well,' Michael said. 'That is all.'

'That's all?' Firbank cried.

'Thank you for your time.'

Firbank seemed to want to reach out, to touch Michael.

'I am absolutely astonished.'

'Close the door after you.'

The Commander's face was indeed astonished.

'Are you sacking me?'

Michael turned to Alan with a negligent gesture.

'Alan?'

'Nothing that Lord Hincham has said can be construed in that light. I am sure his lordship will want to speak to you again, and it would be helpful if you would make yourself available for further meetings over the next few days. Your report – the one you mentioned – will be of great interest and usefulness.'

'And now leave and close the door after you,' Michael murmured.

Firbank left much as a man might stagger from a hospital after being told that he has only weeks to live. When the door closed behind him with elaborate care, Alan Rawtenstall let out a whistle of disbelief. Michael smiled at him without humour.

'Life is short, Alan, and time is precious. I haven't time to waste. In Hong Kong, all this was a piece of business. It looks very different now that I'm here. Firbank is likely to be inconsequential, whatever he's done. Not irrelevant, but of lesser importance. I want to know more about these local barons.'

'I was whistling at the work you've put in.'

'That's nothing. I shall need your help. I know next to nothing of this country – I mean, as it is now. It's all strange. I need to get a picture, and quickly.'

'And the sale?'

'Is stopped. That's definite. I'm afraid you and I are going to have some hard work on our hands.'

'Very well, suppose I get you a short lease on a flat in town, as a base of operations. I realize you may have to go back to Hong Kong.'

'Maybe. Tomorrow I am flying to Paris.'

In Paris that night, Virginia made love to Keith with an urgency that surprised him. She had made him stay over from his visit to the Bibliothèque Nationale until she returned from the funeral. They ate at home in the apartment and went to bed long before the last light had fallen from the sky. It was warm, and she was bathed in sweat. Too much wine made the room spin slightly. She held on to him with all her strength.

'You're safe,' he said. 'You're perfectly safe and free.'

'Nobody is free.'

'Yes they are. There's nothing to be afraid of.'

'And that isn't true either.'

He sighed. For a long time they lay side by side in this embrace until it grew too uncomfortable for Keith. He moved his supporting arm away and rolled over. Within a little while he was asleep.

Virginia rose in the middle of the night and ran a bath. She opened the long narrow windows of the bathroom and shivered agreeably in the clean air that was drifting from the south-west. It was not yet four o'clock, but the sky was already lit. She stepped into the bath and lay back, watching the dawn break, thinking as the tears rolled down her cheeks.

Five

Firbank waited outside his car in a favourite courting spot for young Hincham couples. It was a disused railway bridge, where you could see for miles across rolling countryside if you were to climb the embankment, but could hide from the road if you had other things on your mind.

The familiar red BMW drove up the flank of the hill just after eleven, and Firbank walked to greet it.

Inside the car, Ewan Chivers burst out laughing.

'You look woebegone, old love,' he jeered. 'Haven't been given a wigging, have you?'

'Pull your car over,' the Commander suggested.

'Won't that look a bit iffy? What's on your mind?'

'You can't just leave the car in the middle of the road,' Firbank protested. 'At least pull over and switch off the ignition for a moment.'

Chivers touched the accelerator and made the engine growl.

'I'm not going into the bushes with you, sweetheart. I've heard about you sailors. Best tell me what you want to tell me now. I'm heading for the London train, so make it snappy, there's a good chap.'

Firbank's anxiety was replaced by a sudden hot anger.

'Look, I worked hard for you over your bid for the estate. I've done some dangerous things on your behalf.'

'You've also robbed the place blind in your own right,' Chivers reminded him. 'There was nothing illegal in asking you to represent us to the late Earl as the best offer. I believe we were. You conveyed your advice, I am sure, with your usual scrupulous attention to ethics.'

'I need your help now, Ewan.'

'Don't shout.'

'You know the new man's not going to sell at all.'

Chivers shrugged with good humour.

'That's up to him.'

'He's going to turn the place over. I have that sense of him. The bugger's one of these hard men.'

'Bad luck,' Chivers said, with a sardonic smile.

'Look, there are things between us – between you and me –'

Chivers raised a warning finger.

'I wouldn't say any more, if I were you. You took your profits out of that place, and I haven't suffered from your presence here amongst us. But – and it's a big but – I cover my tracks, Robert. You had better get a hold on yourself. Your plea for help sounds a bit like a threat to me. And I don't like to be threatened.'

'Really? Well, if I go, you go too.'

'Um, no, actually. If you go, it will be well merited, and I shall be the first to say so.'

The window came up, and the red BMW began to move.

Ewan had indeed been on his way to the station for the London train, but changed his plans and drove back to Roman Arches. He got out of the car and walked into his house without seeing it. Pilar, the Filipino housekeeper, was dusting in her slow, absorbed way. Ewan waved her away and flung himself into a sofa, thinking hard. He glanced out of the picture window. His wife Barbara was swimming in the pool. She clambered out, water streaming from her. When she saw him she looked startled for a moment, then wrapped herself in a huge cotton towel and padded off to find a place to sunbathe that was away from the brisk southerly wind.

Ewan thought of asking for a drink, but then ordered coffee. He lay back on the sofa, reviewing what had passed between him and Robert Firbank. It was a question of damage limitation. The trick was to try to predict what the Commander would do.

He knew the answer to that: Robert Firbank, the master of a lee shore, was heading for the rocks. He would lose his nerve and leap overboard.

'Damn,' Ewan said aloud.

Barbara had walked back into view, her breasts naked, the rolls of fat under them making creases that he had grown to know by heart. She looked in his direction and he waved vaguely. She stuck out her tongue in response. When she bent to retrieve her cigarettes and lighter, the breasts that he had once, long, long ago, kissed with such absurd passion fell down towards the terrace like heavy sacks.

Ewan picked up his cell phone and dialled the number of Russell Fairless, MP. But before it could ring out he cancelled the call.

Pilar, patient, mute and miserable, waddled in with his tray of coffee. On most other occasions it amused him to see how much she hated him and despised her mistress, who was now rubbing sun-oil into her jiggling front.

Ewan rang Firbank at Pear Tree House.

'Where is he now?'

'Paris,' the Commander said.

'Keep your nerve,' Ewan murmured.

Virginia chose the most expensive restaurant she could find for lunch, with exquisite mirrored rooms overlooking the Palais Royal, and from the menu she chose the most expensive dishes. Michael sat patient and imperturbable.

'You have a damn cheek,' she said, very angry indeed. 'We haven't actually met for four years and you calmly turn up here with what is really one of your more preposterous ideas. And what is to say, when you have tired of it – and us – you won't simply disappear again?'

'Let's order another bottle of this,' Michael suggested. 'I haven't been to Paris for ages.'

'Well, I live here, and I am extremely happy here.'

'I don't think so.'

She stared at him.

'You are really quite incredible. What gives you the right to say that?'

'It's an observation.'

'A mistaken one.'

She pushed back her plate and threw down her napkin.

'There are also other considerations.'

'Keith,' Michael said. 'Yes. I know about Keith. I am not asking you to give him up.'

'That's very white of you, Michael,' she said bitterly.

'I am asking you to observe the forms of marriage with me, in that house. Look. When the millennium comes round – I mean on that particular New Year's Eve – I shall be sixty-five. Very well. What do I want to have happened to my life? It's late, I know. But this, the thing I have just explained to you. I want to spend that New Year sitting at home, perhaps with a modicum of grandchildren –'

Virginia laughed in spite of herself. Michael reached over and took her hand. The gesture startled her more than anything he had said, more than any of his preposterous plans.

'I have found something worth doing,' he said.

They walked in the Place des Vosges, near her apartment. She could not bring herself to ask him back; and it touched her that he saw that, and was careful not to comment. They walked side by side along the gravel walks, attracting glances from the tourists.

'You are asking for the impossible all over again. I don't now mean me, especially, but the children. You haven't even seen Jamie.'

'He flies into London tomorrow night.'

'What is to attract him to Chelworth?'

'He is Viscount Winterbourne since a few days ago,' Michael suggested.

'Does that count for anything?'

'I don't know.'

'Suppose we all turn you down flat?'

'I shall live there alone.'

'You never have lived alone. What about your girl in Hong Kong?'

'She is very young, Virginia,' he protested mildly.

Virginia glanced.

'Poor Rosie. And your businesses there?'

'Can continue. The investments will work for me. And to head off a possible question, I was actually very happy.'

'And clearly retain an intense loyalty for the people there.'

'Rosie again? I was a rich European – a millionaire boyfriend. Quite old enough to be her father.'

'It's already in the past tense?'

'Something happened when I saw that house, Ginny. I need a purpose. Isn't that something we all need? Any fool can make money, once he *has* money. Money isn't everything. I need to feel I belong somewhere.'

He had accidentally said the one thing that might convince her to join him. He had said what she most often thought about herself. She hoped very much she had guarded the expression on her face; but in fact he was looking away, with that tall man's idle quizzery of the park, and the sparrows in the dust, and the elegant little trees. It encouraged her to find her nerve.

'You have a bad record, Michael. Of belonging, I mean. What are we to do: pig it with you in the country and pretend it doesn't matter that the roof leaks? I hate that side of England, all that impoverished nobility.'

'I'm not going back to pig it. I want that house to live.'

'All very romantic. And all very impractical.'

'Look, I am filthy rich. You are filthy rich in your own right. I don't think practicality is an issue here. I want to sink the rest of my life into believing in something, and belonging somewhere. And I want you to be with me.'

About that, she simply could not speak. More than anything else at that moment, she wanted Keith. Keith the good listener and patient analyser; Keith the safe and soft option, with a taste for wool ties and overlong hair, early jazz and foreign movies. For Keith, the countryside was the green space between secondhand bookshops.

Russell Fairless, MP, sprawled on the cushions of Alan Rawtenstall's ridiculous Italian sofa and felt content with life. This Hincham fellow, for all his dark good looks, was a bit of a wet, he concluded. He was also amazingly ignorant of the delicate balances, the trip mechanisms and little intricacies of modern English conversation. He might, Fairless supposed, be unused to dinner parties. What *did* people do in Hong Kong, except whore and drink and get absurdly rich? He plucked the end of his nose in good humour and let his wife do the talking. If there had been danger signals ringing in his head, their clamour had died down.

'Are you by any chance a student of local history?' Eileen Fairless was asking. 'I am. I think it's sweet. You have an Iron Age fort on your land, and only last year Bristol University excavated a sort of wharf or jetty on the river that dated from medieval times, with just buckets of pottery that came from the Rhine or somewhere.'

'I imagine,' Fairless murmured, 'you're more interested in how to offload your property in what seems to be an uncertain market. You have a problem. There's such an enormous amount of money tied up in London properties. That's the quick-kill area.'

'Oh, I'm sure Lord Hincham knows his own mind,' Eileen said with her studied artlessness. 'Your wife lives in Paris, I believe.'

Michael smiled.

'She has lived in Paris for some years, yes.'

'How lucky she is.'

'You like the city?'

'Oh, everyone loves Paris. What a shame Chelworth has to go. It shouldn't be, that a wonderful house like that should have to go cap in hand to the twentieth century.'

Alan Rawtenstall passed round a bowl of cheese straws.

'I think my client actually has an embarrassment of offers,' he said.

'I think I would still rather have a half-acre site in West London,' the MP responded. 'Eileen is a bit of a romantic about architecture.'

'Or continuity.'

'Maybe,' Fairless said, after a moment's reflection.

When the doorbell rang, Frankie Rawtenstall went to answer. Standing on the threshold was the last of her guests, a good-looking woman in her late thirties. They embraced.

'Sticky?' the newcomer asked in an American accent.

'No shrieks of laughter,' Frankie admitted. 'You look extremely glamorous. We need that. Eileen Fairless is dressed as if for the nuclear winter. Russell is doing his modern-dress Julius Caesar.'

'What's his lordship like?'

'Sexy.'

The American hugged her hostess.

'You're crazy, Frankie.'

Deenagh Long was from Queens, the last New York borough on the road out to Long Island. At least, she had been raised there. She worked at the University of London as an art historian, and was an expert adviser in nineteenth-century drawings to auction houses in London and New York. The moment she walked into the drawing room she felt Michael's calm appraisal of her, and characteristically resented it. At dinner they sat opposite each other. Eileen Fairless was running away with the conversation. Her husband made a few laconic interjections.

'It's a curious thing, really,' he said. 'Houses like yours have such a colossal reputation. They're like little centres of magic. I know for example that Deenagh's compatriots – and not at all stupid people either – angle for invitations to what they call stately homes. Not to ogle, but to be put in touch with something.'

'The past,' his wife said. 'The magic of the past.'

'Perhaps, but why?'

'Maybe because the present is unbearable and the future uncertain,' Alan suggested. 'If people can't get a sense of horizon, don't they begin to languish? If they can't look forward, there's no place to look but back.'

'What do you say to that?' Fairless demanded of Michael.

'Alan may be right.'

Oh, terrific, Deenagh thought. An Englishman playing hard to get. She had met men like Michael a good deal since coming to England: men who fulfilled the definition of a gentleman as it had once been described to her. A gentleman was either there or he was not. He was either in the room or not present at all. He manifested himself without explanation, and his absence required no apology. His rank was his sole justification. He carried with him no story, nor did he require anything of another. Until he was on top of you, Deenagh thought. And to hell with this civilian sense of the past, she added silently. Eileen with her goddam post-holes and majolica fragments, Russell with his comfy Winnie impressions and carefully burnished philistinism. She looked up, and found Michael staring at her frankly.

'All this stuff about the past freaks me,' she found herself saying.

'Well, dear, you're the expert, I suppose,' Eileen simpered.

Deenagh refused to meet Michael's gaze.

'Lord Hincham may have, as Russell wants to indicate, a little potential stake in this heritage business – the room where Charles I cracked walnuts and jokes and all the rest of it – but the truth is that Chelworth, through no fault of his, is pretty much a disgrace.'

There was a moment's silence, greeted with delight by Alan and Frankie Rawtenstall. Michael inclined towards her.

'Please go on.'

'Forget I spoke.'

'Nonsense,' Alan laughed. 'That's breaking the rules, Deenagh. Disgrace is a wonderful word. Scandal would be even better.'

'Well, scandal isn't far off it, either.'

'I think it's a dreadful word,' Eileen protested.

'Perhaps we're talking of an artistic scandal,' Russell murmured. His wife shot him a glance.

'Of course we are. But I think Deenagh ought to explain.'

Deenagh at last looked into Michael's eyes. She was surprised to find they were smiling at her. They seemed to offer complicity. The idea annoyed her.

'Okay,' she said. 'I happen to know a little about drawings. You have four Fuselis that are quite unique – or you should have them. They were photographed in 1924, since when they've just disappeared. You have a couple of Chardins that have never been exhibited, you have a whole raft of good portrait painting across three centuries that nobody ever sees. Maybe you don't know where they are, maybe they're rotting on the walls down there. You have a cultural history that goes a little bit further than 'Legend has it' and all that stuff – and you don't give a damn.'

'Nobody has given a damn in the past,' Alan proposed. Deenagh nodded.

'That's a truer way of putting it, maybe.'

She turned back to Michael.

'Now, you know, what's yours is yours and all that –'

'– But isn't that true, also? If we want to let our paintings rot, can't we do that?'

'Noblesse oblige,' Eileen cried.

Deenagh saw that same air of secret complicity in his expression and was filled with the urge to hurt him.

'You can do what the hell you like, and maybe that's what got you the paintings in the first place. You can just sell the place and all its effects, and maybe you'll do the world a good turn.'

'How?' Frankie asked. The answer was supplied by Russell Fairless.

'Because,' he said, 'the Fuselis will turn up, some American will buy them and have them kept at exactly the temperature and humidity prescribed by Deenagh. Little post-graduates with braces on their teeth will write learned articles on them, the world will roll on, everyone will be happy. And our friend here will have enough money to buy new paintings, or more superior examples of the old masters.'

'That's the possibility,' Deenagh agreed.

'May I ask,' Michael murmured, 'what your father did for a living?'

She hesitated.

'My father sold furnaces out of an office in New Jersey.'

Michael nodded.

'And did he want to remember and cherish his sense of identity by keeping, for example, photographs of your grandparents, or maybe furniture they had passed down to him and so on?'

He was sitting forward, his forearms resting on the table.

'You were quite right, Miss Long. What's mine is mine. I may dispose of it as I choose. But you are also right that what has happened to that house is a scandal. And I choose to conserve it – the house and its heritage. I shall doubtless make a lot of mistakes.'

'You're *not* selling?' Fairless asked slowly, too slowly.

'The house was bequeathed to me, let us at any rate pretend, as a place to live. Or my home.'

'I hope you know a lot about farming,' Eileen said.

'Nothing,' Michael replied. 'I know nothing at all about farming.'

'You'll live there alone? How grand!'

'Not alone, Mrs Fairless. With my wife and children.'

Deenagh stirred uneasily. He said this with his frank, calm eyes on her face.

She made a tiny shrug, and threw her coffee spoon into the saucer with too loud and too large a gesture.

Ewan and Barbara were going to a black-tie party to celebrate the first million of a boy called Gifford. Gifford was twenty-two, six feet four, had four O-levels and in the previous calendar year had earned himself a million pounds in the City. For Gifford, who was in Barbara's opinion a prat of the first water, she wore a suit that cost £380.

'How do they do it?'

'It isn't difficult,' Ewan said dryly.

'A far cry from little Ewan scraping and slaving at the same age.'

'I didn't have the advantage of a Conservative government like this one. And if you will smoke in the car, please open the window.'

Barbara yawned.

'When's it all going to stop?'

'One day.'

She sat forward suddenly and pointed across the fields.

'Isn't that Bob Firbank's place?'

It was almost dusk, and the flames from a fire seemed consequently redder and more menacing. Ewan glanced, and for a second the car slowed. He let the revs die away and then changed gear.

'Barbecue. Or bonfire or something.'

The Commander tripped on the ledge of the French windows and went sprawling on to his office carpet. It was an Indian carpet which had once been the glory of a study in Chelworth. He cursed and staggered to the filing cabinets for another armful of files. These he carried with elaborate care to the fire he had made on the terrace – and flung them in. A huge swarm of sparks flew into the night sky. Firbank found the vodka bottle from which he had been drinking and poured some down his throat. He coughed it back out again and threw the bottle into the bushes. The stereo was still playing in the house, and he reeled his way back inside and tore the whole bang shoot from the wall with the most satisfying explosion of noise. Tapes and compact discs rained down on his head from sagging shelves. Good. It was good, this orgy of destruction. It was a bit of a flourish at the end of a damn good run.

Six

So it was that in late June, to the surprise of all the neighbourhood, the seventh Earl of Hincham took up residence at Chelworth House. With him came his family – the Countess with her alert, intelligent grey eyes, and both children. Of these, it was said that the girl had blonde hair and brown legs, with a hoity-toity way of conducting herself. The boy – Viscount Winterbourne as he now was – seemed quieter and more serious. Unlike his sister, he was seldom seen outside the house and grounds. A little further afield, in the small town of Hincham, and in Salisbury, the re-occupation of the house was hardly news, for there exist round about stately homes of overwhelming magnificence, of a grander order altogether. But, taken together, the family was a source of almost inexhaustible gossip locally, made all the spicier because of the disappearance of Commander Robert Firbank, the agent to the estate. On that matter, police had been called in. There were strong whispers of fraud. For those for whom a story is not a story without police and ambulances, Chelworth suddenly became a rich quarry of secrets and rumours.

Jamie Anstey marvelled at his father's skill and energy in persuading the family to join him. He had been afraid of his father as a child; or perhaps overawed would be a better description. He had supposed, on the model of other boys and their fathers, that there exists in the world an affection and a complicity between men that stands apart from the love owed to women and mothers. Most of the men to whom he subsequently explained this idea were childless; while they found the thing touching, the brightest of them were also amused. Jamie's views on his father were bound up with absence, and silence. In other words, he theorized a great deal about someone he hardly knew.

He looked nothing like Michael. Though he was tall, he had a faintly round and soft appearance, which he shared with his sister. The two together were indisputably from the same stock and might even have been mistaken for twins. Jamie was reserved and cautious, but he had nothing of his father's icy calm. The little boy that lay buried in Michael was much closer to the surface in his son.

As to Chelworth, Jamie had never seen it in his life before arriving there one evening from Denver via Heathrow. Michael immediately showed him the library.

'If you want a job, and I mean salaried employment, you can try to make sense of what we've got, on the arts and artefacts side. It's a mess, and I've no idea where it will lead you.'

Jamie looked around the cluttered shelves and piles of books. He picked up the volume nearest to hand. It was *Erinnerungen aus dem Feldzuge des Jahres 1812 in Russland*, published in Breslau in 1846.

'There should be another two volumes of this,' he said uncertainly – information he got from a glance at the fly-leaf.

'Look, Jamie, I have no idea what we've got, or what we are owed. I don't know what has been stolen, or lost. I do know that in better-regulated houses, such information is important. Maybe there's even a national importance, for people who care about these things. Somebody was saying something about some Fuselis we own, for example.'

'What about them?'

'God knows,' Michael said with an encouraging grin.

There was a surrealistic touch to the library provided by a vintage train set that wound its way in and out of the books and papers strewn across the huge walnut table. Jamie rubbed dust and fluff from the track.

'Are you talking about valuations?'

'That'll come,' Michael promised. 'You'll be hounded up hill and down dale. You can well imagine how the insurers view the decamping of the Commander.'

'But . . . what I'm asking, I think, is what you want to happen in the end.'

'In the end,' his father said, 'this will all be yours. Think of it that way.'

It was a job Jamie took on from first principles, and one in accord with his unaggressive nature. Old Murdoch found him a kettle and his own tea-caddy and so on, and he cleared a space to work in, using the floor to file things and a tea-chest for rubbish. At first he was chary of using the tea-chest at all, but necessity made him throw away some things. Did the estate want (for example) a wartime pamphlet on how to dig for victory, when fifty years on you could see from the cellars to the bedrooms in one part of the house, through broken ceilings shored up by local carpenters now dead and in their graves? Was a 1954 copy of the *Field* part of the heritage of the house? Or a bill from Lockwood and Julian for the repair of a carriage clock, on which had been scrawled in pencil, 'Given to Duddy Walmsely's girl'.

He slept in a room leading off the long corridor that ran across the house on the second floor. During the day, if it was fine, he opened the two windows wide to let out some of the smell of damp and decay. Annie Murdoch laboured up the stairs twice a week to clean his room and that of Tish, who slept in the old nursery. Late at night, Tish played Europe One. She slept until eleven each morning. Michael and Virginia had separate rooms, and though his father proposed they eat together as a family, this seldom happened. Although it was June, the main topic of conversation was the coming winter. This could be divided into two subjects – the renewal of the roof, and what to do about the central heating. Of this last, it was Murdoch's opinion that if charged up, the boiler might quite easily explode. He had this on the authority of the last man to inspect it – 'the gentleman from Southampton', a fabled animal Murdoch never tired of memorializing.

The flat Alan Rawtenstall found for Michael overlooked Chelsea Bridge. He had phoned Deenagh Long a few times since the dinner party, but this was her first visit to his London lair. It also happened to be the first occasion that he planned to stay overnight there. For a while he stood looking out at the river and the traffic pounding past, waiting for her and thinking about her.

Michael knew nothing of feminism, although everywhere else in London, in places of comparable wealth, it was a common enough topic of conversation. Accordingly he thought about Deenagh in a straightforward, acquisitive way, and made the assumption that since she had accepted his invitation, other things followed.

One of the pleasing habits Deenagh possessed was punctuality. She arrived on the dot with a bottle of Bulgarian wine, and the smell of early-evening gin on her lips.

'No etchings?' she asked in her flat, sardonic Queens voice.

'In the bedroom,' Michael said. 'Can you eat pizza? It comes in a box from the King's Road.'

'What am I doing here?'

'Having a meal.'

'A bite to eat.'

'If you like.'

She pushed the bottle into his hands.

'Trash the pizza. I'll cook.'

'You don't have to do that.'

'Look, Michael, you persuaded your wife to live with you again. You fixed up for your children to do the same. You're doing the big number down there on the farm – "a man and his heritage". At the same time you express the kind of interest in me that goes with love in the afternoon and secret phone calls. And if I bitch, you're going to tell me that really you want me for my mind. At least let's eat good while we contemplate the rich possibilities.'

He watched her open the fridge and rummage around in the vegetable drawer.

'I have no idea what's there,' he murmured.

'Your designer's idea of a well-stocked larder. Or maybe your wife's.'

'Virginia has no interest in this place.'

'That's handy,' Deenagh said. 'While I cook, you can tell me what in hell you want.'

'Easy. I like you.'

'In fact, the manners that go with old money – terrific. Do I look as if I was born yesterday?'

'Eating alone is no fun. I take it I won't get an argument there.'

'You won't.'

They drank her Bulgarian Merlot while she prepared a meal. She drank quickly and with an indifference that proclaims the regular drinker. When he asked what wine she would like with the meal she shrugged carelessly.

'Oh, any premier cru you have to hand. And don't let's spoil an occasion by talking about what is screaming to be talked about.'

'You live alone?'

'I do, but isn't it a little late to ask me?'

'You work hard, you're an expert in your field, you have no false modesty. And you've answered my calls with a mixture of derision and encouragement.'

'Derision and encouragment,' Deenagh repeated. 'Just let me run that past again. I'm being called up by a guy who uproots a bunch of perfectly happy people and tells them, "Now you're my family. Forget the life that once you led." Like the man who walks into the saloon and hollers, "Who was the best man before I got here?"'

They ate.

'Virginia has not been asked to give up Keith,' he said after a while. 'We have quite separate arrangements.'

'You're a pretty wonderful guy,' Deenagh scoffed. 'What am I, a way of evening up the score? A little symmetry?'

'You're someone I desire,' Michael said simply.

She examined him without smiling.

'And what you want, you get.'

'I may not get. I always ask. Ginny and I don't have fights. We don't quarrel. We used to have battles; I mean big stately occasions from prepared positions. But not any longer.'

'You're civilized people now.'

There was a limit to the amount of tart rejoinders Michael could take. He challenged her with a serious, unsmiling gaze of his own.

'You asked me what I wanted from you tonight. I could ask you why you are here.'

'Suppose somebody signals something and you can't quite believe the guy is serious. Suppose you never met that particular combination of vanity and need before? In your bathroom, which is refreshingly neat, there is a used toothbrush and another still in its wrapper. This may be because the aristocracy always buy in twos; or it may be a vain man's attention to the small details of a seduction.'

Michael waved his hand around the room, irritated.

'Is *this* a seduction?'

'I don't know. I came tonight because I needed to find out more.'

'And have you?'

'I don't know. I'm an American. I'm not trying to play cute: I just don't know a thing about people like you. You may just be angling for some free expert advice.'

'I may also just want to know you better by making love.'

She looked up, biting her lip.

'That would be easier to understand.'

'And enjoy?'

'Yes. And enjoy.'

He woke several times in the night, as happens sometimes in hotels, when the mind tries to cope with the unexpected disposition of the doors and windows. But of Deenagh, who slept naked in his arms, he had no uncertainties. It seemed good and necessary. That she displaced not Virginia but Rosie was something he could not expect her to understand.

Michael was not a fool. Needing to make love was something not to be analysed, insofar as he sought to understand the workings of his own life. Taking on Chelworth, according to Olivia, to Alan Rawtenstall, to Virginia herself, was an act of quixotic stupidity, to be repaid only by heartache and disillusion. Deep in his heart of hearts, he thought the same. It was in any case a quick way to destroy the Michael Anstey who had made the decision. How often does anyone get the chance to obliterate the past so dramatically? And what else could follow but despair? The self-destructive streak in him was laid wide, even with this stranger in his arms. The more so, perhaps.

In the morning, Deenagh showered first and then walked through the apartment wrapped in his towelling dressing gown, making coffee and fetching orange juice. She brought the coffee and juice to the bedside, set it down and took off her robe. She folded one arm loosely across her stomach.

'You'd better be serious about me,' she said, standing watching him.

'I am serious about everything.'

'No. Understand me. It was terrific – *this* is terrific – and people cleave to you because you're strong, Michael. Because you know what you want. So to be wanted by you is flattering. But –'

He reached up and pulled her by the wrist until she fell into bed on top of him. He kissed her on the lips.

'I am serious about everything,' he repeated.

Roman Arches was the kind of property that leaves the visitor with an uneasy feeling of having strayed quite a long way from home. The general design was taken from a house in California that had once caught Barbara Chivers's fancy on a visit to San Diego. As provided from the drawing board of a bemused English architect and set down in Hincham with a fake Cotswold stone manor house for its neighbour, its effect was stark. This mattered less to Barbara than that it was clearly very expensive and, as the architect gallantly put it, choice. It got its name from the heated outside pool, which had at one end a little colonnade and a terracotta bust of (as it happened) the Emperor Vespasian. Barbara had found this on a shopping trip to Milan. Cuddling up to Vespasian was a favourite snapshot subject of hers, and she had a selection of photographs of herself thus, in a variety of bikinis.

Tish was swimming in the pool at Barbara's invitation. She tanned easily, and the warm spell had deepened the effect of two years in Portugal. Roman Arches was a scream of a place and Barbara Chivers as common as muck, but the pool was pretty warm, and it was anyway something to do.

Ewan watched her in secret for a moment before stepping into view. She was a vain little bitch, and he speculated idly on what she would be like in bed. But Ewan's speculations in such directions had no great thrust; putting it humorously, he would always say that Barbara was enough for one man. Of him Barbara would always say that he was at his best fully dressed. Which he was now, in a tailor-made suit and a dazzling white shirt.

'Good morning.'

He reached out and pulled her by the hand from the pool in a single shimmering action. Tish plucked at her bikini.

'There are towels and so on in the little hut. There's a phone there. Ring the house for what you want.'

The house was all of thirty yards away.

'Your wife said I might use the pool.'

'I'm happy she did. You obviously enjoy swimming. Will you have a pool up at Chelworth? How are things up there?'

'It's an absolute tip,' Tish said immediately. 'I mean it's a complete mess. The roof is going to cost more than most houses.'

'So I've heard,' Ewan said.

'I actually hate big houses. I think it's deadly to have one.'

'Go and find a towel.'

He was amused to see her flirt a little as she walked away. She reached up behind her and unclipped the top to the bikini. She shook the water from her hair in a toss of the head. Ewan laughed aloud.

'What's funny?'

'It was a cry of pleasure,' he lied.

Barbara walked from the house in a sun-top and toreador pants.

'Don't laugh,' she said, 'but her father's just arrived by bike.'

'By *bike*?'

'I met him wandering about in the road and asked him back for coffee. Perhaps he can't ride a horse. They have lots of bikes in Hong Kong, don't they? Or somewhere out there. Perhaps he ran a rickshaw company.'

Michael seemed surprised to find Tish; and Tish went into a freeze when she saw Michael. Ewan logged this information while at the same time acting the smiling host and proposing that they might talk business.

'Do we *have* any business?'

The two men sat a little way from the pool. Their coffee was brought by the Filipino.

'I'd no idea we had such grand neighbours,' Michael said amiably.

'I'm sure you don't mean that. We've been told a hundred times the house is a vulgar insult to the landscape. But then we can't all live in wonderful houses. You intend to farm, I imagine.'

'Know nothing of it.'

'I see Minton has put his farm up for sale. Will you buy that?'

'Will you?' Michael countered.

'I know nothing of farming. It would be an expensive specu-lation.'

'Unless . . .'

Ewan smiled.

'Yes, unless I could slam down thirty or forty houses. That might not please you.'

'It wouldn't help the view,' Michael admitted.

'There we are, however. Views round here are very expensive. Increasingly so.'

'Could the land use change? I mean can you foresee a change of planning policy?'

'The government surely can't have an acute housing shortage on the one hand and an agricultural slump on the other without some change of direction. We live in hope. Those of us with land, I mean. Golf courses and nature reserves are all very well, but you've only to walk round Hincham. People want houses.'

He took Michael's glance unflinchingly, having led him to a question he knew he had come to ask.

'Are you going to buy Minton's farm or not?'

'Don't know,' Ewan smiled, triumphantly. 'How about you?'

The detective investigating Firbank's disappearance was called Williams. He showed no interest in the books that scattered the library, but some fondness for the train set. Jamie sat and waited for him to get to the point.

'These old locos, they're worth a bomb. A little mania of mine, railways. Now, this Firbank character. Was paid a salary of £16,500 and so far we've turned up another three accounts worth a couple of hundred grand. I don't suppose you've had time to find out how this could be?'

Jamie indicated the mass of papers.

'The inventory is a mess. He could have got the money from the sale of a single picture, or in dribs and drabs. I can't tell you yet. You say you've found his car.'

'In Swanage. With a boot full of your silver. Did you know the Commander personally?'

'We never met.'

Williams glanced.

'Not even in New York?'

Jamie felt his throat tighten. Williams smiled gently, but with the confident smile of the police.

'I'm afraid we found his diary.'

Jamie considered. Williams was watching him with the same amiable alertness. If the Commander had kept a diary, he had no way of knowing what it might contain, nor in what detail. Jamie had never mentioned to anyone in the family that he had met Firbank in New York. The reasons, Williams's smile seemed to be saying, were all too clearly laid out in the diary. But what kind of a diary, and how damaging? He remembered talking to Firbank on the telephone and meeting him a couple of times, apparently by chance, in certain restaurants. He remembered all this with a sick feeling flooding through him.

'It might help to say that the bloke was a bit of an inquisitive bastard if the diary's anything to go on,' Williams murmured.

'Firbank rang me in New York while he was over there. Two years ago.'

'Uhuh. What did he want?'

'Money.'

'He was blackmailing you.'

'Have I said that?'

'You were living with a man called Stuart Doblehofer.'

'I shared his apartment.'

Williams licked a shred of tobacco on to the back of his hand.

'Just so. Mr Doblehofer was your patron, shall we say?'

'Which is not a cause for blackmail.'

'Mentioned your living arrangements at that time to your father?'

'Is that part of your enquiry?'

'Look, Lord Winterbourne, I'm not trying to give you a bad time. You're a student in New York, you live with a man of sixty-eight, a rich man who wants to give you things, who takes you to Jamaica and Mexico –'

'My father knows nothing of these things. Is that what you want to know?'

'But the Commander did.'

Jamie hesitated.

'Apparently.'

'And he tried to blackmail you.'

'He may have had the same idea of the relationship as you apparently do.'

Williams yawned.

'I'm investigating a disappearance. Behind which is a fraud, or a series of thefts, or a possible blackmail. I'm working with dirty hands. But you had better know that Firbank's diary is pretty explicit about you and Mr Doblehofer, and Mr Doblehofer's other friends. And the things they shared in common.'

Jamie felt a sudden sharp sting of tears.

'The man you have been talking about so freely is dead. He was a very great friend of mine, and he is dead.'

'Very sorry to hear it, sir,' Williams said carelessly. 'You'll let me know if you turn anything up that could help with our enquiries? And look after these old locos. They're pretty special.'

He thought about it, walking in the grounds at dusk, the lights of the house almost orange against the deep mauve of the sky. Things that were pretty special had never, in his experience, survived, beyond a few snapshots, a line or two of diary entry, a jolt to the heart when a name or a place that was precious came up in ordinary conversation or on the television. In such a context, to save the house itself was an extraordinary achievement. To save its contents, to cherish its layers upon layers of meanings implied a colossal act of will on his father's part.

On the other hand, suppose it was all allowed to languish? Would any of them be diminished, really diminished? Jamie saw his mother walking at a tangent towards him. The white of her skirt glowed in the dusk. It was too early to quit, of course: they had after all only just arrived. The pieces had been put in place on the board. The game had not yet started.

'What are you doing, mooching about?' Virginia called.

'Mooching.'

When she joined him, she slipped her arm through his, and he in turn held her lightly by the waist. She was warm to the touch. They adjusted their steps to walk in unison.

'This in itself was worth coming home for,' Virginia said.

'Truly?'

'Truly. Be of good cheer, my faithful servant James. We are all engaged on what Grandpa calls a wonderfully wrong thing.'

She glanced.

'That means he approves; and you can generally trust him to get things right. And this seems pretty right to me. This moment. We mustn't be greedy.'

Seven

Michael had eight major tenants, of whom the most interesting –
and certainly the most aggressive – was the Yorkshireman Peter
Thornton. Three years earlier, Thornton's wife had died of inoper-
able cancer. They had no children, and he set out on a mammoth
bout of drinking that soon rendered him friendless. Only months
before Michael inherited, the Yorkshireman had managed to stop
drinking and start living again. He was a big, raw-boned and
apparently uncouth man, who, it turned out, had been to agricultural college and was a considerable amateur expert on Wiltshire
pre-history. It was Thornton, claiming to speak for the other
tenants, who wanted clarification as to the future of the estate. He
was blunt and completely without courtesy, but Michael found a lot
to like in him. He turned up at the house the day after the visit from
the police, looking burly and dangerous. Michael had established a
small office in a ruined room, and Thornton's glance at the
brand-new filing cabinets was ironic.

'This is very businesslike,' he said.

'Thank you.'

'I came to find out how safe we are, begging your lordship's
pardon.'

'I don't intend to sell land,' Michael said.

'So you say now, but you haven't been in the job five minutes.
Bob Firbank doing a bunk has put the wind up people.'

'What has Firbank got to do with it?'

Thornton regarded his landlord with the sort of kindly tolerance
that was actually very insulting.

'You have four thousand acres here, milord. That's enough for
any one man. Properly farmed, things could go along nicely. But
each of those farms is built on a hill of bloody gravel. Let's say the

money runs a bit short for you with the house and that, or we find somebody's had their hand in the till in a big way. And I mean big. Say we get another agent like Firbank. Who's to say my farm won't one day go the way of Nowell Hill.'

'Where is Nowell Hill?'

'Oh, you don't know it? Would you like to see it?'

Thornton took him there. They drove through Hincham and up to what was now the furthest edge of Michael's land. Behind blackthorn hedges a ragged saucer of weeds and alders hid from sight a stone-grey lake. The margins of the lake had been trampled into paths by fishermen, all of whom had made a particular part of the shore their own. It was a dirty and melancholy sight.

'Who owns this?'

'This was yours once. The Commander, as he liked to be called, persuaded your brother to sell off a bit of top land that had no agricultural value, as rough shooting. It was this here. We all wrote to his lordship to protest, and so did the Conservation Society and the local history group. But it got sold. Wasn't very big, and up in London one place in the country is much like another, I dare say. It was gravel, of course, top to bottom. If you want it back, your hill, it's under the motorway now.'

'Who bought it from us?'

'Someone you've met very recently.'

'Chivers.'

'That's the man. He was going to put parties of guns on it, if you've ever heard anything so daft. Oh, but then as soon as he gets the land he changes his mind. This gun syndicate idea of his seems to fall through. He resells Nowell, not without a great deal of heartache, I don't think,' Thornton snorted.

'To whom?'

'Wensley Gravel. And now I can show you a bit of what you're up against. We also have a local MP – Fairless, they call him. You might have met *him* too. He'd be one of yours, so to speak. His wife was a Wensley, and she sold her family shares in the gravel company a year or so before this happened. Guess who got hold of them?'

'Chivers.'

Thornton smiled.

'Aye. With Eileen's shares and what he had already, Chivers acquired the controlling interest. Then Firbank more or less makes him a present of Nowell Hill. So in come the lorries, out goes the gravel, everybody's happy.'

'You say you told my brother this?'

'Nobody – with respect – could tell your brother anything. Firbank ran this estate. It doesn't surprise me that he's done a bunk.'

'Know where he's gone?'

'Far, far away. I don't know where he is, no. I do know he's wanted by the police. No thanks to anything you've let slip, by the way.'

'Then get to the point.'

'Sooner or later I knew you'd be seeing Mr Chivers.'

'And he's not your cup of tea.'

'He doesn't frighten me,' Thornton said evenly. 'But I knew you'd have something to talk about.'

'Minton's land.'

'That's right. And did you?'

Michael studied his tenant with extreme care.

'You don't let much get past you, Mr Thornton. And you have a blunt way of showing it.'

Thornton scoffed, without smiling or flinching.

'I live here, remember?'

'All right. If I buy that land, say four hundred acres, at what? – twelve hundred an acre? – just to keep houses off it, or to stop it becoming another hole in the ground . . . and you think I *should* buy . . .'

'Haven't said so. It's not my money.'

'But you think if I don't . . . ?'

The Yorkshireman shrugged.

'I think you'll be sorry.'

'Is this just pub gossip, this stuff about Nowell Hill?'

'Would I tell you pub gossip?'

'Then what's your angle?'

'You need an agent,' he said. 'A good one. There's a good living to be made here for all of us. But the country's run by greedy buggers nowadays or hadn't you noticed? I'm not one of them. I like this part of the world. My wife talked me into coming here, and she's buried here. I don't want it spoiling by anyone.'

'And that includes me?'

'Well,' Thornton admitted, 'you look as though you can box a bit clever. But you might want some help.'

'So. You're applying for the job!'

'I have a suggestion to make. Buy Minton's place, and then I'll relinquish my lease to you and you can sell mine, if you want. I'll find you someone who can look after it – I mean a farmer, not some bloody businessman. And I'll work for you on a salary. What do you say?'

Michael laughed. He had no hesitation in answering.

'I'm gobsmacked, lad,' he said.

'And where'd you pick that up?'

'I used to play squash with one of your compatriots.'

'Oh aye, where from?'

'Tony Sillins. From Harrogate.'

'Harrogate,' Thornton yelped, outraged. 'That's no better'n Hong Kong to me!'

Michael held out his hand.

'If you want the job, it's yours. By the way, Jim Hodnett and his wife are coming in as butler and housekeeper.'

'I know Jim,' Thornton allowed.

'I know you do. And that's how I know you. According to Jim and Daisy, you're the best there is in this valley.'

'That's not saying much,' Thornton grumbled, highly delighted.

They shook hands.

Virginia had been told she was mad to do what she had done. Michael gave her the master bedroom, which was decorated with a rather fine but faded Edwardian wallpaper and had a canopied bed. There was enough room for her to have a small office arrangement there also, although he demanded nothing of her, and in fact scotched any suggestions she made for making the acquaintance of people locally. Like him, she knew most of the other aristocratic families in the county. There are, after all, less than two thousand in the entire island. Some of those who lived nearby – that is to say in Wiltshire – she knew quite well from the days of her youth; and the grandest of them she knew as a matter of course, not as former friends, but as families with histories, whose names cropped up wherever Virginia and her kind gathered.

The bedroom was hers exclusively. He slept elsewhere. He wanted – but was unable to get – an evening meal each night when they met the children. They very often ate on trays at different times. Annie Murdoch was a timid and dull cook. The best meal of the day was certainly breakfast, which Virginia took out of doors, alone, on the terrace furniture Murdoch had dragged from one of his glory-holes.

To her own astonishment, all this suited her very well. Had Chelworth been anywhere near as grand as some of its neighbours, she might have felt oppressed. But the house had such a wounded character, such promise of what might be if care and love were lavished on it, that Virginia accepted living there more quickly than any of them. She loved to wander through the rooms, and to risk her neck across the scaffolding planks Michael had thrown down to bridge some of the more serious and dangerous gaps in the floors.

She drove to see Keith in Oxford from time to time, and saw her father in London, making that the excuse to stay over for a night in a hotel. Keith had so far refused to come to Chelworth when Michael was away.

'It seems I have a new rival,' he said.

'You mean the house? It's fascinating, yes.'

'Will it be as fascinating when the coaches start to roll up for a quick tour of the ground floor?'

'Oh my dear! Nothing so sordid. He's plunging his entire fortune into this. There hasn't been any word about making it available to the public. Michael only ever meets the public one at a time, if you follow me.'

'And when he has it to his taste, what then?'

Virginia evaded the question.

'The point is, I am very happy to be back in England. And the feeling amazes me.'

She laughed.

'Come on, Keith, don't be such a snob. You can't be jealous of a house, surely?'

The day after Detective Sergeant Williams came, the same day that Michael found a new agent, Virginia went to see Jamie in his library den. She inspected and admired his work.

'What do Sotheby's say about this lot?'

'They're appalled to find things in the state they're in. This library has never been valued, did you know that? I found another forty tea-chests yesterday, up in the roof. Everything from dross to the real McCoy. The girl from Sotheby's has offered what seems to me like a small fortune as a reserve at auction.'

'And will your father put them up?'

Jamie ran his hands through his hair in exasperation.

'He won't even let me weed out the duds. He wants it all exactly as it is, everything the family ever acquired, back in its place. That includes paintings, plate, glass. The stuff is scattered in museums and loan collections all over England. We even have a seascape by Boudin that the Boston Museum of Fine Arts described in a catalogue as 'present whereabouts unknown' which you can find with its face to the wall in Tish's bedroom. She told me it was boring.'

Virginia laughed. She kissed Jamie.

'And then the police yesterday.'

'Yes,' Jamie said.

She held his chin in her hand briefly, warned by something in his voice.

'What did they want?'

He looked into her eyes for a second or so before getting up.

'You had better know, I think. When I was in New York, at the MOMA, I met a much older man. And went to live with him.'

Virginia felt her heart lurch, but not so much as she had expected, for she had waited for this confession, or something like it, for years.

'Was he nice?'

'A mother's first question. Yes, he was very nice. He was wonderful. He died.'

Jamie glanced at her.

'Not in that way.'

'And what is any of that to the police?'

'Firbank tried to blackmail me.'

'Oh Jamie!'

She had virtually to stand on tiptoe to cuddle him, but that is what she did. He hugged her back.

'He was called Stuart. Don't ask me any questions about him. I may be able to tell you about it one day. But the only important thing is that I loved him.'

'Of course,' Virginia said. 'Of course it's important.'

She did not have the heart to say that she had suspected for a long time that her son was gay, without ever being able to say why. And she hated herself, a little, for not having the skill of someone like Keith, who would have known exactly how to handle the moment, and when to apply his massive compassion and common sense.

One invitation that *had* slipped through the net was for tea at Barlow Court. It was owned by Cecily Hollar-Wilson, someone Olivia Esholt knew, and her useful if quite unreliable local spy. Cecily was in unstoppable form when Michael and Virginia joined Olivia and Ronnie for a sprawling, ramshackle afternoon there. They wandered about for a while, inspecting the garden and listening to Cecily in monologue, hurling words a hundred yards. Michael found Ronnie was mordantly bitter.

'Either we shan't get the sniff of a drink, or we'll get nothing else but. And whatever you do, for God's sake say nothing against this little nancy-boy she has on the premises, Adrian or Julian or somebody, who I think is kept locked up with his lipsticks and high heels, but you can never tell with Cecily.'

'Where does he fit in?' Michael asked.

'Ha!' Ronnie barked, believing a joke was intended. 'Very good! Where indeed? The place is a *doll museum*! Did you know? You may remember quite a nice ballroom to the house, not large but elegant, I suppose. That's where she keeps her dolls. And this little pill is the curator or something. It's all perfectly hideous.'

'Why are you here, then?'

Ronnie looked down his nose at Michael.

'The woman is Olivia's best friend. For the time being. She is also, I warn you, the most colossal gossip.'

Cecily was still in full flow when they rejoined the women.

'I mean, my adorable boy has researched the collection thoroughly and written such a lovely brochure, and still you get the visitors trying to touch the things, or pass them to their disgusting children, asking if they are anatomically correct, that sort of thing. Dirty old parsons trying to peek up Dolly's skirt. I don't know why I endure it, except of course that I have no choice. That will happen to you, Michael. You'll walk into your loo and find some coach driver sitting there with his trousers round his ankles.'

'Cecily,' Olivia protested weakly.

'They think they own you. And all the accountants ever say is take the money and think of something else more pleasant. You can't! I really would rather have dry and wet rot than visitors. They're such bores, all of them. And how is Virginia? You look peaky.'

'She is a *grande dame* nowadays,' Olivia said spitefully. 'And haggard is very fashionable.'

'I must say,' Cecily said unexpectedly, with a complete change of track, 'I *would* like to see Chelworth.'

Olivia was undaunted. She curled her lip.

'Michael doesn't permit visitors.'

'Nonsense,' Virginia snapped. 'We can go now if you wish.'

Whether or not she actually meant it, everyone was surprised by the speed with which Cecily bounded up. Ronnie was appalled. He set down his scone with elaborate long-sufferingness.

'Look,' he said, as they walked out of doors. 'I'm driving myself, would you tell Ollie? Wild horses would not get me into that bloody car of Cecily's. I'll see you there, although I shouldn't be surprised to find you all killed in some multiple pile-up. Ginny has played a most awful card.'

'Why does Cecily want to see us?'

'She'll get two months' ration of gossip,' Ronnie promised. A thought crossed Michael's mind.

'Have you heard from Robert Firbank, Ronnie?'

'Certainly not. Did I say I was friendly with the fellow? I don't know where he is. He said he was a member at Middlesex.'

'You don't really believe he's watching cricket?'

'*I* would,' Ronnie said dreamily.

•

Michael and his sister hung behind when Cecily led the cavalry charge through Chelworth. Olivia threw her gloves down on a blue sofa and folded her arms in exasperation. She glanced round at the walls.

'Where are all the pictures?'

'In store, mostly. I'm having someone look at them.'

'Your new girl.'

Michael raised his eyebrows.

'You certainly don't waste any time,' Olivia said. 'God, if you knew what people are saying about this farce. Which is what it is: utter farce. You were seen at a restaurant together, you and the American. I understand you have an enormous flat in Chelsea. Ronnie says the bank rate has had to go down as a consequence of your returning with all your money. It's quite revolting. I mean, you will beggar yourself to no purpose.'

'And does that matter to you, or anyone else?'

Olivia lifted up her shoulders in an expressive shrug.

'You were never popular, for what you did to Ginny. It seems to have left her with her judgement permanently impaired. I can't imagine anything more foolish than the bargain you seem to have entered into together. She'll soon tire of it. Or you'll tire of the whole thing and buzz off somewhere. It's said your American is a bit long in the tooth for someone of your tastes in women.'

'You really do hate me, Ollie.'

'I despise you. I despise all stupidity.'

'Where is Firbank?' he asked casually.

Olivia's eyes glittered.

'How dare you?'

'These "people" – the phrase you use so freely of what I suppose you'd call our class – don't impress me for their honesty or sagacity.'

'Firbank is not of our class,' Olivia said quickly.

'But we let him believe so. And, as a consequence, he's made off with some of our money. I'm sure Cecily is jolly good fun, and the MP – Fairless – is awfully reliable on insider information from the Commons. That silly-ass friend of Ronnie's – Duddy Walmsely. He rang up to ask if he could put the Hunt over our land. They're all lovely people. And I want nothing to do with them. I'm sorry you hate us so much.'

He left her for dead, standing in front of open French windows. Outside, thrushes pecked on the lawn, and the sky was a cloudless blue.

Having accepted hospitality, Virginia felt obliged to return it. Without consulting Michael, she arranged a small weekend party for the Rawtenstalls, Cecily, her father, Keith and – an innocent suggestion from Jamie – Deenagh Long, whom *he* knew only as the expert retained by Michael to assess the pictures in store, and Virginia knew (via Olivia) as the American woman.

The party commenced the day the Murdochs finally left. This added a certain pang Virginia had not intended. Harold Murdoch spent hours rummaging, looking for the croquet set he knew he had once seen on his excursions to the store rooms. At about three the Hodnetts came to take over the duties Harold and Annie Murdoch were laying down. Jim Hodnett slung his arm round Harold's shoulder.

'Don't you fuss, Harold. We'll see 'em right.'

'Don't let anyone touch the boiler.'

'Shan't need it tonight.'

'I've laid out the third set of silver.'

'Good lad.'

'But we must have that croquet set.'

Bill Toller was about to leave for Chelworth when there was a visitor to his Tite Street flat in Chelsea. On the doorstep was a man he recognized well enough, but whose presence left him momentarily without words.

'I would like a few moments,' Firbank muttered. Bill simply stood aside, in his old man's way, and ushered the Commander to his study sitting room.

'This is an unexpected event,' he said in his slow, wavery drawl. 'To what do I owe the pleasure?'

'I am in some trouble with your son-in-law.'

'So I read in the papers,' Toller observed dryly.

'There have been mistakes – misunderstandings. And, um' – he coughed – 'the record could be set a little straighter.'

'I hope this has some relevance to *me*, Firbank,' Bill warned. 'I understand that the police would like to hear from you, as to your safety and whereabouts. Shouldn't you be talking to them?'

'This does concern you, in a way. I would like to make reparation to his lordship. It can't be a complete restitution, but I think terms could be arranged.'

'I am still mystified.'

'Lord Hincham has been exceptionally cruel towards me.'

Bill could not help laughing.

'Has he, now?'

'I have never had a chance to explain my side of things.'

'Perhaps a visit to the police might give the opportunity.'

Firbank looked disgusted.

'Your son-in-law has acted throughout with great vindictiveness. I am an officer, as you once were – a very distinguished one; and I like to think I am also a man of honour. I have not had the chance to redeem my honour.'

'Commander, you must fall out of the habit of supposing that because people are old, they are also simple-minded. As I understand it, the accusation against you is that you have stolen from the estate. Indeed, some of the swag, as we might put it, was found in your car. I don't believe an appeal to me as a former officer will alter the facts in any material way. You clearly came to say something. Why not say it?'

'I have great respect for your daughter. I like and admire her. You have a grandson, Jamie. Your grandson is a homosexual. Of course, that matters very little these days, but I believe the fact is not known to his parents.'

Toller examined Firbank's face much as one would study a child who failed to grasp a simple truth. He pulled on his earlobe.

'Um . . . I may have misunderstood you, Firbank, but can this possibly be an attempt at blackmail?'

'Look,' Firbank said baldly, 'I don't want to go to prison. And I don't need to. Jamie will tell you that he lived a chaste life with his friend in New York, who was old enough to be his grandfather; but I can tell you he was passed from hand to hand among Doblehofer's circle of friends, as their toy and plaything. And he loved it.'

'A few moments ago,' Bill said slowly, 'you used the word honour to me. As it happens I am, as you wish to characterize me, a gentleman. I will now show you the door. But I will speak for both my daughter and her husband. Do your worst. Let this poison out. It is of no consequence to any of us. My advice as a gentleman is different, of course: that you too try to behave like one. When you have gone, I shall ring the police. Please see yourself out.'

'I am in a desperate situation, can't you see?'

'I can,' Bill Toller said, with ice in his voice.

Jim Hodnett passed among the guests for dinner with the best of the light white wines he could find in the cellar, where the miserable remains of a once-reputable collection were stored higgledy-piggledy. At Virginia's suggestion he had added a tiny amount of cassis to each glass. *Bien frais* meant just what it said to Jim – the wine was iced up a treat. He was surprised and delighted to find just how much he was enjoying himself. Tish was outrageous in pink, while her ladyship looked wonderfully calm and collected. The cheerful, giggly little woman would be the lawyer's wife, and Cecily he knew from her forays into Hincham, though seldom before had he seen so much of her redoubtable chest. The rather good-looking bloke with the floppy hair was, he supposed, this Dr Shedden character from Oxford. Jim felt coolly towards him because very unfortunately Keith was seeking an unconscious ally in *him*. There was one missing, and that was Miss Long. The other person not present in the room was his lordship.

Michael was on the phone to a drunk and distraught Firbank.

'You have got to give me a chance. There are aspects to all this – things I could tell you, local business matters that you can't imagine –'

'Commander, I am sorry to say it again, but whatever you have to say should be said to the police.'

In the background, Michael could hear the noise of a pub. Firbank slurred his next speech.

'There are other things. Your son – Viscount Winterbourne – Goody Two-shoes – when he was in New York, was the most wonderful bum-boy to a man who had been a member of the Senate. Who has since died. Little Jamie can't get enough of it, or hadn't you realized?'

Michael registered a jolt like an electric shock.

'Listen to me, Firbank. I have never been threatened in my life. Get that straight. Nor am I threatening you. Go to the police. Tell them anything you wish. I am breaking the connection. Don't ring me again.'

'Don't you bloody hang up on me,' Firbank roared.

Michael threw the telephone into its cradle. He looked up. Alan Rawtenstall was at the door, alert and questioning.

'Firbank.'

'Did he say where he was?'

'Had he done so, I would go there now and smash him to a pulp. And in future, knock before you enter any room in this house, will you?'

Amazed, Alan stood aside to let him pass.

Firbank was discovered at eight the following morning on Hampstead Heath. The elements of absurdity and unreality that had characterized his life were present. It was utterly in keeping with the style of the man that he should have kept, from God knew what ancient naval requisition, a Colt ·45. In his pocket were two shells date-stamped 1944, and with one similar, nearly fifty years old, he had attempted to blow out his brains. This he might still have done without agony. But the evidence was that, drunk and incompetent as he had been, and perhaps never really believing in what he was attempting, he had botched the job and suffered most terribly.

The first person to find him vomited, and so did the policeman who was called to the scene.

Eight

The summer passed. Michael was invited to, but did not attend, the Harvest Festival at the church where his brother lay buried. He pleaded a necessary visit to New York, where in fact he joined Deenagh for a few days in the sweltering heat. While he deceived the parish, he was polite and correct enough to tell Virginia where he was going. She acknowledged this courtesy with a faint wrinkling of the nose. During the past four long vacations Virginia and Keith had toured Europe in a car together, looking at buildings and hunting down the birthplaces of the famous in history. To her surprise, that summer Keith accepted an invitation to lecture in Finland: he went alone. She tried desperately not to be hurt.

In September, Tish moved out of the house and began to renovate the North Lodge. It was an acrimonious departure.

'The place is more or less unfit for human habitation. It's a rural slum,' Michael grumbled.

'Yet your faithful servant Woolaston lived there for over forty years. Leave her be. You can afford it, can't you?'

'I don't know,' Michael said, startling Virginia.

For the fact was that the cost of renovating Chelworth was open-ended. Repairs to the roof alone cost over a hundred thousand pounds. In order to render the wings structurally safe – and the survey revealed some alarming faults – Michael would need to find money of a lesser order, provided he had no intention of ever restoring them to use. However, a builder's estimate for shoring up the West Wing lay on his desk unheeded for six weeks. This was not because the task was less than urgent. The fact was, Michael wanted to bring the whole house back into operation – all of it. At this, the architects simply threw up their hands. The bolder of them pointed out that very little of the central part of the house was adequately heated; that many of the ceilings were in danger of falling; that on the ground floor parquet had lifted in all but one of the rooms; that there was no real kitchen in the modern sense; and that Murdoch had been right – the central heating boiler was in danger of blowing up in their faces. Beside this list of priorities, the full renovation of the wings was almost unimaginable.

Michael had spent just short of half a million pounds on acquiring Minton's farm. He commissioned Peter Thornton to find ways of making the estate more profitable, short of commercializing the house itself. Thornton proved to be a brilliant lieutenant, though an argumentative one. He was, for example, bitterly opposed to renovating the Lodge for Tish, when his own plan was to sell it off and let the purchaser bear the cost of modernizing it.

'I need to keep that girl here. That's all there is to it.'

'Suppose she isn't the sticking kind?'

'You talk too much, Peter.'

'You know Chivers is showing an interest in her?'

'Chivers?' Michael said slowly.

'She's thick with Barbara Chivers.'

'And that's part of your business as my agent, is it?'

'No point in faffing about with you. It *is* part of my business, yes. If you haven't worked out that you have an enemy – I mean a real adversary – in Chivers, you've learned nothing.'

'And you think my daughter is trading with the enemy.'

'I think your daughter would be better under this roof; or off out of it altogether.'

'It's the weather,' Virginia told Keith. 'We're all getting scratchy. It really can be most terrifically depressing after four or five days of nothing but rain and wind. The moment it gets dark you feel you are in the belly of the whale.'

'Told you so,' Keith said, but without any satisfaction.

'Why won't you come down? He's away in London very often, with his lady.'

'You tolerate that, do you?'

'What does that mean? He tolerates us, if you want to put it that way. Tit for tat, surely?'

'I should feel more grateful,' Keith said grumpily.

His own little house was a terrace in a student part of Oxford, close to the river. Keith himself was amiably scruffy and dishevelled, but his house was a model of efficiency and quite awesome tidiness. Virginia lay in bed with him, holding his hand, their fingers interlaced, and reflected on how complete things were in Keith's world.

'You have made it beautiful here.'

'It's a little bit smaller,' he said, disengaging his hand.

On the wall of the bedroom was a painting of a nude he had bought in Helsinki. A young girl sat on the edge of a bath, knock-kneed, her feet wide apart. Behind her, the window was crystalled by a savage Finnish winter. Virginia knew that he bought it because of the extraordinary melancholy rising through the tenderness of the subject.

'Don't give up on me, Keith,' she whispered.

Unusually, he had nothing to say. He rose first, and when she came downstairs he was sitting in his tiny parlour, reading by an open fire. She sat in a spoon-back chair opposite him and watched him read, feeling fearful and insecure. Though it was hardly five in the afternoon, it was quite dark in the street outside. It was raining.

It was raining heavily at Chelworth. Tish listened to Robbie hammering and banging and wished for the hundredth time that she was back in Portugal, no matter what the cost to her self-esteem. It was fun, of a kind, flirting with this labourer, but it wasn't life. Robbie was definitely interested; but he wasn't actually very interesting. One of the things that Tish thought a scream was that he very much wanted her to take him seriously. There was a range of things Robbie considered himself knowledgeable on – music, football, ecology, green politics – that Tish found just too dreary for words. She liked his hair, his colossal arms and broad chest. And she liked best the way he sensed her presence in the house. She could feel his eyes on her all the time. That was fun. But it was very low-life fun.

'Are you there, Master Robert?' she bellowed.

The hammering ceased.

'Putting your plaster board in. Geoff's coming tomorrow, remember.'

She walked to the head of the stairs. He was working in a torn tee-shirt and dusty jeans and he seemed exhausted.

'Well, will you stop now? Make a coffee or something. I'm going to have a bath.'

There were a few final bangs and then, as she ran the bath, she could hear him move underneath her to the kitchen. He was switching on the radio.

'I can see you through the floorboards,' she shouted, and laughed when he looked up. 'Make me some coffee, will you?'

She lay in the bath, soaping her shoulders and breasts, listening for his feet on the uncarpeted stairs. She smiled when he paused at the open door.

'Your coffee's here,' he muttered.

'Pass me a towel.'

He came into the bathroom and stared at her, the mug of coffee still crooked in his finger.

'Put the coffee down, stupid.'

As he did so, she rose from the bath and he lunged for her. His mouth tasted of tobacco. The palms of his hands were like sandpaper on her back. I could make him crawl, Tish thought exultantly, I could make him lick my toes, or bark like a dog. I could make him howl. Her hands unbuttoned the top of his jeans.

They both froze. Downstairs was the unmistakable noise of the front door being forced open.

'Hello, Tish?'

The voice was Barbara Chivers's. Robbie hastily dragged his jeans together and walked out, the front of his tee-shirt wet from Tish's body.

'Shan't be a tick,' Tish called.

She dried herself quickly, listening to the sounds downstairs. The radio went off, the front door scraped open and banged shut. Barbara's high heels mounted the stairs. Tish stood and waited, the towel to her chin.

'I brought the wallpaper you ordered from Salisbury,' Barbara said.

'Thanks.'

'Turn round.'

Barbara took the towel and rubbed Tish's back.

'You bloody little fool.'

'It wasn't serious.'

'Are you mad? You don't *do* things like that. Look at me, Tish.'

'Perhaps two women discovered in this situation wouldn't look too good either,' she challenged.

Barbara stared at her.

'I've tried that too, love, and it's not what it's cracked up to be. I'm not interested in you. I'm just disgusted at you for the trouble you can get that kid into, Tish.'

'Everybody's good at something, Barbara,' Tish shouted.

Barbara slapped her face with the tiniest of pats, a symbolic slap with the tips of her dry fingers.

'Don't be such a bloody fool. And put your knickers on. Get dressed, you aristocratic tart.'

She was smoking in the kitchen when Tish came downstairs.

'Where is he anyway?' she asked.

Barbara pointed with her cigarette.

'Waiting outside for the boss to pick him up in the van. A bit of rain will cool him down. How long has this been going on?'

'We do it about five times a day,' Tish boasted. 'Nothing's going on, Barbara. I was just bored, that's all.'

'Bored?' Barbara asked, incredulous.

'Well, it is boring here. It would be different if you could walk outside and be by the sea, on a cliff or something. This dump would be worth doing up then. But it isn't.'

'Thank God we never had children,' Barbara said fervently.

'If you didn't, it rather puts you at a disadvantage in talking to one,' Tish replied bitterly.

Barbara drew on her cigarette.

'Don't try it on with me, darling. I can talk to you as a woman. And as a woman, I'm telling you, you're heading for grief. Screwing some poor kid who's working in your house is not good news. I'm thinking of him. What's fun for you is going to be no fun at all for him when he gets caught. If you like making an exhibition of yourself, become a stripper.'

'You're talking like a mother now.'

'I don't think so,' Barbara said. 'I like you, Tish. You frighten me, but I like you. I like you coming to the house, and I'm happy to help you fix this place up. But perhaps you should talk more to your real mother.'

'Busy,' Tish said. 'Probably on a bathroom floor in Oxford.'

'My God, Tish,' Barbara said, appalled. 'Don't you have even a shred of discretion? Can you imagine what harm talk like this can do?'

The one thing Robbie and Tish had shared in full was the cost of some really good dope, some Afghani, that he got from a pal in Salisbury. After Barbara had left, Tish sat on cement bags in what would become her sitting room and rolled a joint. She was just poking the roach with the point of one of Robbie's plasterboard nails when the door opened again and Ewan stood on the threshold, bright and clean and grinning. Tish threw the joint into the unlit hearth.

'I passed Barbara on the All Saints Road,' he said. 'And I thought I'd take a peek at what you have here. These are designer cement bags, are they?'

'Ha ha,' Tish said. 'What else do you find amusing?'

'Looks generally awful and uninhabitable. You're not sleeping here, are you? You'll catch your death of cold.'

'Has Barbara said anything?' Tish asked sharply.

'Only that you were in. I hear you bought a car.'

'In dock. Utterly useless. And I'm supposed to be in town tonight.'

'Anything special?'

'Oh, friends. Well, as a matter of fact, someone I know from Portugal days.'

'Want to borrow my car?'

Tish gaped.

'You mean it? The BMW?'

Ewan made an expansive gesture with his arm, showing much white cuff.

'This is all going to be very nice, but it's a bit of a hell-hole tonight. Run and get your things. You can change at our place and take the car on from there.'

She stood on tiptoe to kiss him and ran upstairs.

The moment she left, Ewan bent to the hearth and retrieved her joint with a half-smile. He laid it beside the papers and the film tub in which he knew there was her resin. Then, as an afterthought, he put the lot on the cluttered mantelpiece, where it shared space with cardboard screw boxes and Robbie's empty lager cans. He walked upstairs.

She was rummaging round in her gaping wardrobe. He glanced around and saw that she shared her bed with her teddy. A big old-fashioned electric fire batted out some warmth. The room smelt faintly of deodorant, or possibly hair spray. Ewan watched her, seeing her for a moment as Robbie might see her, sexual and eager, and with a suppressed petulance that only emphasized her essential weakness. The few words he had exchanged with Barbara on the road were enough for him to imagine Robbie in this bedroom all too easily.

'You really hate my father, don't you?' Tish said unexpectedly, breaking into his reverie.

'I don't think so. What put it into your head to say that now, exactly?'

'Nothing. You wear terrific clothes,' Tish added.

My God, she's actually giving me the come-on, Ewan thought, incredulous. If her father could see her, he would break her neck.

'Show me the stuff you're going to wear tonight,' he demanded.

She held up a big white shirt and matching tight pants. Ewan smiled.

'Fabulous,' he said.

Leaving, she did not bother to switch off the electric fire, nor the naked light bulbs in the kitchen or lounge. Nor did she look for her stash. Ewan patted her gently on the back, perhaps affectionately, possibly in congratulation.

'You really don't mind lending me the car?'

'We have a flat in St John's Wood,' he said. 'You can have the keys to that, too. Enjoy yourself. That's what life is for, don't you think?'

Giles listened to all this with an amused boredom. They were lolling on bench seats in a horrendously hot disco. It was hardly eleven, and the place was dead. Giles swept back his hair and yawned a theatrical yawn.

'Sounds like a bit of an idiot, this Ewan. *I* wouldn't trust you with a BMW. Funny to think of you down there in the cabbage, or whatever it is. My mother knows all about Chelworth. She claims she had a fling with your father once upon a time, but she says he was sane in those days.'

'She would, wouldn't she?' Tish retorted.

'I can't imagine anything more awful than to hang around in the country.'

'How long have you been home from Lisbon?'

'A month. I'm into property now. More money. Lots of money, actually. London's gone quite mad. I sold a one-bedroom flat for two hundred thousand today, it's good fun.'

'Did you miss me when I came home?'

'Couldn't sleep, couldn't eat,' Giles lied carelessly. 'This place is the pits. My brother comes here to pick up little girls. They go around in gangs. He has a ketch now, in Corfu, so that takes care of conversation.'

'Your brother's a disgusting pig.'

'He says the same about you. Now, Tish, my precious Tish, would you like to do some white stuff?'

Despite herself, Tish looked round cautiously.

'I don't do coke any more.'

'Of course you do. Everyone does. Sex wouldn't be the same without it.'

Tish felt his hand high up on the inside of her thigh. She hesitated.

'Where?'

'St John's Wood I should think,' Giles laughed. 'Altogether more comfy. You don't mind if I phone a few friends? We can make it a party.'

She closed her legs together, trapping his hand.

'Not a party, Giles,' she pleaded in a whisper. 'Just you and me.'

'You'll love it darling. You shine in such circumstances. Lots of fun all round.'

Walking through New College the next morning, Virginia met an elderly Fellow, a friend of Keith's, called George Wraxall.

'Our steps bend the same way,' he exclaimed. 'I must talk to Shedden about College business, and I can take the opportunity to congratulate you – that is, your husband – for the fine effort he is making with Chelworth. A tremendous house. One of my forebears married an Anstey. I don't know whether Shedden has mentioned this? There is a slight correspondence with the fourth Earl; and a small book of water-colour sketches. Very important that houses like Chelworth remain.'

Whatever business George Wraxall might have had with Keith, the more junior Fellow was surprised and annoyed to see him arrive with Virginia. He looked haggard and tight-lipped. He did not offer sherry, and Wraxall began to purse his lips.

'I was saying to Lady Hincham how very important it is to restore the fortunes of such fine houses as hers. I don't say there's an absolute treasure-house down there, but I believe there are some interesting things. And we have quite enough conference centres and private hospitals and that sort of thing, which is what would otherwise become of the place. I often muse on what a conference centre is, exactly. People hardly ever meet to confer, there or anywhere else. They should be called "prejudice reinforcement centres", or something of the sort.'

'You are probably right,' Keith said, unsmiling.

'Of course you would have it all knocked down, out of socialist spite.'

'I would have it knocked down, certainly.'

'Yes, well your abrasive honesty may stand you in better stead in Canada. Though I doubt it.'

'Canada?' Virginia asked softly.

'Our friend has applied for a Chair in Toronto. Perhaps he hasn't told you,' Wraxall said with a sly glance.

'No, he hasn't.'

'I have not applied for the Chair. I have been invited to talk to them.'

'Oh, you'll get it. They'll mess you about – there's always some damn Yugoslav they like better at first. The seductions of living in Canada would hardly merit a postcard from me. But then you are ambitious, Shedden. Are we not to have refreshment?'

'It's hardly eleven,' Keith retorted, furious.

'I think one can drink sherry at any time in the morning without seeming indulgent. But I plainly see you are not about to offer. I expect in Toronto everything stops for flapjacks and maple-leaf syrup. They were going to call the place York, you know. I believe they did, for a little while. But the Huron word is so much more amusing, don't you think?'

He went off in search of the Chaplain, in a great bluster of umbrellas and books and farewells to Virginia. Keith stood by the fireplace in his rooms, biting his lip. When the door finally closed, Virginia flipped her gloves on to her knee, unable to meet Keith's glance.

'What's a Huron?'

'I was going to tell you, Ginny.'

'Tell me now.'

'He did it deliberately.'

'Of course. And with maximum effect.'

Keith sighed.

'It really is an initial approach. They'll pay for me to fly out there.'

'When?'

'At the end of the month,' he said, utterly miserable. He stroked the cold marble of the mantelpiece and the movement of his hand scythed down a little row of invitation cards.

'You'll need earmuffs,' Virginia said with a very wobbly smile.

'The Huron word Toronto means meeting-place, Ginny. It isn't exactly the end of the world. You could come with me.'

'Isn't that a bit of an afterthought?'

He shook his head and crossed the room to take her by the shoulders. She more or less fell against him, almost unable to stand.

'I love you. I fell in love with you from the first day, and nothing will ever change that. But I can't compete. Michael doesn't come into it. If you lived in the Cowley Road and he worked shifts in a factory, I would still love you. But there would be one important difference.'

'The house.'

'Yes, of course. The house. The place. It's like a destination, a terminus. You have found where you want to be.'

'I always discourage people from telling other people what they're thinking.'

'Possibly. But in this case, it is true. I can't compete with what you have there. And I think you know it to be true.'

'And if I say it is only endurable because of also having you?'

He did not reply, but began to roll a cigarette with hands that shook.

'Perhaps it would be better to say,' Virginia choked, 'that I have just lost the best friend I ever had.'

Nine

Tish drifted in and out of sleep in Ewan and Barbara's bed in the flat in St John's Wood. She had no idea what time it was, and her whole body ached, with the centre of the pain in her lower stomach. Her clothes tangled with her sweaty limbs. For some reason she had dressed again before collapsing on to the rucked sheets; she could remember what seemed like hours and hours of walking about with nothing on at all, and a black girl called Angelica, and half a dozen others. There had been some breakages, and she had tried to stop Giles from pocketing various small things. But then there had been Giles and her on the floor of the sitting room, with the others drinking and watching, and a boy from Radley, a damn schoolboy. She could not remember his name, but only a jagged scar across his ribs, and the fact that he was sick several times. Angelica had got very stroppy with someone, and she remembered the startling damp cool of her flesh, and being interrupted by another girl wearing a dress filched from Barbara's wardrobe. Once or twice she determined to get up and clean the place, only to groan and push her face further into the pillows. The noise! They had played tapes at such incredible volume. But what could she do about it now, when she felt so ill and ashamed? It was a question she had asked before in similar circumstances.

But this time she did feel a deep and genuine shame for all the things that had happened, almost of all of which she could have prevented. That everyone had been stoned out of their brains made no real difference. She remembered now why she had dressed: she had been going to walk out on them. And that had to do with the expression on Giles's face, his little boy half-smile, as she discovered him with the kid from Radley, who knelt naked in front of him, his head lolling, his arms round Giles's thighs, sobbing like a woman.

'Well now, sweetheart.'

At first she thought she was still in a bad dream about last night, but when she opened her eyes she found two young men standing by the bed looking at her.

'Would you by any chance be Mr Ewan Chivers?'

Fuzz. Tish tried to sit up, holding the front of her shirt together.

'Piss off,' she said.

'Not a very choice remark, Mr Chivers. Get off that bed, you tart.'

The young detective reached and pulled her up by her wrist.

'Put your shoes on. There's a lot of glass about.'

His colleague picked up a pair of satin knickers by the tips of his fingers.

'These yours? Not very savoury.'

'Get out of here,' Tish said.

'We have been called to this flat by a complaint from a neighbour. She's coming home from the shops, she finds the door wide open, the bloody place has been trashed like a bunch of rock stars have passed through, and there's you laid out on the bed, Goldilocks. So if you're not Mr Chivers, you have some explaining to do.'

'Now you listen to me, creeps —'

'Name?' his partner demanded.

'I've got a perfect right to be here.'

'Handbag?'

He glanced round and found her bag. He tossed it to her.

'Open it.'

'Piss off, both of you.'

'You said that. You already said that. What was it, drugs and sex? Bit of an orgy? What you flash tarts get up to. Anything left? Or have you blasted the lot? You haven't just been having a quiet game of Trivial Pursuits, have you? Haven't got it wrong, have we?'

The detective who had asked for her name picked up the bag and emptied it on the floor with a contemptuous suddenness. Lipstick and coins, her address book, her keys and driving licence showered down.

Tish made a run for it, screaming.

They caught her quite easily by the lifts, each of them enfolding her and crushing her.

'Now don't be daft. Let's go back in and find out where you keep the stuff, who you are, what little devil put it in your head to screw up the nice man's apartment.'

'Maybe he's the one that's been banging you. You smell awful.'

'Don't mind Barry,' the other one said. 'He doesn't like your sort. We're going to get a dog in, to suss the place, and a nice butch Welsh girl called Wendy to make sure your honour is not impugned.'

She made a second break for it and ran down the service stairs, with the two detectives thundering after her. The one called Barry caught up with her and slammed into her, forcing her against the wall. She felt her spine jar. A neighbour's door opened and a terrified face peered out.

Tish began screaming and screaming and screaming. The policeman stepped back with an expression of disgust. She had wet herself.

Michael lit a cigarette with shaking hands. Jamie watched him.

'Did you ever suspect any of this?'

'What, exactly?'

'Drugs. Godammit, Jamie, you know what I'm talking about.'

'They haven't actually found any drugs.'

'Not yet. Is there anything going on between her and Chivers?'

Jamie simply gaped.

'Or Mrs Chivers?'

'I think you can count on Tish being normal,' Jamie said with a bitter little smile.

Michael made a face.

'Not entirely fair. I wasn't comparing you. I haven't criticized you for what you are, either.'

'What I am isn't a matter for criticism. I am who I am. That might be a more productive way of thinking about it.'

'Thank you for your help,' Michael said, cutting off the subject with an abrupt chopping gesture of his hand. Jamie relented.

'She likes to boast about the men in her life. This Giles is a pretty foul example. Tish is insecure, as you may have noticed. She wants to be loved. For her, to be wanted is to be loved. Has she been charged with anything?'

'Not yet,' Michael said. 'Alan Rawtenstall is there. The police are questioning her. She has asked to see a doctor.'

'Poor Tish,' Jamie said softly.

'Isn't it a case of on her own head be it?'

Jamie looked at his father.

'I was actually thinking how upset she will be to have upset you.'

Michael hesitated, then nodded. He pulled a sheet of paper towards himself.

'What is this?'

'You remember you got power to open Uncle Richard's safe deposit. I'm afraid some of the jewellery is there, but not all. There are minor gaps, but the principal one is a ring – my grandmother's – valued at three thousand pounds in 1970. Here.'

He passed his father a jeweller's valuation report. Michael scanned it quickly. The missing ring was a large cluster of diamonds with a central blue stone he remembered very well. He felt an unexpected sting of tears threatening.

'Do you remember her?'

'Granny? Hardly at all.'

'In the painting of her we have, she is shown wearing it. It was a portrait done for Coronation year. The ring was her pride and joy. It was given to a member of her family by Eugénie of France.'

'I don't know what can be done to hunt it down now.'

'Nothing,' Michael said bitterly.

He walked to the door.

'I suppose everything is just so much water under the bridge in time. Is that it?'

'It seems to be,' Jamie said carefully. 'But then I thought all this was a way to think differently.'

Michael shrugged.

'I take it your mother's in Oxford.'

'Yes,' Jamie said.

Barbara switched on the light in the sitting room and then drew the heavy velvet curtains. She brushed a speck of lint from a particular fold.

'How much damage has she done?'

Ewan shrugged.

'You shouldn't have encouraged her.'

'You seemed all in favour last night.'

Barbara shook her head.

'I feel sorry for the kid. That's a very lonely girl.'

'But with plenty of bounce.'

She studied him thoughtfully.

'You really don't know much about women, do you, Ewan? Or anybody, come to that. You know a lot about opportunity, and hitting the ball on the up, and stuff like that. But things have to be in split seconds before they interest you.'

'This is the philosophical you talking, is it?'

'Why did you encourage her? If you saw she was smoking dope when you went to the Lodge, couldn't you have put two and two together?'

'Be rational, Barbara,' Ewan laughed. 'I didn't send her up to town so that she could smash the flat up and get herself arrested.'

'No?'

'No,' Ewan said, evenly and carefully.

'But you want them suffering, all the same.'

'It's romantic novel stuff, Barbara. I don't owe them anything.'

'But you do, actually.'

He tensed, like a balloon suddenly inflated very hard.

'Be careful how you talk.'

'You owe them one or two things. Firbank brought you the odd thing along from his browsings, didn't he?'

'The only thing I ever bought from Firbank was something you made me buy. Do you remember?'

'I never wear it.'

'I hope to God you never will. Not here, not in this country.'

'Does it worry you?' Barbara asked.

'It could be misconstrued,' Ewan muttered.

She pealed with laughter.

'What an owl you are, Ewan. It could be misconstrued that you have stolen his mother's bloody jewellery.'

He jumped up and seized her by her plump wrist, making her gold watch-band skid along her arm.

'Listen to me,' he said. 'I am very patient with you. You do more or less as you like. You spend more or less what you like. Be grateful. I made a big mistake letting you talk me into that one particular thing –'

' – It was my insurance, Ewie. It still is. Against the day you suddenly decide you're married to a fat cow you can do without. That's why I wanted it, and it was the brightest thing I've ever done. I am grateful. I could be usefully grateful to you in bed, but I didn't realize, when you were climbing over me like a puppy over a sty, that you'd tire of that so quickly.'

'Is this the time to drag all that out again?'

'The very time,' Barbara snapped. 'That girl is a bomb waiting to go off. Leave her alone.'

'You don't seriously think I want her, do you?'

'Not seriously, no. Not at all, in fact. You'd be a nicer man for it. On the other hand, you're not going to interfere with her in any other way, either.'

Ewan bit a tiny jag of nail from his thumb.

'You are very clever and at the same time you're a gormless bitch, Barbara.'

'I'm also fantastic in bed,' Barbara said. 'I can give you a list of good references if you like.'

Ewan wondered, for the hundredth time, whether Russell Fairless MP figured on that list. He spat out the shred of nail. It didn't really matter, actually, but he ought to ring Russell and arrange a little lunch somewhere. Things were moving. The ice was cracking under their feet a little. He rose and kissed Barbara on her full, wet lips.

'Tonight,' he said. 'After she brings back the car.'

'She may be in the clink right now.'

'I'm not preferring charges, on the damage side of things. If they haven't found any drugs there, she's in the clear.'

When Virginia returned to Chelworth it was dark. She had driven in blinding rain down through Newbury and on to the A 303. She was crying so hard that she stopped for half an hour in a lay-by, smoking two cigarettes and staring blankly at the clock on the dashboard, ticking away the first hours of a life without Keith.

Michael told her the news as soon as she arrived.

'She was lucky. Her friends are either experienced or very greedy. They couldn't find anything in the flat. She is being released without charge.'

'How very clever of her,' Virginia said. 'I need a drink.'

'Alan is with her. He phoned to say he would put some food into her and see her home.'

'Good. When she gets back, I will cut her heart out with a blunt bread-knife. With pleasure.'

She took the gin and tonic she had poured and walked into the hall, shouting for Hodnett. He came upstairs, eyebrows raised.

'I want a fire lit in every room. I want anything that will brighten this place up. And tomorrow, I want to order some new lighting. We don't have to live in a Victorian gloom for the next six months, I assume.'

'I'll light the fires immediately, madam,' Hodnett said in his slow grave way. He turned to go, but Virginia called him back.

'I'm very sorry. I have behaved rudely. Please forgive me.'

'A good wood fire is easy to arrange, madam,' Hodnett said calmly.

Virginia walked back into the sitting room. Michael was watching and waiting.

'Don't you want to ask me why I'm not still in Oxford?'

'Virginia . . .'

'I am told by Keith this is my final destination, my terminus. That's his word, and it may have popped into his mind because the place is about as inviting and cosy as a railway station. Things are in a mess, Michael. Tish, Jamie –'

'Jamie seems extraordinarily happy.'

'That's because he's doing something that you value. That makes him content – the fact that *you* are content with him creates the illusion. In fact, blast Jamie for his prissy, *noli me tangere* role in all this.'

'All what?'

'*Tish*. Couldn't he have done something? Couldn't he have . . .'

He took the glass from her hand and refilled it.

'Tell me why you're not still in Oxford.'

'Have a guess.'

He gave a long and sympathetic glance.

'I'm sorry,' he said. 'I really am sorry.'

'He's going to Toronto. For good. That's a very elaborate way of being stood up.'

'You loved him.'

'Yes,' Virginia ground out. 'I loved him very much, and I love him tonight. And the moment he saw you, he froze, the way we all do, like a rabbit in a car headlight.'

'Can you really blame me for Keith?'

'Civilization – of your kind – was just too much for him. He's a working-class boy, remember. We were just too polite and accommodating for words. I used to think he was making a meal of that, but I can see it now all right.'

'Has he asked you to go to Canada with him?'

'Yes.'

Michael poured himself a drink and sat down in the faded blue sofa with the deep, deep cushions.

'About Tish for a moment. I know it hurts you to hear things like this, but she is strictly irrelevant. There isn't anywhere or anyone that can hold Tish. I suppose the only relevance is that she doesn't yet have a Keith. Which, I know, takes courage.'

'It takes luck,' Virginia said, feeling sick enough to faint.

'And courage.'

'It takes chance. Look, I can't stay here to find out what happens. I'm going to bed.'

Michael glanced at his watch.

'It isn't six o'clock yet,' he said gently.

Virginia groaned.

'This isn't really the time, but I want to say it before it sounds trite – I hope you don't go to Canada.'

The look on her face was stony.

'You know damn well I won't.'

Alan Rawtenstall drove Tish back to St John's Wood where the BMW was parked.

'You can count yourself lucky Chivers has good neighbours who don't panic. And you can thank *him* for not pressing charges, though he might change his mind when he sees the flat for himself. Are you going to be warm enough in that?'

'You mean do I want to reappear at Chelworth wearing it?'

Her shirt was torn at the sleeve and the first two buttons were missing. The white trousers were creased and stained. Rawtenstall pursed his lips.

'Your mother and father love you, Tish. I know you well enough to call you that, and to make that point. They'll be angry, but they'll be concerned.'

'I don't want a lecture,' Tish said, dull and spiritless.

'It's not anything that serious. Come on, buck up.'

'You weren't there.'

Alan sighed.

'The place, the people down there, need you. Your father wouldn't have got you all together again if he didn't need and love you.'

'Oh for Christ's sake,' Tish shouted. 'Let me have the keys to the car and let me get out of this shitty little conversation you want to have.'

Without a backward glance she slammed the door and strode towards the parked BMW.

The BMW left the road on a fairly sharp but not dangerous bend. It was raining heavily still, and the next car to pass was perplexed to see the undersides of trees lit as though filming were taking place. The driver was sensible enough to stop. He ran back, peering down the embankment, a sick feeling spreading in his throat. Where Tish had careered off, there was a deep set of wheel-prints that ended in space, and the yellow fracture of winter boughs from the trees round about. The car lay below him, on its back at an angle of fifty degrees. The horn was sounding and the radio was still working.

Climbing down the bank, slithering and hanging on to handfuls of wet grass, the good Samaritan came across Tish face down in the leaves. At first, as he kept explaining later to the police, he thought she was a young man with a flayed back and a leg turned on itself. But as he tried to help, he saw it was a woman.

'I told her,' he said. 'I said to her your face is all right, you haven't a mark on your face. I was trying to help the poor kid.'

When the stringer cameraman for the regional television news-room was dragged away from a golf-club dinner, the identity of the victim was a bonus on a night's pleasure ruined.

'I thought she was a lad until I turned her over,' the witness said to the national newspaper that rang him at two that morning. Though he was in pyjamas and had been given a glass of brandy by his wife, he could not sleep for seeing Tish deathly white and dribbling from the mouth. He seemed not to mind being called up in the middle of the night, and the next day was rewarded by seeing himself described as a hero. So far as he could tell from the report, Tish was still alive.

Ten

Hincham celebrated Christmas without snow. But in February, to the surprise of the locals, there was a blizzard and a fall of nearly a foot, drifting up on the hills to eight feet. The snow confounded the weather experts in the pubs by remaining right where it was. Instead of a predicted thaw, the neighbourhood recorded the sharpest frosts for forty years. Many herbaceous gardens and trees were lost in four hours of one night, when winds from Central Europe came streaming across the Channel and whipped the termperature downwards. On the farms, the cattle could not be turned out and much of the milk was poured down the drains. Schools were suspended for a week, and three people died in the town, of hypothermia.

'That just couldn't have happened, years ago,' Thornton raged. 'You don't *get* hypothermia in the countryside. It's a city disease. Country people look after each other, or they should do. There's more open hearths and chimneys among us, for one thing.'

'Then, what?' Michael asked.

'It's not that people don't care any longer, it's that the bastards actually hate each other. They're like dogs round the one bone. Something is happening in this country.'

'A favourite theme of yours,' Michael objected. 'Was there a time before this that you can remember when everybody was nice to each other? I should have liked to have been there.'

'All right, I spoke out of turn,' Thornton said.

'Don't get sullen.'

'I won't. I've cut down a couple of your dead elms and I'm paying some layabouts to log them and sack them up. If it's all the same to you, I'm going to give them away.'

'Fine. So long as there's no publicity. Do it without a song and dance.'

'Why not a song and dance? Don't we need the publicity?'

'No,' Michael said, 'we don't.'

'You're going to get a lot of interest in you. Folk want to come and see. If you're not going to open the house –'

'– You can take *that* as the one definite thing in my plans –'

'Aye, well. Folks will still want to come and see. Let me call these Chelworth Oaks.'

'They're elms.'

'It's just that you've had a mint of bad publicity since you came.'

For answer, Michael simply gave him what the Yorkshireman cheerfully called an old-fashioned look.

'How is she, your daughter?'

'On the mend.'

For a week, the only wheel-track in the snow that obliterated the drive was Thornton's. To save his own water system, Michael had installed huge industrial space heaters that roared in the corridors day and night. It was still cold enough in the house to wear a topcoat most of the time. The snow that lay hard against the walls and blanked out the lawns and terraces was sharp and glittering. Skiing out to the gates, Michael saw for the first time in his life birds fall from the sky, as if the winter itself had shot them dead. Cars that had been abandoned on Tull Hill stayed slewed this way and that for a week. They were buried up to their roofs.

Virginia thought of Toronto. She missed Keith terribly, though his wry, lengthy letters arrived regularly once a fortnight, typed up expertly on airmail paper. He wrote whether she replied punctually or not. About Tish he wrote:

I am so very pleased that she is not more badly hurt than you have described. A drunken woman at a cocktail party asked me last night why I had never married, and whether it bothered me that I had no children. For this continent, this is an unusually frank (and dangerous) way of putting things, and she was excused to me later by the host as being Italian. But Italian or not, I could not answer either of her questions satisfactorily. I thought of the only time I met Tish. She told me that she considered University a waste of time for students. I was never certain she was not pulling my leg . . . The girl who runs the Faculty Library is a bright spark, a Dane but not a gloomy one, and an expert on Where to Go in New York . . . I shall put her to the test in that area this weekend . . .

Virginia and Michael still slept apart. For as long as Tish was in hospital there were things for Virginia to do. She saw to the completion of the Lodge; and she squabbled with her daughter about the decoration of the rooms. In the house she helped Jamie in an intermittent way, and accepted Michael's invitation to choose colour schemes for those rooms that were merely unkempt and not structurally unsound. During the cold spell she sat by the fire a great deal, reading. Michael was friendly and very easy to live with, on the terms that he had proposed. They saw very few people. If she went to town, she stayed with her father in Chelsea, or sometimes at a hotel. She accepted dinner invitations from French acquaintances and friends who were passing through, and promised vaguely to go back to Paris in the spring. Most of these dinner dates were with husbands and wives. On one such occasion, she was talking animatedly to her companions when a man introduced himself at their table.

'I hope you don't mind. Tony Evrington. We're neighbours, in a way. I met you with your sister-in-law at Cissie Hollar-Wilson's, on New Year's Day.'

Virginia hesitated. The Basonpiers, with whom she was dining, waited expectantly.

'I remember,' Virginia said.

Evrington smiled.

'I have tickets for Covent Garden . . . I saw you here, and I wondered . . .'

'That's very kind of you but I don't go to the opera. But thank you for the invitation.'

Evrington inclined his head and went back to his own party. Madeleine Basonpier blew out her cheeks gently.

'Il est gentil! Virginia, you are too cruel.'

'What does he do?' her husband asked with a practical heaviness.

'I've no idea. He told me, but I've forgotten. The man he is with is our local member of parliament.'

'Ah!' Madeleine exclaimed. Every so often for the rest of the meal she stole a glance at the other table.

Virginia remembered him from New Year's Eve, but knew a great deal more of him than that by reputation. He was a type – what Ronnie Esholt called a parcel-carrier. Good-looking, single, reasonably rich, he made a style of accompanying beautiful women, preferably married women with an itch for adventure. Sometimes he did no more than carry their parcels, in Ronnie's graphic phrase – going shopping with them, taking them to Longchamps for the racing, driving them to Scotland, or whatever. Sometimes (by report) he ended up in their beds, for a few weeks or a few months. It amused Virginia to be approached by him. At the same time she was faintly alarmed. That night, at her hotel, she drank rather more brandy than she intended with Charles Basonpier, after Madeleine had gone to bed.

'Your husband is a fool,' he murmured, holding her hand in his.

'Your wife is not,' Virginia teased.

'Ah, you are such a beautiful woman, Virginia. I wish it were possible for me to make you happy. Who can understand the English?'

They kissed goodnight in the corridor, Charles standing on tiptoe to do so. In the bedroom, Virginia took off her clothes and studied herself in the long mirror for a few seconds before turning out the light. It was only for a few seconds, but that moment made her feel guilty and ashamed. It was the action of a girl, unsure of her sexual appeal.

Evrington rang her at home a week later.

'I was really ringing to find out how your daughter is.'

'She's fine. The cast on her leg comes off next week.'

'If you are in Salisbury today, can I buy you lunch?'

Virginia laughed.

'You're very immediate about these things, Mr Evrington. Now why should you want to do that?'

'I am fascinated by you,' he said. He spoke as if it were a mere pleasantry.

'It was an impulse,' he amended. 'You might respond in the same way, I thought.'

She refused lunch but accepted a drink. They met at a pub called the Flag, where the snow was still piled up in the carpark and a huge coke fire made the room smoky and soporific. Though he claimed to know the pub well, she guessed that he had never been there before. Nor did he often drink in pubs, she thought.

'I don't suppose you are a regular pub drinker either,' he complained good-humouredly.

'We own one,' Virginia said. 'I like pubs.'

He *was* good-looking, in a very obvious way, and he spoke well about things that did genuinely interest her. He was clever enough to keep the tone light and inconsequential. He drank very little. Virginia was amused by him.

'I asked my husband if he knew you,' she lied. Evrington smiled.

'What did he say?'

'He thought not.'

'You realize of course that you are both the subject of fevered speculation.'

'Oh yes?' Virginia asked.

'As to what you will do with the house,' Evrington said, sensing that he might perhaps have gone too far.

'And you're here to gather information, is that it?'

'I'm here because I would like to know you better.'

'Well,' Virginia said, 'I'm averagely unknowable. But do let's talk about the house.'

He rang her a couple of times more, and she saw him at an auction sale in March. Saw him, but did not acknowledge him with more than a nod. He raised his hand ironically, in a little gesture of defeat – or tactical withdrawal, she thought to herself, driving home through the cheerless winter lanes.

Michael continued to see Deenagh. Once a fortnight he stayed over at the flat near Chelsea Bridge. They ate out, or went to the theatre together, where he sat in contented silence or sometimes fell asleep. In the spring they flew to Tenerife for a long weekend and he sat on a balcony watching her swim and sunbathe. At night the sheets were scented with sun-oil. They talked vaguely of an extended American holiday in the summer, when they would rent a car and drive from coast to coast. Deenagh had a fierce pride in her independence and never asked for a thing from him. Sometimes he wondered exactly what it was they needed from each other. They were like well-matched boxers.

'Tennis players is neater,' Deenagh suggested with a yawn.

His hand lay on her naked stomach.

'Are you happy, Deenagh?'

'You ask that a lot. It's a vanity you have, as though you have the power to throw a goddam switch and make me happy. What difference does it make whether I'm happy or not? I'm here, aren't I?'

'Doesn't it make a difference?'

'What am I supposed to say?' she asked. 'That I've never been happier in my life? That only through knowing you have I known happiness? Am I supposed to be grateful?'

She bounded off the bed and poured herself a mineral water, her hands shaking. The sliding door to the villa balcony was open, and she walked out, the moon reflected back from her shoulders and spine.

'If you really want to know,' she said, 'I'm sick with jealousy. This isn't the first time. I've been here before, in moments like this. And maybe the truth is I deliberately find myself men who won't budge from what they've already got, just to have that delicious pain go through me. How about that? Delicious pain – doesn't that make you feel horny, Michael?'

'I want you to be happy.'

'Bullshit,' she said bitterly. 'You want me to be compliant.'

The next day she didn't go to the pool, but disappeared on a bus ride. He found her at six, drinking beer with a young German. The boy regarded Michael with blond belligerence.

'He doesn't speak English,' Deenagh said carelessly.

'Yes, I speak very good,' the boy said.

'I was worried for you.'

'Are you kidding?' Deenagh jeered.

She came back at midnight, contrite, and sat huddled in a chair, drinking brandy. Michael had difficulty in finding ordinary things to do. He took his second shower of the evening and read a chapter of a paperback. Eventually she came into the bedroom.

'I'm sorry,' she said.

'Was he fun?'

'He can dance,' she said. 'That's where I left him for dead. He's down the road at the Paradis, putting *zwei und zwei* together. I was pissed off, that was all.'

'You walked out on him?'

'The kid is twenty-two. There's something wrong with me, Michael. Every relationship I ever had was ruined by jealousy – and I don't mean of the wives. I just want to be part of the other person. I'm jealous that they are separate from me.'

'I understand that very well.'

'But you don't ever want to be anyone else.'

'I understand that it's true of you.'

She threw herself on to the bed, sobbing. When she undressed, the red weals made by the German's fingernails down her back were still there. Michael said nothing.

The spring arrived at last with a glorious flourish of clear, mild weather. It seemed then that these emotional tangles were nothing but an inevitable consequence of short days and long nights. On a single morning, there arrived such a feeling of regeneration and promise that the whole house borrowed from it. Michael opened every door and window in the place. New lists were drawn up of new priorities. Jamie emerged from the library. He and Tish played round the dewy lawns with an ancient set of golf clubs. The balmy weather continued for more than a week.

'It's good to see you goof off,' Tish said to her brother. 'I thought you were going to go straight from adolescence to middle age.'

'I feel like some creature that has just come out of hibernation.'

'The dormouse. Come and stay the night with me at the Lodge.'

He stayed two nights. During the day he painted her bathroom for her, and dug over a little border along the side of the house. At night they sat up drinking and talking. Although Michael and Virginia passed at different times in their cars, they were left alone. Jamie exulted in the season of the year.

'The sap is rising, as they say.'

'I've heard the expression.'

'You are lucky, to have this place. You've made it very nice.'

'With his money. I suppose it's an investment. He'll no doubt sell when I go.'

'Will you go?'

'Lovely though it is, Jamie dearie, I can't quite see myself here in thirty years' time as the spinster Lady Patricia Anstey.'

'Don't go.'

Tish laughed.

'You would like everything to end happily ever after, wouldn't you? Lots of teas out on the lawns during the summer, and – with a bit more central heating – a nice bookish winter. A comfy routine and no quarrels.'

'Have you read any of the books I sent down?'

'Perhaps you haven't noticed, but I am not the reading kind.'

The scar from her accident ran down the length of her shin. She still walked with a limp. Running from her hip bone to the small of her back was a second disfiguring snake of white tissue. He discovered she was secretly exercising with weights; but all the same she looked thin and a good four or five years older since the accident.

'I think you should stay, at least for a while.'

'And you,' Tish countered. 'How about you? Don't you have a life of your own any longer? Don't you have a future of your own? It's not exactly made for lovers, this place, is it?'

'Don't know. Not my area of expertise.'

Tish kissed him on the cheek.

'Well, you can't exactly bring home a friend, can you?'

'I'll tell you if I ever find one.'

Late that night, cleaning his teeth in the bathroom that smelt of paint, he heard her crying on the other side of the wall. He hesitated at her door but went on to his own bedroom, crisp and neat, and empty. The books he had sent down from Chelworth were stacked against the wall in little reproving piles. He tumbled into bed, and dreamed of New York. Not about Stuart, but Tish, in a wonderful apartment on the East Side and with a career in television. She was the most highly paid woman in America. To Jamie's dismay, she had undergone surgery to make a scar on her left side identical to the one on the other side from the car crash. Her lover was Ewan Chivers, a man Jamie had hardly ever met in his waking life. But all this was the grand action of the dream, the drama at which he was no more than a spectator – a fascinated and horrified one. He himself was looking for Stuart, who he secretly knew was already dead.

Eleven

Each year the Hincham Civic Society organized a Festival that took its place in a sprawling annual calendar of fêtes and bazaars, gymkhanas and gala days. The Hincham Arts Festival got most of its support from the better-off residents, the retired, and the artistic fringe of Salisbury. Almost every day in summer when the weather was fine, Michael could find elderly men and women sitting outside their cars on the verges of the roads around Chelworth, or just inside his fields, sketching in water colours. Many of these sketches found their way into mounts and frames and were hung in the mammoth Festival Exhibition. There they joined sullen nudes executed in oils, incoherent abstracts, and portraits of children, grandchildren, dogs and (from a cracked young woman) the Royal Family.

It was a Festival that drew in most of the life of the little town. The Civic Society was perhaps a little dismayed at the range of things on offer, which grew each year. The Committee had some austere ideas in the beginning, but reckoned without the strong energies of the community it wished to enlighten. To the High Art of the original programme had been added over the years martial arts, art for the disabled, a flower and vegetable show, and a dance display. There was a schoolteacher from All Saints who ran the films, and Thornton told Michael of the redoubtable old Dr Wallingford, whose maps and drawings of prehistoric Hincham were a regular exhibit of the Festival.

'Quite crazy, but a fine scholar. I think well of him. You could have him up here at the Hall, perhaps. Nobody ever goes to his exhibition anyway, and it would look nice in your place.'

'I'd rather not.'

'Man after your own heart,' Thornton teased slyly. 'Hasn't got a friend in the world. He's the only man in step. You should see some of the articles he's had printed, tearing the backside out of other prehistorians.'

'Don't I have a friend in the world?'

'A man unto himself,' Thornton amended. 'How does that sound?'

'Not much better. No, Peter. The Festival approached me in the spring, and I sent a donation. Let's leave it at that.'

He mentioned some of this after dinner that night. The file of letters enquiring about the Hall was on his lap.

'I can quite see how the upper class gets its reputation for loftiness. None of these people seem to grasp that we actually live here, and consequently – for example – an exhibition by the Hincham Caged Bird Society in the house and grounds isn't quite an honour bestowed.'

'What else have we had?'

'Some madman called Donatip wants to set off in a balloon from the front pasture.'

'I would like that,' Virginia protested mildly. 'I do think we should begin to accept some of these things. You had the Venture Scouts at Easter, for example.'

'Never again! Tish, what do you say?'

She was sulking, reading a magazine. She shrugged without looking up.

'The Hincham Sun Club,' Michael went on, riffling through the file, 'would like to rent a wood near the river. Jamie?'

'Nudists are a bit boring.'

'Here's another one. The North Wilts Model Aero Club, for a flying display.'

'I would prefer the nudists,' Virginia said.

'The Sarum Game Fair.'

'I would prefer the model aeroplanes,' Jamie murmured.

Tish threw down her magazine.

'I think it's all revolting. All of it. In any other European country they wouldn't dare ask. They'd be shot for crossing the boundary.'

'I didn't know that,' Michael said gravely.

'I would shoot them. Goodnight.'

She jumped up and, still limping a little, walked from the room, on her way back down to the Lodge. There was a short silence.

'Why don't we try this Dr Wallingford?' Virginia asked in a careful voice. Jamie laughed.

'Oh, what enormous breeding, never to be upset by bad manners. Shall I go after her?'

'Do you know what's wrong?'

'Nothing special.'

'I imagine she can't stand it here,' Michael said.

This time the silence was longer.

After Jamie had gone to bed, Virginia lingered. It was cathedral quiet. The room they sat in had been refurbished, and there was a very pleasant man from a local painting and decorating firm who had been engaged by Michael to bring the huge cube entrance hall up to scratch. It was an agreeable feeling, now that the days were longer and the house warmed through, to have signs of change and improvement all about them. She watched Michael working methodically and quickly through piles of bills and correspondence.

'You're enjoying yourself enormously, aren't you?'

He laid down his pen.

'For the first time in a very long time. I love it here. I think it's mellowed me.'

'You seem very mellow.'

'We all do, except for Tish. It was a bad start, I grant you, and having all these to-dos with Chivers and the rest of it hasn't helped. But Thornton's very good, you know. Perhaps we don't entertain enough, but I know you're not that keen.'

'It could be seen as a duty,' she said, mildly enough.

'I don't want you to be dutiful. I want you to be happy. When we have things as we want them, perhaps we can do more. Bill wants me to join him in the Lords, for example. That might change things.'

'All this stuff about the Festival, though. I know it's small beer, but doesn't it seem like an invitation to belong?'

'How can we, Ginny? I mean truthfully? We could make ourselves patrons, we could have the Committee out here a couple of times a year, but where would that get us? I know nothing at all about that side of England, and I'm not terribly sure I'm missing a lot.'

'This is enough, is it?'

The tone of her question made him go to bed feeling troubled. Once Deenagh had suggested that he was interested in her purely out of symmetry, to balance out Virginia and Keith. Now that Keith was gone, there was a lopsidedness, apparent every time they said goodnight and went to their separate rooms.

Michael was in a box. How difficult it was, once the gap was exposed in a marriage, to bridge that gap and make things over anew. The planning, scheming side of him said that he was cautious with Virginia out of respect for her. The more honest emotion was that he was besotted with Deenagh, but had no real plan and retreated into the affairs of the house as a form of escape. In a sense, he had widowed both women out of a fear of failing them. Virginia was a phone call away. So he dialled.

'It's me.'

'You don't say,' she said. 'I was the first to applaud the installation of an internal telephone, but I resent being rung up when the door to my room is only a few yards away. I don't lock it at night, you know.'

The line was disconnected with a click. Michael dropped his own receiver on to the cradle and fell back on to the bed, smoking and listening to the house creak and sigh, a set of little noises he had accustomed himself to, and now could not sleep without numbering.

Virginia rang Tony Evrington the next morning. As she was careful to explain, the call was made out of pure spite. She needed to get away from Chelworth for a day. More than that, she was angry with Michael.

'Does that mean you'll tell him where you're going?'

'If you like.'

Evrington laughed.

'It isn't really what *I* want, is it? I'd like it if you came here. And stayed as long as you wish. Perhaps you'd enjoy that. As well as achieving your other objectives.'

Virginia wrinkled her nose. He had a little boy's impudence that grated. For a moment she thought of making a hasty U-turn and ringing off.

'You don't have to compromise your womanly virtue,' he added. 'I'm quite a good listener, if that's what you want.'

'Where can we meet? And be sensible.'

'I'll meet you in Blandford. In an hour and a half.'

He turned up looking rather dishy in a linen suit. He kissed her cheek.

'We can eat, if you like, or we can walk.'

'Walk.'

They drove in his car to a place where they could walk along the banks of the Stour for a mile or so. She let him kiss her. His broad hand stroked her back. She found herself laying her head against his chest.

'Tell me what is wrong.'

'No,' Virginia said. 'I'm using you, that is what is wrong.'

'I thought Michael had no interest in you. I thought that was the point.'

'I'm still using you. How many times have you done this? Flirted your way into someone else's marriage?'

'Does it matter? I like you very much and I would like to go to bed with you. You affect a certain toughness. I simply tell you what I would like. In that sense, I'm not flirting at all. And so do, please, use me.'

She laughed, in spite of herself.

'What a terrible thing, to be Tony Evrington. Haven't some of your other ladies fallen in love with you?'

'I've no idea,' he said with stunning simplicity.

In the end they did drive back to his house. Virginia reflected that he might have anticipated they would from the very first moment she announced herself on the telephone. The thought did nothing to cheer her up. His taste in decor and furnishings was careful, almost prissy. There was actually a silver cornet laid beside his stereo equipment.

'Can you play this?'

'Of course not,' he said.

'It's just for effect.'

'Is that a sneer?'

'Yes,' she said miserably.

'Listen to me,' he said. 'You're super-intelligent, everybody says so. You're also very sexual. Whatever the word is. Sexy, if you like. Your husband is a fool for not noticing that you still love him. But it's no part of my pleasure in life to help husbands find their wives again.'

'Is this a set speech? Do you make this to all your conquests?'

He glanced at his watch.

'It's six. I'm going to cook, and then I want you to stay the night. I pay myself the compliment, Virginia, of realizing that intimacy has already taken place. With or without the bedroom. That's true, isn't it?'

She looked at him for a long time, unsmiling.

'Yes,' she said.

She left while he was in the kitchen, without saying goodbye. She stopped at a pub on the way home and had a large vodka and tonic. Then, alarmed at the events of the day, and hungry into the bargain, she stayed on to eat a perfectly disgusting chicken Kiev in the restaurant part of the pub, where some idiot called Nino held sway. He came and sat at her table for a moment or two.

'Now, my darling, have you enjoyed your meal?'

'Did you cook it?'

'Yes, I cook. Everybody who comes to Nino's, I give them a rose to remember him by.'

'I shall remember your cooking for a very long time without your having to trouble with the rose,' Virginia said. 'Perhaps you would be happier as a florist.'

That night, the Hincham Memorial Hall burned down. People going to school or work in the morning, under the huge banner reading 'Hincham Arts Festival', that spanned the streets, saw one of the prime venues reduced to a pile of ash and charred wood. Michael was called away from a meeting in the office with Jim Hodnett, where they were discussing wines, to meet a woebegone figure standing with Jamie in the hall.

'This is Mr Gordon Padgett, the Chairman of the Arts Festival.'

'We've met,' Michael said with hearty politeness. 'How are things? Everything getting on like a house on fire?'

It took a little persuading to convince Padgett that he had not heard the news, and that the remark was not an ill-judged joke.

'Just a week to go, you see, and the Festival depends on that place. I mean we have long ago sold tickets to stuff that was going to be in there. The Kalashnikov Theatre, for example.'

Michael inclined his head quizzically.

'From London,' Padgett explained. 'Prior to their appearance at Edinburgh this year. The Fringe, and so on. Then there's Radical Paratroop Troupe. They're women, of course. They were also in there.'

'It all sounds very . . .' Michael searched for the right word.

'We have more than a few new departures this year,' Padgett said stiffly. 'But there was an Evening with Marvin Hamlisch booked there too.'

'Marvin Hamlisch!' Jamie exclaimed wonderingly.

'The W I Choir. We may be able to put them in the Three Bells, if Mrs Harper agrees and we can shift the darts to an away venue. But one way and another, we're in a bit of a state.'

'How dreadful for you. What can I do?'

When Virginia went to town, she was one of the many to inspect the ruins of the Memorial Hall at first hand. There she met Mr Blackwell, the gentle and dotty old man who was decorating for them up at Chelworth. She offered him a lift. He spread a newspaper on the seat before slumping down in utter dejection.

'This is a tragedy for the arts in Hincham, milady. There's no other word for it.'

'It must be. Are you connected with the Festival, Mr Blackwell?'

'I was Secretary of the Hincham Concert Society for eight years, before the thing was wound up.'

'That's why you are always whistling Mozart!'

'That you recognize it does you credit, if I may say so. Though of course I would expect it from you. But elsewhere I might as well be whistling anything at all.'

'How fascinating. Do you play?'

'Self-taught. I play the viola. I also made the instrument myself. But I'm afraid to say that things have taken a sorry turn in Festival affairs in recent years. We are shabby custodians of the classical in

Hincham nowadays, no doubt about that. Folk would rather have a bit of a film about Turkish peasants, like the star offering last year, than listen to chamber music.'

'Is there none, then?'

'Oh there is. The Leopold Quartet. There always will be some music for as long as I draw breath. But it's a battle. There's a man called Padgett –'

'I think my husband sent him a donation.'

'That was gracious,' Mr Blackwell said to the floor of the car without enthusiasm. 'Padgett is a schoolteacher. I've heard it said he's competent enough. But he doesn't have the feel for the thing. Let the Turks watch their own films, I say.'

'I think I saw the film you're talking about in Paris,' Virginia said weakly.

'Ah well, France! They're all film-barmy there, aren't they? Well, I don't consider Mozart to have been surpassed in any art, in any age. And that has put me at loggerheads with Gordon P. Padgett.'

With nice timing, they passed Padgett leaving the grounds of Chelworth. He goggled in at the car, but Mr Blackwell looked away, his chin on his hands, staring back through the centuries. Virginia was delighted, and laughed.

'They want me to put some awful theatre lot on here,' Michael complained when she left Blackwell stirring his paint and went in search of coffee.

'You could have Marvin Hamlisch,' Jamie objected. 'He was on offer.'

'They've got *Marvin Hamlisch* to come to the Hincham Festival?'

'As rendered by the W I Choir.'

'I'm not sure that wouldn't be preferable to the Kalashnikov Theatre,' Michael groaned. 'Anyway, the answer is no! No to the lot of them! I gave a donation to the thing, and I'll donate to the rebuilding of the Memorial Hall, if it comes to that. But I don't want to get involved in any other way.'

Tish swam her twentieth length in the pool at Roman Arches and stopped abruptly. Her legs felt like lead. She waded to the steps as Barbara Chivers watched her thoughtfully.

She had come out of the crash with a broken arm and leg, three cracked ribs and lacerations. For three days she was suspected of having broken her back. Nor was she a good patient. In the side ward where she was nursed the other women did not like her because of her disinclination to communicate with them in any way. Tish refused her father's offer of a private bed and toughed it out. Only when it came to physiotherapy did she find someone to whom she could respond. She exercised until she was fit to drop. Barbara went to see her more often than anyone, and when she came out of hospital bullied her into being positive. And Tish was changed – quieter, less sulky, tougher. The old assertiveness was there, but with a new direction. Barbara knew what all that cost in pride.

'Want a hand out?'

'I can manage.'

Barbara rose and poured out two orange juices.

'You're tough, kid, I'll give you that. You don't give up. The scar on your back looks much better. In fact you look pretty wonderful, top to toe. Ewan will be sorry to have missed you.'

'Where is he, exactly?'

'He's halfway up Mount Kilimanjaro by now, or should be. Shooting things and buying things. Quite a property speculation, Mount Kilimanjaro, as it turns out. Although he'd be better at selling than buying. Come and flop out.'

'Do you love him?' Tish asked suddenly.

'Of course I do, darling. It's my job.'

'Don't joke.'

'I'm not joking. Anyway, it's none of your business. But you've stopped liking him, haven't you?'

'He never speaks to me,' Tish blustered.

'It's all right,' Barbara said. 'Relax, Tish. I know you've seen him in London a couple of times since the accident, and I know without asking how it went. Ewan isn't chasing you because he's a randy old devil.'

'He isn't chasing me at all.'

'What you have to realize is that everything's an investment with Ewan. Including people. I should know. I may be turning into a bit of a drunken old cow, but when Ewan was starting out and looking for what impressed the boys, he looked no further than these.'

She bounced her breasts cheerfully.

'That was in the days when blondes were supposed to be dumb, of course. He picked the English National Champion, or thought he did. And I thought, what the hell. A couple of kids, a house to look after, I'll have plenty of real things to occupy my mind.'

She looked back at the childless house she owned now, where the Filipino maid was moving languorously behind the reflected image of the garden, and sighed.

'Are you training for the fun of it, or are you getting ready to sling your hook?'

'You're ten times as bright as he is,' Tish said.

'He knows that, darling. That's why I get such a hard time. But it's nice to have him out of the way for a while. I'm not exactly at a loose end in the evenings.'

Tish cycled back from Barbara's with her costume hung over the handlebars of the bike. Her body ached, but she had the pleasant feeling of having cheated boredom and despair. As soon as she got in, she took out the plain postcards she had stolen from Michael's office and began writing. And that is where he found her, a bottle of wine in his hand.

'I came to see how you are.'

She pushed the cards away and laid down her pen.

'I'm sorry I was so stuffy last night. Would you like to go for a walk?'

'Yes,' Michael said, surprised.

They climbed into a tussocky field and strolled together. Tish bent and stuck a crow feather upright in the ground.

'Who taught you to do that?'

'You did,' she said. 'Look, you might as well know — I'm scribbling to everyone else. I've been offered a job on a boat. Well, I haven't actually been offered it, but I'm meeting the owner in Paris. It's a ketch, in Marseilles. He wants a crew to sail it to Antigua. It was advertised in the yachting press, and I've made a few enquiries. It seems all right.'

Michael took her hand.

'Would that make you happy?'

'I do like it here. I know you don't believe me, but I do. It just isn't for me, yet. Or I'm not ready for it or something. Perhaps one day. I'm not rejecting you, is what I'm trying to say.'

'I couldn't really blame you if you did.'

'Yes you could. I have this horror of joining in.'

Michael had a lump in his throat.

Before Mr Blackwell put away his dustsheets for the evening, Virginia told him that the Hall would very much welcome the Leopold Quartet in any reorganization of the Festival schedules caused by the fire.

'In fact,' she said, 'I would rather insist that we are considered.'

Blackwell studied his fingernails.

'That would be a very difficult thing to arrange,' he muttered. 'The problem is that Gordon Padgett and me are not what you might call bosom pals.'

'But you used to be Secretary of the Concert Society. Talk to them.'

'I was sacked,' Blackwell said miserably. 'On an issue of musical taste. A Liszt recital.'

'Mr Blackwell, I am offering what I hope might be thought the perfect venue for the playing of chamber music.'

'Just so,' the painter said.

At that very moment, Gordon Padgett was trying not to look down the front of Barbara's blouse at Roman Arches, a glass of white wine held like a time bomb in his fingers.

'What sort of music does this lot play?' Barbara asked.

'They're very highly regarded.'

'You're looking at a woman who thinks Barry Manilow is pretty okay.'

'It's just that we need to find them somewhere nice,' Padgett said desperately. 'They're playing Haydn, Mozart and Shostakovich.'

Barbara gazed at him fondly.

'Are they? And you think they'd knock that off in here without trouble, do you? What about Chelworth? I bet you've been up there first.'

'Lord Hincham didn't want to know.'

'Showed you the door, did he?'

'More or less.'

'I see,' Barbara said slowly. She smiled. 'What do you make of him, Mr Padgett?'

'Um, how do you mean, exactly?'

'Drink your wine. You can have them here if you like. I take it they're house-trained?'

'They've been on Radio Three.'

'That probably means more to you than it does to me. Sold any tickets yet?'

'It's always a last-minute rush with this sort of thing,' Padgett said, bringing his nose out of his wine glass. Trying to visualize the Leopold in this room playing to forty people in a week's time, vied with a vision of Barbara Chivers without her clothes on, swimming with him in the pool outside, and to hell with the arts for that year or any other.

Virginia wrote to Tony. It was a difficult letter and involved many drafts. However she phrased it, the sense of fairness and obligation to others that had driven her to write came out as feminine weakness. This annoyed her but was also faintly alarming.

'What I would like you to see,' she wrote, 'is that some of me is very lonely. When I think about you in a positive way, I realize you understand that. I came to Chelworth with my eyes wide open and what finally happened between me and Keith was also easy to predict. All the same, I miss him terribly and it does not seem fair to punish you for that. In a way, that's what I have done. I apologize. You're a nice man in your own right and it was bitchy of me to walk out on you. I'm not asking to be taken back or anything of that sort, but I would not want to end on quite such a sour note. Thanks for the various offers . . . Take care . . .'

As often happens, the moment she posted it she was filled with an urgent regret for having written the letter at all. But after a day or two, when nothing happened, she heaved a sigh of relief, for she was honest enough to realize that it was not Tony Evrington she was trying to punish, but Michael. This was an uncomfortable truth about which she could speak to no one, least of all him.

Twelve

The Leopold were performing in Alnwick, in Northumberland, and so remained in happy ignorance of the storm that was breaking three hundred miles away as Virginia and Barbara wrestled over who should have them when they came down to play at the Hincham Festival. Virginia's agent in the matter, Mr Blackwell, invited Gordon Padgett to his cottage for a conference.

'Thanks to you,' Padgett said bitterly, 'the situation couldn't be worse. It's all very well saying they want this thing up at the Hall, but I have already offered it to Barbara, to Mrs Chivers,' he amended hastily. 'And I'm going flat out, remember, with a hundred other things. This isn't the only item in the Festival programme.'

'But it is the most important.'

'It is to you,' Padgett said, exasperated.

'This Kalashnikov lot will put you behind bars, by all accounts.'

'What have you heard?' Padgett demanded.

'Jack Freeson's boy is helping with the lighting. He says it's a hundred-per-cent pornographic.'

'What would Roger Freeson know about pornography?'

'Pretty well everything,' Mr Blackwell asserted mildly. 'Bit of an expert in that line.'

'Oh my God,' Padgett said.

'I think the Leopold should be asked where *they* want to play. They're not students, you know. They're professional musicians, who deserve the best acoustics.'

'Mrs Chivers has sent cards out.'

'Lady Hincham has ordered chairs.'

Michael recounted these episodes to Deenagh at the Chelsea flat.

'What makes it worse is that I had already hired a madman called Donatip to make a balloon ascent from the front pasture, as a sort of sop to Ginny. She then wins the battle with Barbara, and we have both on the same evening.'

'Terrific,' Deenagh said sullenly.

'What's the matter, Deenagh?'

'I just love all the village gossip. It puts me in the picture. I feel – I almost feel – I live there myself.'

Michael gave a rueful little shrug.

'I'm sorry.'

'What's to be sorry about? It's all such jolly fun, and terribly English, don't you know it?'

'We're going to quarrel.'

'You think so? I flew to Amsterdam last week, to authenticate a drawing. Stayed out, did a lot of walking. Did a lot of thinking, Michael.'

'You really are angry.'

'Yes. But that's not what I've been thinking about.'

'About us.'

'About *me*,' Deenagh said. 'What is this us? I haven't seen you for three weeks. Us doesn't figure. I've been thinking about myself . . . and if you politely offer me a drink right now, I'm going to scream.'

An hour earlier they had made love. This present mood startled Michael. He felt a flutter of urgent wings in his chest.

'Say what you want.'

She studied him. Her gaze was sombre, and also somehow, weary.

'You're a very nice man, a bit of a collector's item for the present age. We've had a year. It's been a year of Sundays. But I can't go on any longer. I know what you like to eat, what you like to do in bed, what you want out of life. But knowing isn't having. I know you very well, and have you maybe once a month. You're very scrupulous – you never talk about Virginia, and you try not to talk about Chelworth all that much. But you're growing roots there.'

'That's pretty inevitable.'

'Sure. But when I first met you, you were a man in a hurry.'

'I have asked you, always, to be patient.'

131

'If you think I haven't been, you should try another mistress. Maybe you're at your best with orientals: they like things to be inscrutable, don't they?'

'Would that count as a cheap shot?'

'Yeah,' Deenagh said, aggressively. 'Sure. I feel sorry for that Rosie kid. I feel sorrier for your wife. I feel sorriest of all for myself. It's over, Michael. I don't want to see you again.'

Michael shook his head.

'No.'

'That's always been my only card. You don't tell me. I tell you.'

'Listen, I can make it work.'

'It works now,' Deenagh said. 'But I want out.'

She fished in her handbag and dropped the keys to the flat on the coffee table. The gesture seemed to upset her and she picked them up again and laid them gently on the sofa.

'If you're looking for cheap shots, there's one. I'm ashamed. I wanted to hurt you like hell, to make your teeth ache with it, and then suddenly I'm ashamed.'

'Please don't be,' Michael said with a sudden rush of formality to his voice. He walked to the kitchen to open some white wine. When he came back into the room, she had gone. The key was where she had left it. He stood at the window, watching and waiting. Eventually she came into sight on the pavement below, tall and slim and desirable. She hailed a cab and one slewed to the kerb in an instant. She climbed inside and it was like stepping through a magic mirror. The cab pulled away into the anonymity of the traffic and he knew he had lost her for ever.

The enormity of it all was muddled up in his mind with the brevity with which it had happened. He pushed away the wine untasted and poured himself a large whisky. When he walked to the bedroom, the sheets were still rumpled, still warm to his touch. In the bathroom there was the scent of her perfume. He opened the airing cupboard. A little tangle of her bras and knickers sat on top of the hot water tank. He pulled them out and flung them to the floor. On the back of the door hung her dressing gown. He ripped it from the hook and flung it down. He found himself in the kitchen, as if he had been teleported there from the bedroom. He opened the overhead cupboards and, with his forearm, swept her herbs and spices on to the work surface. A bottle of wine vinegar rolled, hesitated, and then crashed to the floor.

He walked into the West End. It was one of those overcast evenings when London looks at its least appealing. Wind stirred the grit on the pavements and there was a tide-mark of litter against the advertising hoardings, as though the world had eaten the soft promises of the advertisers and then spat out the rind. Michael walked swiftly, too swiftly. The whisky he had drunk burned his throat. He might have found a safe haven with Bill Toller in the Tite Street flat, where the old man was undoubtedly at home in surroundings of calm, but it was not the right night for that. Some of Lord Toller's special concern, the homeless and the utterly bereft, were about on the streets, some of them reeling towards this tall, elegant man who was unaccountably walking amongst them as though he had a great and urgent purpose.

The West End was crammed with tourists. London girls with impossibly short skirts and bare legs clattered past on cheap and scuffed high heels. In their wake were Americans, Australians, Japanese, Italians, all races of men, in a travesty of promenade. Every so often music would blare out of shops and clubs, and there was always a lunatic about with a huge portable tape machine, drifting along to the sound of rock and roll much as Donatip and his balloon were at the mercy of the winds. The attractions of the city – its pleasures – were a set of cheap thrills, impossibly marked up in price. People like Michael, from his class or with his money, were nowhere to be seen on foot. They were carried about in cabs or limousines, insulated from the scene by glass, as they might be underwater explorers scudding through the shallows of a lagoon. Michael was with the shoals of little fish, swimming this way and that, flirting with their predators, moving aimlessly.

He started drinking at a pub in Orange Street, behind the National Gallery. There was no room to sit down, and had he wanted to fall into conversation with anyone he could not have been heard for the noise of the juke-box. In this pub, some of the little fishes had found what amounted to a hole in the rocks. Young people – some of them very young – stood about with pints of lager in their hands. One whole table was piled high with backpacks and sweaters. The boys were well on the way to being drunk. Their girls wore crisp white cotton tee-shirts and baggy trousers, and looked about them. At one end of the bar some of the regular drinkers, older men, sat watching without humour, their eyes cold and expressionless.

He walked across to Long Acre, where he knew a pub from long, long ago. He talked to a former market porter. They drank steadily and peaceably and then Michael's new friend rolled him a cigarette.

'This bleeding country is on its knees. They give you the stuff about how rich we are an' how lucky we are. Don't you believe it. We're on a technical k.o. decision here.'

'Did you box, as a boy?'

'I was boxing before you was born, my son. I got six kids, I got eleven grandchildren, and if I couldn't drink this stuff, I wouldn't have a reason to get up in the morning. Know what I mean?'

'Is your wife alive?'

'She was this morning,' Michael's companion said humorously. 'And your wife, how's she?'

'Fine.'

The old man rapped on the bar counter once with a coin.

'I gave up trying to understand it long ago,' he said. 'You can have a few moments, like, with what you've got between your legs, and the rest is a bloody mystery.'

'That's the biggest mystery of all.'

'I dare say.'

It was appreciably cooler out on the streets. He felt the sweat dry on his back. He wished he had eaten something, but could not bring himself to eat alone now. On an impulse, he caught a taxi in Cambridge Circus and gave directions to his club. For thirty years he had been a member, without ever staying overnight or making more use of it than as a handy rendezvous on his business trips to England. Since coming home he had gone there for tea on a couple of occasions. The porter nevertheless greeted him as though they had met the previous day. Michael felt himself sway a little. He signed the day-book and laid down the pen.

'Is there anyone in tonight?'

'None that you know well, milord. Mr Stuyvesant, the American gentleman, was through here as the guest of Lord Rougemont a week or so ago, and asked to be remembered. Lord Toller dined tonight with Lord Stanedge.'

'Are they still here?'

'I believe they had business in the House of Lords, sir.'

The porter kept up a wooden face as Michael nodded and made his way to the cloakrooms, a little unsteady on his feet. Once there, he splashed cold water on his face and drank a mouthful from his cupped hand. He accepted a towel passed to him by an elderly attendant.

'A change in the weather, sir. They say it will rain for Wimbledon tomorrow.'

'Wimbledon?'

'Yessir. The Men's Quarter Finals.'

'Do you follow it?'

'One has a passing interest,' the cloakroom attendant said equably.

The club's main room was deserted, save for a man Michael did not know who was reading a paper. He tugged on a bell-pull and ordered a large whisky. When it came and he had signed for it, he wandered through to the card room.

'Bloody hell! Hincham! A drunk Hincham!'

Michael peered through the gloom and frowned.

'Hullo Toby.'

Toby Marchness was sitting with two others, one of whom Michael recognized as a man called Watson, a racehorse-owner he had met in Hong Kong. The third man was introduced as David Marbeck.

'Hincham's drunk,' Marchness said. 'I know that because I am plastered myself. My senses are alerted. We have been trying to play three-handed bridge, d'you see. A cruel and not very exacting way of passing the evening. Where've you been, Hincham?'

'Nowhere special.'

'That's it, be outgoing and friendly. Hincham hates his own class, did you know? Was that way inclined at school, I remember.'

'Were you in my class at school? I don't remember.'

Marbeck laughed. Toby Marchness blinked for a second or two.

'And then he inherited. This is the man I was telling you about, in fact. We've been talking about you. Your damn fool brother-in-law was in here a few nights ago, telling us all about you.'

'To what end?'

'He was saying what a shit you are,' Marchness said. 'The village Lord Bountiful, the panto Baron, that sort of thing. Hincham has a rather ordinary house near Salisbury, you know.'

'You are neighbours in fact,' Watson supplied.

'Oh Christ, he's far too grand to have neighbours.'

'Would you like to play cards?' Marbeck asked.

'That's for money,' Toby said.

'Poker.'

'Bit of a cad's game, what?'

They played for an hour and a half, and Watson won a thousand pounds while Toby Marchness kept up an incessant monologue. Michael remembered him well from school days. Marchness had then been a scratch golfer and a good middle-order bat. Those days had long fled. He was now an out-of-breath, overweight braggart with a second wife half his age, and a huge house so completely turned over to commercial exploitation that he was really no more than a fractious and meddling tenant in it. His new wife had two children under three years of age.

'And you, Hincham. How's your whore? The American one, not the Chinese.'

Michael's mind swam back into focus. He looked up from his cards. The other two men exchanged glances.

'He is very drunk,' Watson said quietly.

'Let him say what he wants.'

'Bloody decent of you,' Marchness sneered. 'I wouldn't touch it with a barge-pole myself. Don't like the arty types. You're a bit of a loser in that respect. She's a damn good poke, I understand, if you can get her to stop talking.'

Michael threw down his hand as Marchness looked around him, grinning.

'But, while you have been clamping turnips and gazing in wonder at the family silver, old darling, your whore has been much engaged with Eddie Picton-Ellis. He's been banging her for years, when it suits. She can't get enough. Or didn't you know?'

Michael pushed back his chair.

'Excuse me,' he said to the other two. Marchness threw down his own hand of cards.

'Oh bloody hell,' he said in drunken triumph. 'Don't go.'

When Michael walked through the main room, the man who had been reading the paper was still there, still engrossed. It seemed incredible, surrealistic. Michael brushed a table with his knee and stumbled slightly. The member looked up in quiet disdain.

He asked the porter to fetch him a cab and waited in the foyer. Watson joined him there.

'Toby is quite exceptionally drunk. If you would come back in for a few moments, he will make amends.'

'I don't think so.'

'Marbeck and I would appreciate it.'

'Thank you for the game,' Michael said.

In the cab, he held on to the plastic seat with both fists, the streets slurring past the windows.

There was music coming from behind the front door of the flat and he thought for an irrational moment that it might be Deenagh. It was Tish, looking sheepish.

'Jamie lent me his key,' she said. 'Is that all right?'

Michael leaned back against the wall.

'Is that Louis Armstrong? Turn the volume up.'

'Are you all right?'

'Turn up the volume and fetch me some bin-liners from the kitchen.'

He went into the bedroom and stripped the wardrobes of anything that was Deenagh's. Tish watched him from the doorway.

'Do as I say!' Michael bellowed.

He sat in the ruination of Deenagh's clothes, sobbing. When he went into the little sitting room, Tish was huddled with her legs under her, terrified.

'You can probably see I am drunk. I'm sorry, I didn't mean to frighten you.'

'Do you want to talk?'

'No. Rosie – the girl you were so keen to know about – my Chinese whore – had parents, of course. He was a clerk in the police headquarters, she . . . worked in a shop. You can imagine, we met seldom. Whenever we did there was great politeness and, on both sides, the most terrific disdain. I was always good at that, but Rosie's parents were experts. Well-qualified experts.'

'I'm your daughter. Remember? I've no complaints. Who taught me to pick up loose feathers in a field and stick them in the ground?'

'See a feather, pick it up, all the day you'll have good luck.'

'You taught me that. I swim because you taught me. I'm not afraid of the dark because you taught me not to be. I can keep going until I drop, because you taught me.'

Michael felt a wave of misery breaking over him like a salt sea.

'I am most incredibly drunk, Tish,' he whispered.

He did not see the hurt in her eyes. But even if he had, there was nothing he could do. He stumbled into the bedroom, kicked off his shoes and slept. Where she slept, what she knew, what she thought, he did not know.

Thirteen

Tish was on her way to Paris. She left behind her what at first seemed a minor problem of etiquette. Just before setting off to spend the night at Michael's flat she had been interrupted by a knock at the door of the Lodge. Standing on the step was someone she instantly recognized and instantly embraced.

'Dibs! What on earth are you doing here?' Her eye caught sight of Dibs's car. 'And a 2cv! Wonderful! Classic!'

She had been at school with the plump, painfully shy Dibs and, as sometimes happens, they had become unlikely but inseparable friends.

'I'm playing at the Festival.'

'You are? How fantastic!'

'I wrote to you,' Dibs objected faintly. 'And my name's on the programme.'

'But Dibsy dearest, I'm just on my way to London, and then to Paris.'

'Crumbs,' Dibs said.

Tish made her tea, and they sat on the floor of the living room, dunking chocolate biscuits. Dibs was very plump and round-faced. A small head and baby lips gave her an expression of perpetual innocence. She wore smocks to hide her weight, and high-heeled shoes to add to her height, but no make-up to improve her looks. The frames to her glasses were round. She looked like an awkward schoolgirl. Nothing about her seemed to have changed since she was about fourteen.

'Tell me about the Festival.'

'I shouldn't have come,' Dibs mumbled. 'I'm playing Messiaen. It's fiendishly difficult. I shall probably be terrible.'

'But what instrument, O Fat One?'

'The organ,' Dibs said, sending Tish into gales of laughter.

'But what are you doing here? Now, today?'

'You invited me. I wrote to you in the spring saying I was engaged to play at the Festival, etcetera, and you wrote back saying I could stay.'

'But you never replied. Or did you?'

'Yes,' Dibs said, miserably. 'Twice.'

'Dibsy, I'm so sorry!'

'It doesn't matter.'

'Come and talk to me while I have a bath and we can decide what to do.'

'I'll go home again, of course.'

'Oh no you won't. You can stay at the Hall. They'd love to have you.'

'No!' Dibs said in alarm. But two hours later she clattered the 2cv up the drive to Chelworth, her knees knocking, and met a bemused Jamie.

'I'm Deborah Harper. I was at school with your sister.'

'Tish is – I think she's going to Paris or something today.'

'I know,' Dibs said. 'I've just driven her to the station. You don't remember me, do you?'

Jamie stared.

'Um –'

'You came to stay once, when we had Beveley Manor.'

Jamie stared even more intently and then his face burst into a huge grin.

'You're Dibs! Your mother let us run around stark naked.'

'We were only ten.'

'I didn't recognize you,' Jamie laughed. 'How wonderful! How are you?'

'Fine,' Dibs said uncertainly.

'You were the first completely naked girl I ever saw in my life.'

'Oh, good.'

He kissed her cheerfully on the cheek.

'I hope you've come to stay. What are you doing in these parts anyway?'

Dibs sighed.

'I'm playing Messiaen on the Parish Church organ, for the

Hincham Festival.' She smiled wanly. 'I can see that news of my recital has got everyone at fever pitch.'

Jamie took time off to show her round. He was curiously happy to do so. There was a ruined church at the foot of the home pastures, close to the river. It was theirs, but it had been deconsecrated thirty years earlier. The windows and doors were secured with huge timbers. Dibs was fascinated.

'Haven't you been inside?'

'No. Why, do you think there's treasure? Or skeletons? Tell me about Beveley – what happened to it?'

'My father couldn't afford to keep it up. We live in Blandford Forum now. He has a small farm survey business.'

'And you play professional recitals?'

'Oh,' Dibs said. 'Not really. I mean I'm not really good enough. I started a design course, but . . . Your mother is nice. She's very kind.'

Jamie shrugged.

'They're under a bit of pressure.' Jamie hesitated for a moment. 'My father isn't unkind.'

'I realize.'

'But he can be intimidating.'

'Pretty well everything is,' Dibs said.

He studied her carefully while she poked about the walls of the church, standing on tiptoe to peer in through the cracks in the boards. Dibs was squeaky clean. She wore her clothes well, but was never completely happy with them. Like a child, her fingers plucked at the cotton, smoothing and touching. In his honour, perhaps, she had on a very expensive pair of sandals. Her legs were bare and tanned. She was certainly no sylph, but Dibs was young, and some of her bulk at any rate was strength, pure animal good health. Jamie liked her a lot.

'You have the most terrific feet,' he found himself saying, causing a huge blush to flood down into her chest.

'My best feature, or my smallest, anyway.'

Jamie had embarrassed himself.

'What's it like in Blandford?'

'You've been there. I've seen you there, in the bookshop.'

'Why didn't you introduce yourself?'

'I don't really do things like that. Besides, you're very grand now.'

Jamie laughed.

'Grand's not exactly right.'

'Pretty grand.'

'I'm so pleased you're here, Dibs. Can I come to your recital?'

'Crumbs. I'd rather you didn't. Perhaps you could buy a ticket, though. I think that would astonish them.'

'Who?'

'The organizers. There's a Mr Padgett in particular. It has crossed my mind that he thinks he's getting the *Messiah*.'

'And he isn't.'

'Um, very much not so.'

That night, at dinner, Jamie drank more than he usually did, and talked quite wildly in order to cover the black silence at Michael's end of the table.

'Mrs Harper let us all run round around stark naked, with lipstick for warpaint. And they had a coracle on the lake.'

'It was a pond, really,' Dibs said in a tiny voice.

'You enjoyed that, did you?' Michael asked.

There was a moment's awkward silence.

'Very much,' Jamie said.

Michael looked up for the first time when pudding was served.

'What is it you're doing at the Festival?'

'You have an exceptional instrument in the Parish Church. It's a Renatus Harris. I don't know how much you know about it.'

'Nothing,' Michael said. 'Who is Renatus Harris?'

'He's very important.'

Virginia came to her aid.

'Do you do many of these recitals, Dibs?'

'Oh, I'm not really that good. I'm a bit of a mess, or so my father says. I'm very undecided about things, as you've probably noticed. I envy Jamie.'

'Do you indeed?' Michael said.

'Let's take our coffee on the terrace,' Virginia proposed. 'It's such a lovely evening.'

'We'll join you in a moment,' Jamie said.

Michael looked up, surprised.

They went to the library, while Virginia and Dibs sat on the balustrade of the terrace outside, waiting for Hodnett to fetch coffee.

'Right,' Jamie said. 'I would just like to make it quite clear, if it isn't already, that she is here as my guest. She's been dumped on us by Tish, but that is beside the point. She is my personal guest.'

'I have no objection.'

'You have been absolutely foul to her.'

'I have been polite until my teeth ache. She herself confesses to being a mess, and I'm not going to quarrel with her. Does she know about you?'

Jamie froze. He set down the glass of brandy Michael had poured him.

'Does she know *what* about me?'

'She seldom takes her eyes off you. Does she know about you? It seems a reasonable question, I'd have thought.'

'Yes, it would strike you like that. Look around you. This is your library, and in it, a year's hard work on much else besides books. A year of my life. Is it to your taste?'

'I don't want a quarrel, Jamie.'

'We are having a quarrel,' Jamie shouted. 'If I can do all this and not have you take the slightest real interest, and do it as who I am, and what I am, should it bother you – is it any of your damn business – how I entertain a friend of Tish's, or what I tell her about myself?'

Michael said nothing, but looked at the fingers of one hand in the palm of the other. The effect was maddening.

'I like her,' Jamie said bitterly. 'Mummy likes her. That's feelings, our feelings, emotions that exist outside you, and what you want, and who you are. I am sick of dancing to your tune, or marching to your drum. Tish has gone. She can't stand it here. It's only a matter of time before I follow. Can you get that through your head? And then Mummy, perhaps. Won't it be wonderful here for you then?'

'How long have you felt this way?'

'Since a minute ago. I want you to be pleasant to that poor girl,' Jamie said, trembling with anger. 'Do you want to know her word for us? Grand. She thinks we're terribly grand. Doesn't that make you cringe with shame?'

'No.'

'It does me.'

Michael drummed the library table lightly with his fingers for a moment.

'Very well. I apologize for being . . . preoccupied.'

'Don't tell me, tell her,' Jamie said. He walked from the room seething, hardly able to contain himself.

When the young people had gone to bed, Virginia stayed up. All night she had been matching Michael drink for drink.

'What was all the shouting in the library?'

'To answer a question with another question – an unrelated one – did Tish ring you from London this morning?'

'Yes,' Virginia said, after a tiny pause.

'And?'

'It is none of her business. I don't think it's any of mine either, actually. What about Jamie and you?'

Michael smiled wryly. He acknowledged the change of subject with a nod of his head.

'We discussed Dibs.'

'I like her. Don't you?'

'I asked Jamie if he had said anything to Dibs about himself.'

'Oh, *Michael!*' Virginia wailed. 'He's not a leper. He's not unclean. What a ridiculous thing to say. She obviously thinks he's lovely –'

'Yes, indeed.'

' – and it's for her to find out, isn't it?'

'Find out what?'

'Whatever,' Virginia said, exasperated. 'And she may not be the greatest in the world at what she's doing, but she does deserve an untroubled and calm rehearsal for this concert, or recital, or whatever it is. I have asked her mother to the Leopold.'

'My God, the Leopold!' Michael remembered.

'Blackwell is delighted with us. Since we poached it for here, the sale of tickets has trebled.'

'Has Thornton said anything about the balloon ascent?'

'He's calling it the Chelworth Air Show. Listen to me, Michael. It was foolish of Tish to ring me, but now that she has, all I can say is that I'm sorry about Deenagh. It's all I want to say. But try to put it in context. Haven't we done rather well here, in the house, by working all the hours God sends? In just one year? And isn't it good that a day from now we shall have people here, doing something pleasant, like listening to music?'

Michael dredged up a smile from nowhere.

'You sound proud of yourself.'

'I was sharing a compliment with you, I thought.'

She rose and nodded good night to him. Her back expressed disappointment.

He yawned and stretched, and opened the doors to the terrace. Outside, the solstice sky was peppered with stars. Huge cream moths flew haphazardly towards the light. Over on the ridge, towards All Saints, a fox barked.

That there was someone called Evrington; that Virginia had been seen with him in Salisbury and London; that Michael was no closer to her now than he had ever been, for a whole cascade of reasons – these reflections kept him out in the dark, smoking, until the first birds began to sing.

On the morning of the quartet recital chairs were set out in the Hall under the direction of Mr Blackwell. Donatip arrived at noon with his balloon and humped it into the front pasture, assisted by his partner and an unexplained young woman called Sharon, dressed in white. At two a jazz band turned up on a flatbed truck, sent by a distraught Padgett, who had banished them from the town centre. The band obliged by playing 'Beale Street Blues' for openers. After a while they sat in the grass by the side of Michael's drive, drinking cans of lager, watching the delectable Sharon and cheering Donatip. From time to time news came in from the Festival proper. Cecily Hollar-Wilson was an afternoon visitor.

'How amazingly jolly. I'm quite sure nobody expected to see Chelworth *en fête* in this way. Who is that girl without a brassière?'

The enquiry was directed at Dibs, who had been landed with looking after Cecily.

'She's called Sharon. She's Mr Donatip's friend and mascot.'

'I think *she* needs rather more support than he does,' Cecily mused. 'You wear a bra, my dear, don't you?'

'Always,' Dibs said.

'Well, anyway, I have managed to get the WI Choir to Barlow Court, and they are absolutely thrilled. And as makeweight I have a couple of poets; no trouble at all really. One is quite black and the other is a Scotsman. You, of course, are doing the fiendishly difficult organ recital. You can be absolutely certain of one dedicated auditor – my Scottish poet. He is very difficult to understand, but the gist was that he didn't believe it possible, Whatsisname in the Parish Church. Who is it again?'

'Messiaen.'

'Was that it? Hamish is very dubious about it. What a pretty thing you are, Dibs. How are you getting on with Jamie? He's like a little orphan, isn't he, with those hungry eyes? They all want so desperately to be loved.'

'Who do?'

'The members of this family. It's quite a thing with them. You see the band, by the way? That boy playing the trumpet is my butcher.'

Virginia watched Cecily and Dibs from a window with Jamie.

'She's very sweet,' Virginia said. 'Do you like her?'

'Lots.'

'That's good. Because she likes you.'

'Oh, God, Mums, please . . .'

'It can happen, Jamie,' Virginia protested gently. 'I mean . . .'

'You should try the idea on my father. That Dibs is a possible cure.'

'That's not what I wanted to say at all. She likes you, that's all.'

'I like *her*,' Jamie said.

That evening, guests arriving for the Leopold concert were bemused to find the air filled with frantic jazz. At the last moment Sharon had given up her place in the balloon basket to Dibs, and to the strains of 'King Porter Stomp', augmented by blasts on a hunting horn from Donatip, the ascent commenced. Thornton and Jamie stood watching.

'You think she'll be all right?'

'Ask Sharon,' Thornton suggested slyly. 'Or do you mean will she fall out?'

At the entrance to the Hall, Bill Toller greeted Barbara Chivers.

'I know all about Mozart,' she said cheerily. 'I got a book from the library.'

'You're what I believe is called a good loser, Mrs Chivers.'

'They deserve something like this here. It could be like this a lot more.'

'I think so, too,' Bill said.

Blackwell had been the first to enter and seat himself in the recital room; in fact he had been there an hour before anyone else arrived. Michael and Virginia were the last to go in.

'I think it's lovely,' Virginia said. She pointed. Donatip and Diba were a multicoloured blob two miles away. Jamie had driven after them in the 2 cv.

'Well, happy anniversary,' Michael said.

'That's the ticket.'

Walking into the Hall to take their seats, they passed Tony Evrington, lounging in his chair with an amused smile.

Fourteen

Tish got her job with the charter boat. She sailed in it to Turkey, and thence to Athens. For a time there were laconic postcards, and then a long silence. When Virginia next heard from her she was in Antigua. There was a veiled reference to a man, and otherwise she was working in a restaurant. Then the cards ceased altogether.

Michael appointed Dorothy Wild as his secretary. She was dark, and even sensual-looking, but had a no-nonsense quality that subtly altered the mood of the house. As everyone had predicted, the flow of money was beginning to dry to a trickle. From being a crusade, or a quest, the rehabilitation of Chelworth was changing to a much more prosaic set of balances. Dorothy Wild was the perfect choice of employee for this situation. Once she was installed, lunch became the central meal of the day, and at lunch the energies of the family were translated into business. She sat with them, a notebook beside her plate, forcing Michael – forcing all of them – to make lists and keep schedules. She was offered the Lodge to live in, but turned it down. At night she drove home to Salisbury, to private circumstances which were never mentioned. At nine punctually each morning she drove up in her battered Renault, fresh, alert and impassive. Within a couple of weeks she had wrought a mighty change in all of them.

This change was made all the more urgent by the international money crisis that came along that autumn. In a single three-day period Michael had eighteen per cent wiped off his remaining share-holdings in Hong Kong. His personal fortune was now in rags. The house, and the external events outside his control, were threatening to beggar him. Though Dorothy knew nothing of this in detail, or no more than Michael chose to reveal, what she brought to the affairs of Chelworth was an office routine. In this she was enthusiastically supported by Peter Thornton. There began to be immediate horizons, close objectives, in place of cloudy dreams.

'About bloody time too,' Thornton said cheerfully.

Russell Fairless had been given a knighthood in the Queen's Birthday Honours. It was a thing he liked to make a great deal of, to the amusement of Ewan Chivers. One Friday, Ewan asked him to a photo-call in the constituency: he was selling off a three-acre site beyond the industrial estate. He had acquired the marshy strip of land twenty years ago, when he was a county councillor; now it was being resold at ten times the value to a supermarket chain. Russell – Sir Russell – lent his jovial presence to the symbolic bursting of the wire fence by a contractor's bulldozer, gave an interview to local radio (in the person of a nervous trainee in her early twenties); and was photographed shaking hands with Ewan and the supermarket supremo standing on the tracks of the bulldozer.

'Another victory for enterprise,' he boomed.

Ewan walked with him back to the boundary fence. Russell saw an elderly man shouting and shaking his fist. Something stirred in his memory.

'Wasn't this designated some sort of nature reserve?' he murmured.

'Now would we be here today if it were?' Ewan chided.

'But there were plans. Or protests. I can't remember the details.'

'Why should you?'

Russell stared about him.

'They paid a damn good price, I understand.'

'Their flagship operation in the South West will be right here,' Ewan said comfortably. 'I forget how many thousand square feet of pet food and chocolate biscuits: but big.'

'You have great patience, Ewan.'

'Can't see any point in killing oneself for it. It had to happen.'

'They say it's made you a money millionaire.'

'And why not?'

'Why not, indeed? I have some vague recollection of some idiots trying to get it designated as a nature reserve, that's all.'

'The place to be patient,' Ewan suggested, 'is standing on the bridge. That way you see all the water pass underneath. I bought this for a hundred and ten thousand in the teeth of almighty opposition, when I didn't actually have that sort of money at all. Barbara thought I was mad. I remember you pursing your lips. It was just a matter of time. You could have done the same.'

'But the fact remains, I didn't and you did!'

Ewan laughed.

'You are altogether a nobler sort, Sir Russell. You have given your life to protecting the people from swine like me, remember?'

Russell fussed with a twig, scraping mud from his shoe.

'There's a bit of a do this lunchtime at that old hag Cecily Hollar-Wilson's. You'll come, of course?'

'I've always been the most admiring of your public.'

'Don't be so bloody cynical,' Russell snapped.

'Was that taken as cynicism? Seldom has a knighthood been better merited. I'm just Ewan Chivers, while Sir Russell Fairless is a household name.'

'You'll cut yourself on your own tongue one day,' the new knight muttered as they walked towards their cars. In the background the yellow bulldozer was churning scrub and saplings and the site of a small colony of bog orchids, one of the last to be found in that part of Wiltshire. Later in the day, to his great amazement, the driver was to discover a snake over a foot long, a thing he had not believed to exist in England. He beheaded it with a shovel and took it home in a plastic bag to show his wife and children.

That day, Cecily gave a party at Barlow Court in Russell's honour, attended by some minor political grandees. Central Office had sent a very bright young man in a startling violet shirt, and Russell's agent was present with some of the more senior county councillors. Included in the guest list were Olivia and Ronnie Esholt. Virginia had accepted for Michael.

Olivia looked at her sister-in-law without enthusiasm.

'My God, she flatters herself,' Olivia drawled. 'I wish I had the confidence to dress as many years younger than my age as she does.'

'Diffidence was always your besetting sin, darling,' Ronnie muttered, peering into his glass. 'Not a bite to eat to be seen anywhere. I suppose we must all drink this muck until we drop. The bloody man Fairless could do us all a great favour by leaving early. That way some of us could stay alive and unpoisoned.'

'He's only just arrived.'

'I was talking to some chiropodist who is the constituency party chairman. Scraping the barrel a bit there.'

'They take anybody these days,' Olivia shrugged.

'What does a chiropodist know about anything except feet? I understand he intends to make some fatuous speech or other. He seems rather simple-minded to me.'

'The chiropodist.'

'And the other fellow. Fairless.'

'Oh, shut up, Ronnie.'

'I am merely saying —'

Virginia was across the room talking to Ewan Chivers.

'I hear from my spy Hodnett that you are suddenly very rich.'

'Jim Hodnett? What does he have to say?'

'That you sold some land by the railway.'

'Marsh Lane. Yes. To a supermarket. To the supermarket, as they intend to be known. How is your daughter, by the way?'

'Very well. How is Barbara?'

'The same.'

Ewan smiled, and smiled a little more broadly when he saw capitulation in her eyes. She laughed.

'What is it?' he asked.

'You amuse me, that's all. I really can't help liking you.'

'I am greatly flattered.'

'I suppose you're here to trawl for gossip. What have you found out?'

Ewan looked at her quizzically. The remark was uncharacteristically direct. He smiled and shrugged.

'Your sister-in-law tells me she is selling up. That the sort of thing you mean?'

Virginia looked relieved.

'That sort of thing, yes. It seems she and Ronnie are going to live in Majorca. Everyone is taking their profits, apparently. They're selling the house in London.'

'Would Majorca suit you?'

'I shouldn't think so,' Virginia said. 'How about you?'

'Oh, I'm just a local bumpkin. I'm as English as New Zealand butter.'

'You wouldn't want their house in Holland Park?'

'Too grand. And no fishing.'

'Then we shall stay neighbours.'

Ewan inclined his head gravely.

'That will be a pleasure, of course.'

He was surprised to see her attention stray. He followed her glance.

Standing in the doorway, talking to Eileen Fairless but looking directly at Virginia, was Tony Evrington.

'Would you excuse me?' she murmured.

Tony greeted her with a handshake and a peck on the cheek. They walked out into the garden side by side, watched by more than one pair of eyes.

'You are quite mad to come.'

'You knew very well I would be here. Anyway, one has to be loyal to one's chums.'

'Is he a chum?'

'Russell? I think he's the most odious little pill I ever met. How are you? Did you get home safely from Bristol?'

'Look, we are being watched. I can't talk now.'

'Everyone is talking to everyone else. This is all perfectly innocent.'

'No it isn't,' Virginia said.

'Did you enjoy Bristol? You didn't ring to say so.'

They stood apart as the chairman-chiropodist walked past with two empty glasses. Virginia caught sight of Olivia watching her from some topiary hedges.

'You're just a naughty little boy, aren't you? Such a philanderer.'

'I love you,' Tony protested in a genial voice, pitched loud enough to be heard by the chiropodist's wife, who was sitting nearby on a bench, holding the notes to her husband's speech in her lap. Virginia turned a laser-intense stare on her until she dropped her gaze, startled. When she looked back, Tony was smiling.

'Can we leave? I really have heard Fairless waffle on about his knighthood four or five times already.'

'How can we leave? Be sensible.'

'I'll go first. I'll meet you at Tadderton, on the gated road. I'll wait for you.'

Virginia made a bee-line for Olivia the moment he left.

'That was Tony Evrington,' she said brightly. 'I wonder if you know him? I was going to introduce him and he just upped and went.'

'How awkward,' Olivia said down her nose. 'Ronnie has gone off to sleep on the grass. He's quite right, this woman has no sense of what is what. As far as one can tell, there isn't a scrap to eat. And the people are quite beyond belief.'

'I thought she was a friend.'

'Oh, friend's a very elastic word, darling, don't you think? I wonder why you think I should know that Evrington man. He's quite common. That cleft chin and all that little-boy grimacing. I suppose he thinks he's being irresistible.'

'When do you go to Majorca?' Virginia asked.

'The sooner the better. There's so much inexpressible vulgarity about these days. Michael's girl was in the paper, did you see?'

'What has she done?'

'She has married that Picton-Ellis man in Scotland.'

'I hadn't seen that.'

'Disgusting family,' Olivia said. 'And a revolting mock castle for a house. Daddy was asked to shoot there once, drove to the front door and departed again without switching off the engine. I should think she is well suited. How lucky for you, my dear, that things are so smooth and untroubled between the two of you these days. You must be so happy. I can't begin to imagine how relieved you must feel. How grateful.'

Virginia looked her sister-in-law square in the eye and said something to her in French that made Olivia blush deep down into her neck. Then Virginia walked round to the front of the house and got into her car, shaking with anger.

Tony was waiting for her on the road above Tadderton, sitting on a rock and smoking. He tossed away his cigarette and they walked, following sheep-tracks through the bracken. Black flies buzzed round Virginia's head.

'I want to sit down somewhere.'

They found a glade of grass. Virginia beat about her face with her hands, exasperated and hot under the collar.

'First of all,' she said, 'you can stop playing the fool as you did at Cecily's. It isn't amusing and I don't like it.'

'Ginny . . .'

'And stop phoning me at home. I'm not some shop girl. I won't be pursued. Do you understand?'

'I've told you. I want you.'

'And what does that mean? It doesn't help very much to say so.'

'I think it helps enormously. I am telling you what's in my heart.'

'You don't have one. I don't want to be courted, or hunted down. Perhaps you think I'm unfulfilled or something. Unhappy.'

'I'm telling you what I want,' he said evenly. 'I want you.'

'Go to hell.'

At Chelworth, lunch had ended in acrimonious silence. Dibs was staying, and she and Jamie went for a walk. Dorothy watched them out of the window.

'You should eat some fruit,' she said to Michael absently.

'Dorothy, I really had no idea when I engaged you that there was a deep well of mothering waiting to surface. I don't want any fruit.'

'She's afraid of you.'

Michael glanced at his son and Dibs walking side by side in the tall grass.

'That's not for you to say either. It's strictly none of your business.'

'It's true, all the same.'

'I haven't time to think about it.'

Dorothy turned her dark eyes on him. Michael sighed and picked up an apple.

'I am in some financial difficulty, as you may have realized.'

'The dollar collapse.'

'Indeed. The dollar collapse.'

'Do you need to go to Hong Kong?'

Michael hesitated.

'Probably. I don't know.'

He held out the apple for her inspection and bit into it.

Jamie and Dibs walked downhill towards the river past a little ruined pavilion. Dibs had her hands in the pockets of her skirt. The wet grass made the hem black.

'I suppose we ought to get back.'

'To hell with it.'

'It's not very popular, my coming here, is it?'

'Oh, Dibs, please.'

'He seemed not to want to talk about anything.'

'Look, what is happening is exactly what everyone warned him of. This little exhibition that you've helped me arrange, of some of the things we have, that's a debt paid, if you like, to people who understand and appreciate these things, and whose interest in Chelworth is genuine. That's one path forward for him. Thornton wants him to find the money to clean out the river for a mile or so and sell the fishing. There's talk of a trout farm, a gun club, all sorts of things. But he won't act.'

'Why?'

Jamie shrugged, helpless.

'I don't know. Something's preoccupying him.'

'He and your mother are terribly formal, aren't they?'

'I don't know what you mean,' Jamie said evasively. Dibs blushed.

The exhibition was laid out in the library. When she got back from Cecily Hollar-Wilson's via Tadderton, Virginia found Michael in there, sombre and uncommunicative.

'You were sorely missed this lunchtime,' Virginia said.

'I can imagine.'

'Olivia and Ronnie were there.'

'Good. You see what is on this table? According to Jamie it is priceless.'

'Then stop glowering at it.'

She flicked a page of botanical illustrations from the eighteenth century.

'This is pretty enough.'

'Who else was there today?'

Virginia glanced.

'Oh, nobody special. Where are your father's stamps? Shouldn't they be displayed? I thought they were something special.'

Michael examined his fingernails.

'Dibs turned up again.'

'Good.'

'Does that girl know what she's letting herself in for?'

'I don't know. Does she, in your opinion?'

There was a long silence. She could hear her heart beat. Michael jumped up.

'Yes, where are those stamp albums. And where is Jamie?'

That evening, at dusk, Virginia walked out along the drive. She sat on a felled tree trunk and smoked a rare cigarette. She was surprised by a footfall. It was Thornton, who touched his cap.

'I'm afraid I frightened you. I smelt the tobacco smoke.'

'Did you think I was a poacher?'

He held out his hand. In it was a small flint. Virginia took it.

'What is it?'

'You can pick them up in the fields. It was probably used for scraping hides. This was all forest, once.'

'Is it very old? Before Stonehenge?'

'Oh yes,' Thornton said. 'I sometimes wonder, you know, when I put my foot down, whether it isn't in exactly the same print of a man who walked that path long before me, with something very different on his mind.'

Virginia shuddered in spite of herself.

'I'm not sure I like that idea.'

'The man who used that flint you have in your hand would perhaps have sat on a fallen tree in just this spot. It isn't frightening,' he added gently. 'Or it shouldn't be. I find it comforts me, to tell you the truth.'

'Walk back with me to the house,' Virginia requested. Thornton nodded and took off his jacket.

'It's cold. Put this round your shoulders.'

The jacket smelt of hay and sweat.

'The fields look wonderful,' Virginia said politely, and Peter Thornton smiled.

'Nice of you to notice.'

'You think we're not serious people, don't you?'

'I wouldn't work for you if I thought that.'

'Perhaps you would, though.'

'No,' he said.

Impulsively, she took his hand.

'Thank you for the flint.'

When they drew near the house she gave him back his jacket and ran up the last of the drive.

Michael was waiting in the *porte-cochère*.

'Who was that with you?' he asked.

She was astonished, and of course fearful.

'It was – does it matter?'

'Was it Evrington?'

'Who?'

'I asked you a question, Virginia.'

She gave him the flint.

'Here. Peter Thornton gave it to me. It comes from your fields. It's prehistoric, so you can wave it about outside your cave and bellow, if you like.'

He threw it into the gravel of the drive and walked back inside the house without another word.

Fifteen

Often, if the morning was too wet to walk, Michael would clamber about in the West Wing of the house. He rose early from habit. So many missing floors and ruined ceilings, so many rooms filled with furniture that had once shone with polish and was now piled piece upon piece, greeny-grey and forlorn. To begin with, these excursions were a form of beachcombing: he stumbled across things of value that had lain forgotten for nearly a century. As time went on, and the shattered rooms offered up fewer surprises, the journeys became a kind of ritual. At the very top of the building, where servants' attics ran, he had set a velvet spoonback chair by a window, and there he would sit and smoke, gazing out on to the early morning. At this time of year, the trees of his own estate and those on the neighbouring hills rose in billows beneath him like clouds, or vast underwater corals. The floor of his makeshift observatory was littered with cigarette ends.

The morning after the scene with Virginia he was to be found there, bathed and shaved, smoking on an empty stomach, and decidedly edgy.

Once, his life had been so direct. The collapse of the dollar put this past life much in mind. Then, his energies had a focus, and his pleasures too. He was very good at what he did, and to a certain extent the envy of others became necessary to his existence. The indulgent side of him went into the relationship with Rosie, in playing golf and cricket, in gambling in the Macao casinos. While he lived richly, the indispensables of his life were quite small and could be bought at any shop, by any schoolboy, even: a calculator, a computer, a secure briefcase. All the rest was himself, his will, his determination. His unforgivingness.

The strength of the dollar, he thought ruefully. It seemed to him in the present crisis that the decision to live in England, and at Chelworth, and the plunge in his dollar fortune were somehow connected. One had occasioned the other. So it was that the morning after revealing to Virginia that he knew about Evrington, he sat in his spoonback chair, one corner of which was supported by bricks, and tried to review things. There was quite a menu of items to think about.

It went without saying that Virginia topped the list, no matter how he tried to order things. It seemed to him beyond belief that she was serious about Tony Evrington; in which case why was he so seriously jealous? She had been the first to respond to the matter-of-fact and orderly atmosphere brought into the house by Dorothy Wild; she had gone out of her way to insist, too, that Jamie adopted it. In many ways, the affairs of the house and Virginia's presence in it were becoming linked in just the way he had hoped. The Evrington business, seen from this perspective, was like a rock thrown through a window, an act of vandalism. He also found, not for the first time, and not without a feeling of rue, that he wished Tish were in England. He missed his daughter more than he could admit.

He stood, and ground his cigarette into an empty tobacco tin. The plain fact was, he decided, he was in a mess. Inside him was that dangerous rising that was the overture to action. He could not let things stand as they were. He paid a last look from the window. The fine misty rain had ceased and there was a watery sun breaking through.

Virginia was driving her car along the avenue of trees that lined the approach to the house. Michael glanced at his watch. It was not yet seven-thirty.

He met Alan Rawtenstall in London, at the offices of De La Haye and Co. in the Strand. The solicitor was amused.

'I had no idea you were coming up to town. What is it this time?'

'My grandfather and father were considerable philatelists. Jamie has an exhibition – I think he calls it an eclectic show – of some of our stuff for arts journalists and a party of visiting Americans at the end of next week, but we can't find them. The stamps, I mean.'

Alan looked faintly pained.

'Did you need me present to talk to this chap?'

'Possibly. De La Haye's were our dealers in grandpa's time. They sold him the stock. I thought they might have records.'

'Where do I fit in?'

'You'll see.'

Simon De La Haye was brisk, burly and businesslike. He was in his late forties, and ran a highly efficient suit of offices on the river side of the Strand.

'Your son's call to us yesterday afternoon rang some alarm bells, Lord Hincham. He wanted to know, of course, whether we kept records of what was sold to your grandfather the Fourth Earl, and subsequently to your father. We did; but unfortunately all that was destroyed in the Blitz. However, as I told you last night on the phone, there is more to it than that.'

'You have seen the stamps in recent times.'

'In 1980, yes. They were brought to us for valuation.'

Alan and Michael exchanged glances.

'By my brother?'

'By his agent, Commander Firbank. Six calf-bound albums with the family's crest embossed and really rather a spectacular collection of mint British and American: I think you may have seen them yourself as a child.'

'It was a special treat to view them.'

'Just so. You might wish to know that we put a valuation at auction on the collection of close to three hundred thousand pounds.'

Alan Rawtenstall whistled.

'For stamps?'

'For those stamps. Had they come to auction in this country the sale would have been a major sensation – among philatelists,' De La Haye added with a tiny smile. 'I wrote to your brother immediately, advising him of the value, and suggesting that at the very least he allow us to re-catalogue them and keep them in a place of safety. There was no reply.'

'This was in 1980?'

'Yes.' De La Haye straightened his desk blotter and then looked directly at Alan. 'I do read the papers, you understand. Firbank's suicide caught my eye, though I'm afraid I was no more than curious. Then the most surprising thing happened. I mean quite astonishing. His lordship rang us, concerning these self-same stamps. I thought it only right to invite you both here as a matter of urgency.'

'I'd be grateful if you told my lawyer why.'

'The stamps are on the market. They form part of the estate of John Joseph Goodrich, a very distinguished collector from Florida. They're being offered at auction in New York at the end of this month.'

'Comment,' Michael demanded of Alan. The lawyer thought quickly.

'There is absolutely no doubt they are the same stamps?'

'None. We, ah, took quite extensive notes in 1980, you can imagine. Among the American stamps were Buchanans, Lockports – these are Postmasters' Stamps of great rarity. There are many other pieces of evidence. They are unquestionably the stamps I valued myself when Firbank brought them to me.'

'I see,' Alan said slowly. 'And Goodrich?'

'He died last spring. He was a very rich and extremely highly respected collector. This auction of his collections is quite the biggest event in American philately since the Centenary Exhibition in New York in 1947.'

De La Haye studied his desk for a moment.

'There is of course a dark explanation of how he came by them, but I think I ought to say, too, that philately is a hobby of secrets. It sometimes – forgive me – happens that a collector will conceal from his family, from his closest relations, the extent of his commitment. Your brother, milord, may have sold these stamps to Goodrich. On the face of it, that is the more likely proposition.'

'My brother was a fool,' Michael said, 'and a trusting one at that. But in no case did he sell anything from the house. On the other hand, we do know that Firbank stole from us.'

'I think you might have discovered such a huge theft before now,' De La Haye suggested.

'Are you going to the New York auction?'

'Yes, of course. Any service I can do you there I shall be only too happy to discharge.'

Michael and Alan walked to a wine bar in Covent Garden after this interview. It was at Alan's suggestion. He chose his words carefully.

'We haven't spoken together for some time. Is everything all right?'

'This stamp thing is annoying me.'

Alan shrugged.

'Pretty obvious what's happened there.'

'That seems a remarkably flip judgement,' Michael retorted sharply. 'I don't find it obvious at all.'

'I beg your pardon.'

'You think it's Firbank. I don't think so.'

'It may have been your brother himself.'

'I think not.'

'Then –?'

Michael pushed his glass of wine away in distaste.

'I have no idea.'

'Michael, forgive me, but is there anything else troubling you?'

'If there were, would I tell you here?'

Alan bit his lip and said nothing. A few minutes later, after some desultory remarks, they parted. Michael walked up to Long Acre and caught a cab.

The sea had that mirror calm that happens only a few times a year. It stretched away in a taut sheet of silver, lit by a fitful sun. Virginia sat watching it, watched in turn by Tony. They were at the extremity of a small promontory of land called Burland Point, with a bottle of wine and two glasses, carried down from the car along sandy tracks. The sun was warm enough for her to have removed her jacket. She stroked her bare arms.

'This is the life,' Virginia said with glum irony.

'It could be, yes.'

'What do you see, Tony, when you look at me? Truthfully? I shouldn't have come today.'

'I'm glad you did.'

'Do you really paint here?'

'When the mood takes me. I'm not a painter, however.'

She sipped at the warm red wine without pleasure.

'Perhaps you still don't realize that part of our relationship is an attempt to spite Michael. It's not about you at all.'

'You're here, nevertheless. And I still don't know that we have a relationship. Not in the sense I would like.'

She glanced at him. Tony tossed a stem of clover at her.

'What do you want me to say?' he asked. 'That we are just good friends? I hope we are. But we can be something better than that.'

'With just a few little obstacles in the way.'

'Yourself, principally.'

'Yes?'

'You're very like Michael.'

'That hadn't occurred to me.'

'You're a romantic.'

He stood and pulled her up by her wrist.

'I'm a hedonist. I think that's a philosophy which could do you some good.'

At the back of the bay were some low dunes scattered with marram grass. Tony sat and watched as she walked in the sea, her skirt hitched up. The water hardly broke its mirror calm, except where she had trodden. After a while she came and sat beside him, the sand clinging to her feet and calves. He lit her a cigarette. She examined it for a while without drawing on it.

'In Paris I had a complete life, minus the children, but then the children weren't children any longer after all. I had Keith, and I ran really rather a good gallery. I knew some interesting people – including some devoted hedonists – and I avoided situations like this like the plague.'

'Go on.'

'That's all. Keith was very good for me. We were happy. You want to tell me that I bottle up emotions, that I'm lofty or something. That I'm ungiving.'

'I love you.'

'Oh, don't be such a bore,' she snapped. 'That doesn't mean anything. We're not children. When you say you want me, that I can understand. Another scalp to your belt. This is quite the most elaborate way of going to bed anyone could devise.'

'We haven't been to bed. You seem to have a pretty comprehensive amnesia about that.'

'But that's what you want.'

'Among other things, yes.'

'As a trophy,' she suggested.

'As a pleasure.'

He leaned over and kissed her. It passed through her mind, with a kind of surreal justice, that she was doing no more than being polite. But as the kiss persisted she began to return it, at first against her will, and then with an abandonment that surprised them both.

Michael caught the three-fifteen with moments to spare and walked through the first-class carriages looking for a seat alone. To his surprise, he met Barbara Chivers. She was surrounded with bags from shops in South Molton Street. She put up her face to be kissed.

'What a lovely surprise. Where've you been? You look like thunder. I've been looking for those wonderful shorts that look terrific on the girls in the colour supplement, but made me look like some Bulgarian grape-picker with a hormone problem.'

'So you came back empty-handed.'

'Not exactly, no. Tell me about *your* day.'

'I've been talking about stamp albums. A hobby of mine.'

'Not another one! Ewan was –'

She stopped suddenly and for a few moments they rattled through the grimy and forlorn factories of Southwark in silence. Michael could feel his own heart beating wildly.

'Ewan's a collector, is he?' he asked as casually as he could manage.

'Oh bloody hell!' Barbara groaned. 'Why do I always put my foot in it?'

'I don't suppose you have. What does Ewan specialize in?'

'He was thinking of investing in them. You don't think he'd sit up at night with tweezers and hinges, do you? The only thing Ewan collects is grudges.'

'But about the stamps?'

'There were some kicking around, once. He bought a book on it. Oh God, why don't I learn to keep my mouth shut?'

'You haven't said anything you shouldn't, Barbara.'

'I bet.'

'When was this? Earlier this year, about February?'

A look of intense relief passed across her face.

'Years before that! Yonks.'

'1980,' Michael said.

She realized she had been tricked and flushed.

'He decided against it,' she said. 'If you're trying to find out whether he has any, he doesn't, I'm certain. He decided not to go ahead with whatever it was. And that's the truth.'

'Let me get you a big gin and tonic,' Michael suggested.

'As a reward? I don't betray people knowingly, Michael. Ewan's a fool, but he's not a criminal.'

He was surprised to see tears start up in her eyes. When he took her hand she squeezed it hard. The tears suddenly ran down her cheeks.

'I don't know what I've told you, but it's clearly something awful. I like you, and admire you. If you want to know the truth, you're worth ten of him. But he's my husband. Can you understand?'

'Of course.'

'You're bigger than he is, in personality and everything. Please.'

'Don't beg,' he murmured. 'Dry your eyes.'

He had a Salisbury taxi drive him home and found Jamie. His mind was now racing, and he outlined what he wanted at breakneck speed to a son who gawped at him in amazement.

'Are you quite mad? You want me to fly to Florida tomorrow? With the show coming up in six days' time?'

'That's exactly it.'

'Do you realize how much work I've put into making this thing a success? Look, next Friday you'll have a film crew, Lydia Lytton of the V and A, the English Heritage people, the National Trust, the Americans . . . No, I won't go! You go.'

'I cannot go for the very plain reason that I have to watch the markets. To save what I can so that, among other expenses, I may pay you to look after the arts side of the house.'

'All this, on the strength of some chance remark by Barbara Chivers on a train? Go to hell.'

'I really don't want to argue with you, Jamie. I'm not asking you, I am telling you to do as I say.'

'You're mad. You realize that, do you? Supposing you find Chivers bought the collections from Firbank and then resold them? Then what? You can't get your money back. Would you really ruin him? Is it all as easy as that?'

'You'll go to Florida tomorrow, and you'll go alone.'

Jamie looked up sharply.

'What does that mean?'

'Alone. Without Dibs.'

'I see. While we're on the subject.'

'Yes. While we're on the subject.'

'You disapprove,' Jamie said bitterly.

'Does she know about you?'

'Does she know what about me?'

'Does she know you're gay?'

'You guess.'

Michael glanced at his watch and then poured himself a whisky.

'The girl is young, she is very impressionable, and she is probably in love with you. You are fond of describing her to me as your guest, just as you speak about your exhibition, your hard work, and so forth. This place, however, happens to be mine. It is an expression of my will. When the time comes to explain to the Harpers –'

'Explain what to the Harpers?'

Michael drained his whisky.

'Does she think you might marry her?'

Jamie studied his father with open contempt.

'You bloody fool. What an incredibly vain bastard you are. Dibs is suddenly your concern, is she? How touching. You're the moral expert in this house are you? You know all about love and marriage?'

When he turned to go, he bumped into his mother standing in the doorway.

'You talk to him,' Jamie said.

Virginia let him go. She stayed on the threshold of the room. Michael did nothing to invite her in.

'I've spent the day by the sea,' she said.

'I hope it was pleasant.'

'With Evrington.'

'I imagined so. Was he on good form?'

She watched him pour a second whisky.

'Isn't it a little early to start drinking?'

'What did he want? Or is that a foolish question?'

'I don't know,' Virginia said. 'Is it?'

'You know about him, of course.'

'You mean his predilection for safely married women with money of their own? Yes. He hardly makes a secret of it. May I have a drink, too?'

Michael gestured towards the drinks table.

'You're going to say it's no concern of mine. And it isn't.'

'Let me ask you something, Michael. Are you truly jealous? I don't mean offended, or with your nose put out of joint, but sexually jealous?'

'I have asked Jamie to go to Florida tomorrow,' he said. 'See that he does, will you? It's quite important.'

He set down his tumbler and walked from the room. Virginia sat down suddenly, as happens sometimes when the blood seems to rush to the head, and the room spins. She kicked off her shoes. Sand ran from them on to the wine-coloured carpet.

Sixteen

The bonfire was placed very prudently, away from the trees of the drive and a hundred yards or more from the house; and this was just as it should have been, for sparks rose high enough in the air to be seen from the main road. The fire was made of fallen boughs, some of which took Michael all his strength to drag through the meadow grass. Every so often he would pitch headlong and stay prone in the dark. From the house, where Virginia and Jamie watched, he seemed to have been swallowed up by the earth for a minute or so. But always he would rise and stagger back to the fire. He was drunk.

'Thornton's gone to talk to him,' Jamie said quietly.

'Why not me? Why not you?'

In front of Jamie, Virginia tried to affect a casual bitterness she did not feel. Her actual mood was one of fear. Michael drunk was not an uncommon event: once or twice a month since they had moved to Chelworth he had gone on drinking past the point of conviviality. Michael utterly out of control was a new thing. She glanced at her watch. It was past midnight. The bonfire suddenly roared and lashed out its tongue of flame. She could see Peter Thornton ambling across the pasture, his hands in his pockets. Michael was a furious silhouette.

'Where is Dibs?' she asked.

'Gone to bed. There's no sense in her seeing this.'

'What a little prig you are, Jamie.'

He stiffened, and moved away from the window.

'You think so? I have worked bloody hard for that man. I have put in long hours and taken a great deal of criticism that should properly have been directed at him. You think what he wants is easy? Let me tell you he is a laughing stock in the fine-arts world, let alone to his insurers and the accountants. This show –'

'This show, this show!'

Jamie looked at his mother. He walked to a side table and picked up a Chinese vase. When he inverted it, the keys and pencils she herself kept there fell on to the floor.

'This was excavated in 1860, and sold to us in 1891. I found it still in its crate in one of the cellars. According to the V and A, it is irreplaceable. You at least keep your keys in it. So far as I know, he hasn't even noticed its existence. If it is knocked off the table one day, Hodnett will sweep up the pieces and that will be that. Do you want me to go on? I have spent a year calling in all the pictures and plate we have on loan to museums. In some cases, they are only too pleased to be rid of them. But have we made any provision about exhibiting them? He doesn't want them to go into storage: it is quite out of the question that they come back here. And so on, and so on, and so on. Look around you, for God's sake.'

'Enough, Jamie.'

'Something has got to give. It won't be him. He won't alter. Something will give, though. First Tish, then you, then me. That's how it'll work.'

'Speak for yourself.'

'You feel you're very close to him, do you?'

Virginia clapped her hands together with impatience.

'No, I don't!'

'I can imagine,' he said in a low voice. 'I don't want Dibs involved in any of this any more than she has to be. She doesn't deserve it.'

Virginia made a small nod of acknowledgement.

'She's in love with you, of course.'

'Do you think so? She's a loyal friend.'

'Oh, Jamie . . .'

'In a house where loyalty counts for rather a lot. Or should do.'

'Have you talked to Dibs? I don't mean about any of this – us – but you. The two of you?'

'What should I say to her? She has eyes. She can see it for herself. We walk about this damn great house, ringing bells for service, and trying to behave like people in a play; and for what? Ever since he found out I was gay, or had been gay –'

He stopped suddenly. Virginia looked at him in the dark of the hall.

'Go on,' she said.

'We're all in pigeon-holes. I'm gay, Dibs is dumb, Chivers is the villain of the piece, you are the unapproachable wife, icy cold on her pedestal –'

'That's enough!'

'I am ordered to go to Florida this weekend.'

'Then go! You're being paid. What is so awful about doing what you are paid to do?'

Jamie drained the last of his brandy and wiped his lips.

'I thought I had an ally in you,' he said.

'You do. But not when you talk like this.'

'What should I do? Wait until you leave, or he decides for the good of common humanity to kill Evrington first?'

'Get out of here,' Virginia said with trembling rage. 'How dare you? Go away and nurse your wounded ego.'

'Mums –'

'Get out of my sight,' Virginia said.

The heat from the bonfire was quite colossal. Michael drank from the neck of the whisky bottle and waved Peter Thornton away.

'Clear off. You're in no danger, I'm in no danger. It's none of your damn business, any of this. Go to bed.'

'You're blind drunk,' Thornton said.

'I really don't see that is any concern of yours.'

'Come away from there before you fall in, you barmpot.'

He caught Michael by the sleeve and with no more than a twitch sent him flying. Michael lay on the grass laughing.

'I bet you enjoyed that!'

Thornton sat down beside him and began to roll a cigarette.

'Now you listen to me, my lord. You've had enough. You've made your point. I've had the police on the blower; you can see the damn fire from Copps End. Here, smoke one of these and give it a rest.'

'Tish was right about you. You're an impudent bloody Yorkshire-man.'

'Happen so,' Thornton said laconically.

Michael sat up and wiped the sweat from his hair and forehead. He took the roll-up and leaned into Thornton's cupped hands for a light. He seemed suddenly to make a supreme effort to be calm.

'Walpurgis Night,' he said. 'You shouldn't have come out. I'm fine, really. Not happy, but not desperate. Look, we've done some good things here in a short space, wouldn't you say?'

'No question,' Thornton said.

'We have. I know how much you've contributed. A lot. A hell of a lot. I know it would all get on even faster if I could see it as a business, just a business. And I should be able to do that. But it fascinates me, hypnotizes me. The truth is, Peter, I never really owned anything in my life before I owned all this. I don't know how to handle it.'

'You were a rich man.'

'Money. I made a lot of money. I don't think you can really own that. You can't eat it, or drive a nail into it. I suppose you can take it out of the bank and look at it or something. I made lots of lovely money, and left it all dressed up and nowhere to go. And then this.'

'So. What's the problem?' Thornton asked. When Michael shook his head, he frowned.

'Listen to me, my lord. There can never be a second conversation like this between master and servant, I know that, and I'm risking my arm, but it happens that I like you. Your son works damn hard at what he does, and I like him too, though I never thought I would. And your wife's one of the best.'

'I am not that drunk,' Michael warned.

'You're drunk enough. I'm telling you, the family's hundred-per-cent behind you. Only you can't see it.'

'You're an insolent beggar, Peter.'

'All that kind of language went out with horse-whipping. If I were you, I'd put some cold water over my head and go and mend some fences there in the house.'

'Mend some fences.'

'I think you know what I mean.'

Michael threw away the cigarette.

'Go to hell.'

Thornton rose, massive and calm.

'As you say, milord. And good night to you!'

He lumbered off, vaulting the stone balustrade that divided the field from the gardens. It occurred to him to walk towards the house, to see if Virginia was watching and waiting, but when he peered through the windows to the great cube entrance hall, the area was deserted. A single standard lamp burned in one corner. Thornton crunched away across the gravel.

On the top floor, Jamie sat drumming his fingers and trying to think. He picked up the internal phone. His mother's voice was sharp and fearful.

'Michael? Are you all right?'

'It's me. Tell him I'll go to Florida as he asks.'

There was a long silence.

'Thank you,' Virginia said, and the connection broke.

Jamie walked down the corridor and tapped at Dibs's door. Though he hardly dusted the woodwork with his knuckles, she called him in immediately. He slipped into the room, closing the door behind him with elaborate gentleness. He felt the whole house could hear his heart beating.

Dibs sat up in bed, wearing a tee-shirt nightie, her plump arms outside the sheets. The only light in the room came from the moon.

'Were you asleep?'

'Of course not. Is your father all right?'

Jamie laughed in spite of himself.

'We're talking as though he's been struck by the curse of Chelworth. Yes, he's all right. He'll have the most massive hangover tomorrow. You don't mind my being here?'

'No,' Dibs said. 'I like it.'

'I have to go to America tomorrow.'

'For long?'

'No.'

He could see her only as a pale shape against the bed-head. The light in the room seemed to swim and eddy. He felt emotionally exhausted. Physically it was as though he had been running for hours.

'Dibs.'

'Yes?'

'They think I'm – they may think I'm leading you along. You

know what I mean. That I'm not being fair with you. I wanted to say –'

'Yes?'

'I just wanted to say –'

There was a sudden soft whoosh as she turned back the sheets.

'Come here,' she said.

He walked to the bed, trembling. Dibs held out her arms. It was so unexpected he knelt, his lips on her outstretched hand.

'Come into bed,' she said, in the smallest voice imaginable. 'Don't catch cold. Come in with me.'

When Dorothy Wild opened up the office at nine the next morning she was surprised to see her employer, brisk, alert and finishing off a tray of egg and bacon, coffee and orange juice. Michael greeted her heartily. Dorothy hung up her coat and took the covers from the word processor.

'You're very bright and bushy-tailed this morning.'

'Jamie has flown to Florida, or at any rate he will do later today. He's scribbled a list of additional people he wants to ask to this show of his. And ask Chivers and Barbara, will you? And could you make a special point of inviting Fairless, the MP? Tell him the cameras will be here; that will bring him along. Then, if you would, sort out a buffet menu with Mrs Hodnett for me, Dorothy.'

'Shouldn't her ladyship –?'

'You do it. See that Hodnett gives us something good to drink.'

'Is there any news from Hong Kong?'

'Um? Oh, no. We'll have to see what happens at the close of market in New York. I was going to London this morning, but I've changed my plans.'

'Your brokers!' Dorothy wailed. 'I moved heaven and earth yesterday –'

'They can wait. Do you happen to know if my wife is going anywhere today?'

Dorothy flicked the pages of the huge dark diary.

'I don't think so. She was going to talk to Peter Thornton on your behalf about this trout farm idea. Do you want me to find out?'

'No.'

Michael drank the last of his coffee standing. He hesitated for a moment and then pulled out his cigarettes.

'I want you to tell me something in confidence, Dorothy.'

She shook her head.

'No, I can't do that. I can't keep secrets, true enough, but neither can I divulge them. Whatever it is you want to ask, or say, I'd much rather you didn't.'

'All right, I'll put it as a statement. I have been pretty beastly to Dibs – Miss Harper. Not since yesterday, but generally.'

Dorothy's face showed a certain amount of relief. She made a small smile.

'Miss Harper's a lot tougher than you think.'

'I don't doubt it.'

'Very well. Just as a statement of fact: no, she doesn't deserve it. I think she's a very nice, very loving girl. Your wife is talking to her in the drive. I think she's going home. If you ask me' – Dorothy made a rueful face – 'if you ask me, she needs encouraging to come back. She's very good for this place. And whatever appearances to the contrary, she's no fool.'

'Good,' Michael said. 'Well said.'

'All of which it has been no part of my duty to say.'

'Well said all the same.'

He was just in time to see Dibs driving away down the avenue of oaks when he went in search of her. Virginia was leaning against a pillar of the *porte-cochère*.

'I was hoping to catch her before she went,' Michael said.

'She's coming back for Jamie's exhibition. He is quite extraordinary. He drove up to Heathrow without saying goodbye. I think she's a bit upset. She seemed specially quiet.'

'I wanted to apologize to her for being so ratty these past few days.'

'She understands.'

'May I apologize to you also?'

Virginia seemed taken by surprise. She straightened up and dusted her hands gently.

'Yes, of course.'

'I lost my way for a day or so. I'm very sorry, Ginny.'

'You sound horribly back on target now.'

'I think I am.'

Virginia thought of saying something, then changed her mind. Instead, she laughed. Michael raised his eyebrows.

'What's so funny?'

'You. In this mood, we are all in danger.'

'Not everybody,' Michael protested gently.

Tony Evrington arrived at the Hall at eleven. He was received by Hodnett, who applied his most glacial manner to the situation. Evrington was kept cooling his heels for what Jim Hodnett considered the correct number of minutes before looking up to find not Virginia, but Michael.

'Hullo,' he said uncertainly.

'Before you see Ginny, I wonder if we can walk in the grounds for a few moments?'

Michael led him out in a blaze of cheery inconsequentialities. Though they had met before, it was only to nod across a reception or the like. Michael marched him along briskly.

'I called to invite Virginia to lunch in Salisbury,' Evrington said, having to stride out to keep pace.

'I'm sure she'll be delighted. You'll have to remind me what you do, Mr Evrington.'

'Tony,' he corrected gently. 'I think you know well enough. I'm a marine architect. I live on the coast. Virginia must have told you.'

'I think she did mention something. Shall we walk across the fields here? Tremendous day, don't you think?'

Evrington looked back at the house. Michael had already climbed the stile and was waiting.

'There's a purpose, is there?'

'One should never need an excuse to go walking. But I can find a purpose, yes. I wanted to ask you what you're doing here.'

'I think I said: lunch with your wife.'

'Yes. And more broadly?'

Evrington studied Michael, trying to gauge how far to go.

'I imagine it is obvious. I'm in love with her.'

'Ah, yes!'

He smiled and walked on across the field, forcing Tony to follow him across the stile.

'You seem to take that without comment,' he called.

'You're in love with her, eh?'

'And I think she could fall in love with me.'

'Do you? How fascinating. I should have put it as highly unlikely. But we'll see.'

'I thought it was more or less understood that Virginia was free to do as she chose.'

'More or less. Shall we cut down to the woods? I have started to get quite interested in ornithology. I can show you my barred woodpecker if you like.'

'Damn your ornithology.'

'I will say this, Evrington, you're the most impudent bastard I've met since coming home to England. You're in love with my wife, are you? And what are you going to do? Marry her? Why not. The least I can do for the pair of you is to divorce her, naming you. I'm quite fond of her myself, d'you see? I mustn't stand in the way of her happiness.'

'Michael –' Evrington began.

'No, please don't call me Michael. I have taken the trouble to find out a little about you. You've had quite a few affairs. Diana Walton Watson lived with you for a few months in your little seaside idyll before going back to David and the children, I believe.'

'It depends who tells you the story.'

'I rang her up. She did. She says you ought to be castrated with a pair of rusting garden shears, but that's just her jealousy, I imagine. No, in the light of what you've said, I'll start divorce proceedings immediately.'

'I can't quite tell whether you're joking,' Evrington said.

'I wish you both every happiness. Where's the joke in that?'

They had reached the edge of a rambling wood. Michael walked in under the shade, and after a moment or two, Evrington followed, less certainly.

'Look, just a minute,' he said.

'You leave me hardly any other choice,' Michael replied.

'Of course there are other choices.'

'There are, yes, but do you know I have never thought about them. One does grow an old-fashioned skin with a title. I would hardly have believed it, but it's true.'

'I don't exactly know what the hell you're talking about, but there is an alternative to divorce.'

'There is,' Michael said. 'That's really very civil of you, Evrington. Perhaps you're not as modern as you seem after all. So let's try the other solution, shall we?'

He hit Evrington with a colossal right swing that any boxer could have seen coming. Evrington himself saw it coming but couldn't really believe it. Michael's fist connected with the side of his face and sent him flying backwards as if on elastic ropes. He was actually lifted off his feet.

As to Michael, the pleasure of the event was quite outweighed by the appalling pain to his knuckles. He walked back up towards the house with his right arm across his chest, the fist tucked under his armpit.

Virginia received him later in her bedroom. She had been doing the household accounts and trying to make sense of one of Peter Thornton's schemes, laid out erratically in biro on ruled sheets of paper.

'All right,' she said. 'Explain.'

'I'm afraid I enjoyed it. Never done it before, not even as a boy. It hurt like hell, but it was worth it.'

'And that's all the explanation that's necessary, is it?'

'In a way, yes.'

'He thinks you're mad.'

'Oh yes. Mad. But a bit dangerous, too, I trust.'

'And do I get any say in these goings-on?'

'Yes.'

There was a silence, and Virginia gave him a long look.

'What are we saying, Michael?'

'That I love you myself.'

She made a face, and Michael blew on his knuckles.

'That I want you myself.'

'Not quite in the way he does.'

'How do you know that?'

She threw down her pencil and walked to the window.

'You're no good at this sort of thing.'

'Listen to me, Ginny. It could quite easily come crashing down, all of it. We've all worked bloody hard for over a year, pushing a rock up a mountain. It could just roll back and flatten us.'

'Money.'

He thought about that.

'Money, yes, I suppose. But other things too. You. Evrington, perhaps. Jamie.'

'What has Jamie got to do with it?'

'I want him to stay. I want him to be happy. Unfortunately, he is beginning to hate my guts. That may be true of you also.'

Virginia turned back from the window.

'You look absolutely awful. You know that, don't you?'

He said nothing for a moment, but shrugged.

'If everything else goes under, I want to be left with you. That's from the heart.'

They stood motionless in the silent room for what seemed a long time, a few paces apart, a few paces from her bed. Virginia, who had asked for choices, had one to make now. Evrington had gone back to his house by the sea, and was waiting for her. And with Evrington she could be assured of romance of a kind, adventure of a kind. Michael regarded her with calm, dark eyes.

'I do have a heart,' he whispered. 'And it is speaking to you now.'

With a little sob, she ran into his arms. Although she was crying, when she spoke it was apparently without emotion.

'Lock the door,' she said.

But then it became a frenzy on both sides. As if a dam had burst, all that had been pent up between them since long before Chelworth flooded out. She lay on the bed with her arms outstretched to receive him, realizing that something in particular had given way in her. What had been, even with Keith, a lake, had become a torrent. He must have seen some of this in her eyes. Michael made love to her with an urgency and passion that broke down all the barriers of the years. Without speaking, he declared a need that she had perhaps pretended to herself he could not feel.

On her part, the sensation of release was utter. It went beyond pleasure. She was filled, she realized, with joy. It was the kind of joy that sits in the heart next to terror, the joy that hardly dares announce itself. She was the first to speak.

'More,' she said. 'More.'

Seventeen

You knew people by their capacity to describe the world. What was familiar in what they said – their geography of the capes and bays – was what made them understandable. Or perhaps, putting it another way, you sought a reflection of your own mind in another, and when you found it declared that person appealing. Virginia lay beside Michael and stared at the cracks in the ceiling. He was asleep, face down on the bed, sprawled almost like a tiler who has fallen through the roof and landed by accident beside a naked woman. She tugged gently at the sheet that was caught at her hips and pulled it over herself. It was still quite light. Her watch was on the floor and the radio alarm was obscured by a pillow. She guessed it to be about eight, or maybe nine.

She felt a sensation of almost pure relief, of a weight lifted, that things had at last come to this. Before that afternoon, she could not remember when last they had made love. It seemed too long ago to bother thinking about. She slipped out of bed and found a robe. Moving as quietly as she could, she unlocked the bedroom door and walked down the creaking boards of the corridor to the bathroom. She had taken to leaving a portable radio tuned to Radio Three there, and after she had drawn her bath she switched it on. She stepped gingerly into the water to the sound of Brahms, and lay back rested and content.

Virginia began to think of Chelworth. She was happy there, happier than she had supposed possible. Part of the joy was in living out the four seasons. From every window she could look out on to trees and lawns, fields and hills. She hardly ever looked at clocks these days – the landscape itself was a gigantic clock. And if it meant (as it did in practice) that you could barely distinguish Thursday from Sunday, or late July from early August, there was the compensating pleasure of submitting to the rule of the sun. Not until she moved back to England and took up residence in Chelworth had she to ask bank tellers or shopkeepers for the date, a thing she did quite regularly now. All this was from the bewitching of time by the house and its location.

It could not last. Though Michael had yet to realize it, she already knew they must come to their senses. It simply could not be that they continue in never-never land. One day, quite soon, the time she had been picturing would have to stop. Jamie would see to that.

Because, when Michael spoke of Jamie and his marriage as a way of continuing the inheritance, Virginia had already looked ahead to the time when she became a grandmother and Jamie's child was playing on the lawns outside. To imagine that child himself inheriting at some time in the twenty-first century, with nothing altered or abated, was a wishful folly. In her heart of hearts, Virginia knew they had been living in a dream.

She rose from the bath and dried herself on a huge pink towel. When she went back to her bedroom, Michael had dressed and was gone. The bed was made, expertly and crisply. Her watch, which she had torn off in abandon three hours before, had been picked up and was staring at her from the bedside table. It was twenty to ten. She dressed in a white button-through dress she had not worn for ages, and went in search of him. Along the corridors it was very dark, but as she walked downstairs the last of the light of day was still pouring in, miraculous, faithful and abundant. Michael came to greet her at the foot of the stairs.

'You are wonderful,' he said.

'I'm famished.'

By the side of the quay in St Pete there is an astonishing inverted pyramid that turns out to be a shopping mall and restaurant. The sharp, crisp Florida sunshine reflects back from its windows; in the restaurant there is a sepulchral gloom. Red is a colour without which Americans could not eat and feel themselves pampered. Jamie wandered into the place feeling as if he was walking across the tongue of some cartoon dog. The windows were of tinted glass and a stiff, air-conditioned breeze rustled the paper table-cloths.

He was looking for Mr Calcavecchia whose name he had picked out of the phone book on arrival in Florida. The private investigator made it easy for him by raising a huge ham of a hand in greeting. He wore a floppy golf hat, a shirt with palms, and bright yellow trousers. He weighed at least half as much again as Jamie.

'Siddown, kid,' Calcavecchia said. 'I'm drinking Bourbon. Wanna join in?'

'I'll have a beer. Did you find anything?'

'First off, what's with this viscount crap? You're a viscount?'

'Yes.'

'Live in a castle?'

'A house.'

'Big house? Like the Ringling place in Sarasota?'

'Slightly smaller than that.'

Calcavecchia shook his head wonderingly.

'No kidding? That must be really something.'

'You come from Philadelphia,' Jamie said.

'I come from New York City,' Calcavecchia corrected. 'I was a cop in Philadelphia.'

'Nice town.'

Calcavecchia looked at him as though studying a child.

'You see my lips move when you said that? They didn't move, did they?'

'I thought it was a good place.'

'Yeah,' Calcavecchia said wearily. He had been half sitting on a big yellow envelope, which he threw on to the table.

'Photostats,' he said. 'The hotel register, a letter from the hotel to him saying he had left his camera behind and did he know. A letter from him to the hotel saying, shit, yes, he knew, but to give the camera to charity. They cracked up over that one. They're still talking about it.'

'Well done.'

Calcavecchia removed the toothpick from his lips.

'God bless you,' he said. 'The desk clerk retired four years ago, lives in some shithole place in Largo. Your man asked the guy to fix him up with a girl. He was upset. It's a class hotel. You ask the room-boy for that. His address is inside. He's a corroborating witness, and a hungry one.'

'How much do I owe you?'

'Two fifty,' Calcavecchia said.

'Would you like it now?'

'Now is fine. What'll you do with this guy? Stitch him up? What's he done to you?'

'He's given my father the surprise of his life.'

'Is your father another fucking viscount?'

'More or less,' Jamie said.

Michael examined a wine-label with a wry smile.

'I keep forgetting how well you live.'

Ewan Chivers waved his arm negligently. The two men sat by the pool at Roman Arches, their chests and faces lit by the water's reflection. It was a fine evening.

'Barbara likes wine. She's actually very good at choosing it. Thank you for your invitation to this do on Friday, by the way.'

Michael made a little gesture with his hands.

'It's what Jamie will insist on calling an eclectic show. Bits and pieces. It's a way of testing the water, I suppose. We might turn one room over entirely to works of art.'

'I thought you didn't want to do that,' said Ewan.

'I don't.'

He watched his glass being recharged. Ewan was very much at his ease.

'I suppose you've been hit badly by the stock-market panic.'

'Things could be better.'

'It's hurt everybody, of course. But then, there's a tradition of aristocrats strapped for cash, isn't there? I imagine you always jump clear.'

'Our kind, you mean?'

'Your kind.'

'In novels, yes,' Michael said drily.

And he was waiting all the time, waiting. At last Ewan played his shot.

'I think Barbara may have said something to you on the train recently.'

'About your wishing to buy Barlow Court? I was startled, yes.'

'Not Barlow Court,' Ewan said. 'She tells me you were hunting down some stamps.'

'Oh, that! Yes, I was curious. But now I know where they are.'

Ewan looked surprised.

'You do?'

'Yes.'

'Well, good. The point is, and there's no reason to deceive you, Firbank did offer me some stuff in 1979 or 1980, I can't remember which. That may be the thing you were chasing up.'

'1980,' Michael provided amiably.

'Was it? Anyway, he pitched up here with them, and I turned them down. It goes without saying he claimed them as his own. But . . . well, he was a funny chap.'

'He was, wasn't he?'

'I thought it best to keep out of it.'

'I'm very grateful,' Michael said negligently.

'You don't believe me,' Ewan decided. Michael laughed.

'Why should I not believe you? I don't suppose they were very valuable. It was just an idea, that we should show them. Quite a fun thing. Something a little different, perhaps. Jamie approves.'

'How is he?' Ewan asked. 'Butterflies in the stomach over this show of his?'

'He's away for a day or two,' Michael murmured.

'Look,' Ewan said. 'It may need saying. I'm not in any sense an enemy of yours, you know. I wish you nothing but good.'

Michael smiled, and the remark died on the air.

He and Virginia dined from the best service that night in the room decorated by Cipriani. They ate by candlelight, with the curtains drawn, though it was still light outside. She cooked the meal herself.

'I want you to tell me what's in your mind,' she said.

'A man comes home to a strange country, with rather fewer virtues than he supposed he had. He is in mid-life, and while he's hardly with one foot in the grave, he has done a great many things, worked extremely hard, and he is tired. For the first time in many years, he can admit that he is tired. It frightens him, a little.'

'What will he do?'

Michael shrugged.

'He knows enough about life to know that he hardly has a choice. He must do what is immediately in front of him. He must take the first cab on the rank. But perhaps he's wrong about that.'

'Michael, nobody who loves you could point to a soppy side in you. I mean you've mellowed unbelievably just by being here, but whether you start smoking a pipe and wearing slippers, or decide to give golf a real go isn't actually in question at all. You can't do any of those things. It isn't in you.'

'I would like Jamie to have all this when we go, and it frightens me sometimes that he may not want it.'

She considered that carefully.

'Are you serious about being tired?'

'I think I'm most serious about having fewer virtues than I once thought. Perhaps fewer talents is a better way of putting it. Handling Jamie isn't one of them. Loving you. I've made quite a mess of that, too.'

She reached across the table and held his hand for a moment.

'Look, if it never worked out with Chelworth – no, listen to me – if it never really worked out, you would have done something just by coming home,' Virginia said.

'But just what, we don't know.'

'I do.'

The exhibition went ahead on a gloriously sunny day. Jamie and Michael were closeted together in the office for an hour and broke off only as the first guests arrived. A huge buffet lunch was laid out, and people were given a glass of very good wine. They slowly spread themselves round the house: Americans who had fitted this visit into their itinerary of Wilton, Blenheim, Oxford; arts writers; officials from museums and the National Trust. Regional television sent a camera crew, and Russell Fairless soon had them cornered. He leaned against the wall of the corridor and did his act of plucking common sense from the air just above his head.

'I do think, and I know the government thinks this also, that great treasure houses as these are must survive – indeed will survive – for as long as the will is there to preserve them.'

He smiled ingratiatingly at his interviewer, someone he had just described, off camera, as an incompetent little shit who ought to learn his business. Russell touched his bow tie with a tiny gesture of aplomb that had become his trademark on television.

'I mean, let's look around us.'

The reporter gave him a vehement thumbs-up for the chance he had made to cut away from his talking head.

' – This is a colossal endorsement, don't you think, of Britain, of the heritage we fight to preserve – I mean not just now, or in this place, but across the board.'

He came to a sudden stop with a winning smile. The moment the camera ceased running, the smile vanished. Russell looked vaguely about him as if bored with the whole thing.

'Is that okay? I could do it again.'

The young reporter all too willingly took his bored act for the truth of the matter.

'That's great, that's all we need.'

Russell frowned, considerably niggled.

'Were we going to do a little piece about the knighthood?'

'Yes, of course, we'll knock that off in overlay. We'll come to you after making it clear who you are. Thanks a bunch.'

'You're very welcome,' Russell snapped. He glanced round, and found Michael watching him. Russell rolled his eyes.

'I haven't congratulated you myself,' Michael murmured, as the camera crew trailed away after their reporter.

'Oh, I don't have to pretend to you.'

'You must be very proud, all the same.'

'Well, do you know, I suppose I am. Aren't you on parade, sort of thing? I must say the stuff you've put out is quite fascinating. I'm green with envy.'

'There's something in particular I want you to see.'

'Oh well, lead on, by all means. I should like to get that young reporter's name. I thought he was very casual.'

'We'll go to the Yellow Room,' Michael said. 'That's the only place off-limits today. We can talk. It won't take long.'

'Gosh, secrets!' Russell said in his best flirty voice.

They walked into the room and Russell looked about him.

'What exactly is it?' he asked.

'This.'

Michael passed him a large yellow envelope and watched while Russell opened it and scanned the sheets. The M P did his fast-read, at-a-glance perusal and then read the second and third sheets more carefully.

'I'm not quite on your wavelength,' he said in a low voice.

'It's a photocopy of a hotel register in St Petersburg, Florida. An old whaling port, I believe.'

'Yes, yes, yes . . . But what of it?'

'Russell Fairless, M P. That's you. The letter about your camera is addressed to you at the House, and you replied on House of Commons notepaper. There's no argument there, surely?'

Fairless licked his lips.

'Are we going to say what this is about?'

'Stamp collections. Philately.'

The M P laughed, as if at an uncertain joke.

'I'm afraid I haven't the faintest idea . . .'

'You told Goodrich they were your own property.'

'Who is Goodrich?'

Michael lit a cigarette.

'On June 30th, 1980, you flew to Tampa, via Boston. You booked in at your hotel – that hotel – after a drive across the causeway, and the next day you sold Mr Goodrich the contents of six albums that had been stolen from this house. Where, as you were kind enough to say a few moments ago, there is great pride in being English. And honest.'

Russell put down the papers with elaborate care and quiet.

'I think I would like to consider these allegations in another place.'

'You must take all the time you wish. But I can help – if that's the word – a little. Goodrich knew England. During the war, he had been on Eaker's staff, and then on Eisenhower's as an air attaché. He found you comically vain, he said. He often referred to your flying visit. There is even an entry in his diary.'

'I have no recollection whatever –'

'But you see, Sir Russell, that won't do. Jamie has just come back from Florida. These are the immediate fruits. I can prove without a shadow of a doubt that *you* bought the stamps from my former agent, Firbank, knowing them to have been stolen, and that within a fortnight you had sold them to Mr Goodrich.'

'We shall see what Goodrich has to say.'

'Goodrich is dead. The stamps have come up for auction. Exactly as they were in my grandfather's day, nothing added or subtracted. I'm sorry to add one more nail than is necessary, but the stamps are mounted on paper that was watermarked with my family crest, and there they sit right now, in New York, on the same sheets. To some people, just so many unimportant little bits of paper.'

Russell sat down, and then stood up again immediately. He walked to the window and swore violently at the lawns and ornamental ponds.

'What do you want?'

'That is the question, isn't it? You've been greedy, and stupid, to be sure. That may be your defence.'

'Look . . .' Russell started with tears in his eyes.

'I wouldn't try to think on your feet,' Michael said coldly.

The buffet was eaten, the wine was guzzled down. Jamie took the more hardy of the visitors on a little tour of the house exteriors. Some were amused and touched to see Dibs at his side. The local MP, Fairless, had made his excuses and left. Michael and Ewan strolled, hands in pockets, up the drive, for all the world like agreeable neighbours.

'You really intend to go through with it?' Ewan said, after a glance back to make sure they were out of earshot.

'I think so.'

'If I were to make an offer of full restitution? I'll pay you whatever the stuff makes at auction. Or I'll go and bid for them myself.'

'We seem to be in a difficulty here. The day before yesterday you were offering me your undying friendship. Now you're offering to pay his debts. We can't all three be friends, surely?'

'If he resigns . . . my God, you can't make him do that! These things never stay secret, you know that.'

'Of course. After he has resigned his seat in Parliament, we shall have to see what happens.'

'The bloody man's just been knighted by the Queen, for God's sake!'

'Wasn't her great-grandfather a collector? Let's not have him resign, then. I'll simply make the facts known to her, if you like. That's to say through her Prime Minister. And things can take their course, if you think that's a better idea.'

'You're a cold bastard, Hincham.'

Michael shrugged.

'He's no great loss.'

Ewan walked a few paces and then found something to laugh at, although his pleasure seemed grim enough.

'You expected it to be me, when you sent Jamie shooting off there. That's what you were guessing, that I swindled you out of your bloody stamps.'

'Or a quarter of a million pounds, depending how keen you are on the stamps as stamps.'

'But you thought – you guessed – you would find me at the end of the search.'

'You, neighbour?' Michael protested mildly. 'Would *you* do a thing like that?'

They stepped on to the verge as the minibus carrying the Americans drove away. The occupants waved merrily.

Eighteen

To the west and south of Hincham there is a huge stone-built wall running beside the road, behind which is Nesrigg Hall, the home of Arthur Dullington. Lord Dullington's estate includes ponds, where it is sometimes amusing (as he puts it) to shoot duck. The guns he invites are seldom great sportsmen, and to be truthful the shoot is nothing very special. Arthur Dullington goes to Yorkshire for the grouse, and stalks stag in Somerset. His own duck-shoot is really quite a minor pleasure by comparison, and a way of repaying local hospitality or humiliating local critics.

It was here, one evening, that Ewan Chivers met someone called Harper, whom, after a few moments, he correctly identified as Dibs's father. Charles Harper was, as it turned out, though poor as a church mouse, the best shot ever to be invited to the ponds. This was surprising. He was a wan, abashed sort of man who had fallen in luck and circumstance and was now running a not-very-enterprising farm survey business. The moment Chivers introduced himself more fully, Harper showed his hand.

'You don't happen to know Lord Hincham?'

'Of course,' Chivers said. 'I know the whole family.'

'That's a man I am going to have to meet some day.'

Dullington had also invited his chum Dudley Wolverton, a huge red-necked horse trainer with a notorious passion for women as well as horses. Wolverton had already decided he did not like Harper.

'What's the story about Fairless, the MP fellow?' he interrupted. 'What's he resigned over? Can't make head nor tail of the gossip. Bloody Hincham comes into it somewhere.'

'I think you could say Fairless was hounded out by his lordship.'

'Caught with his trousers round his ankles or something?'

Chivers considered whether or not to tell the whole story. He decided against it.

'Russell was a very good and popular constituency MP. He's taken it all very badly.'

'Know him, Dudley?' Dullington asked.

'Met him. Bit of a fool, vain as buggery, but at least he wasn't one of those grocer's boys, not one of these appalling estate-agent shits. This Cabinet rabble is what I'm talking about. This one played cricket. Got his Blue.'

'In a bad year,' Dullington amended.

'Oh yes! But he was at least part-way presentable. Well, he got his knighthood, etcetera. One assumes people know what they're doing with that sort of thing. As for Hincham, I never liked the brother, thought he was a complete wet, but this one is a complete and utter pill, by all accounts.'

'Harper's girl goes out with the young Viscount, Jamie.'

'Him! The boy's a raving nancy, Harper. Your girl must be a bit slow on the uptake if you ask me. I wouldn't let the unhappy little bugger near my dogs!'

Harper walked away from the three of them, his face white. Dullington laughed.

'Tremendous sense of tact, Dudley.'

'I'm only telling him the truth, for God's sake.'

'Go after him, Chivers, there's a good chap. Can't have the evening spoiled.'

Ewan did as he was asked. There was a strong smell of weed rising from the lakeside. The duck they had shot were laid out on a scrap of canvas and Harper stood nearby. He turned on Ewan mournfully.

'They are friends of yours, I suppose,' he said.

'Dullington wants to sell me a bed of gravel. The other one's a complete caricature. There was no need to speak like that, no need at all. You should ignore it.'

'Is it true, however?'

Ewan studied him.

'I think you already know the answer to that. What does your daughter say?'

'She's a child,' Harper said. He brushed back his hair.

He kicked up a pebble with his shoe. It bounced on the muddy ground and hit the carcass of a duck. Harper picked it off the dulled feathers and flicked it absently into the lake.

'My daughter thinks she can change him. And from what my wife says, she has already gone about it. But the whole idea sickens me.'

'Children these days,' Ewan murmured.

'But you don't have any.'

Ewan laid a hand on his arm.

'Come back to Hincham with me. We'll have a drink.'

Harper, to Ewan's private pleasure, seemed pathetically grateful for the invitation.

'That boy is not going to marry Dibs,' he said.

'Marry? Is that on the cards?'

'That's what he says he wants.'

'You've spoken to him?'

'I won't. He's at the house now. I want never to see him; I think I've made that clear to both of them. To all of them,' he added.

'Poor chap,' Ewan said mechanically, his mind racing. 'I can quite see your point.'

'I dare say you want to tell me he's not actually like that at all.'

'Well . . .' Ewan said.

Harper looked at him sharply.

'You know of something?'

'Look, I would be speaking completely out of turn.'

'There is someone else? I mean he has a man?'

'Let's talk about it over that drink.'

Mrs Harper had something of the blue-stocking about her. She was a faded blonde who spent a great deal of time with her shoes kicked off and her feet tucked under her, reading on sofas. Jamie was not unaware of the type, and there was much to like in her, but all the same she was not easy to talk to. For her part, she was kindness itself; but in a weary, exhausted kind of way.

The whole house had a sunned and dusty feel to it. There were a great many books, and Dibs practised at a scuffed baby grand in a room filled with records and green plants. The one missing element was any real indication that Dibs's father also lived there. It struck

Jamie that the two women lived there as uneasy and squabbling spinsters who had been disappointed by men, and so had no further need of them. But he knew this was an illusion. Charles Harper lived there, all right.

Lydia Harper had been catching up with the Sunday papers. Jamie sat opposite her, glancing at a page she had folded back for him to read, wherein a gossip column featured Michael. He skimmed it, not wishing to tell her he had already committed it to memory on the day of publication.

'My father's not in a popularity contest,' he said slowly. 'And there are aspects to Fairless's resignation that can't be mentioned by him, and will never be mentioned by Fairless. As this particular journalist knows only too well. And so what? It might have mattered once, what the papers do or don't say. But I can't see that it does now. It's trivial.'

'It's also fairly wounding,' Lydia said in her soft, languorous voice.

'I don't think so.'

'Why? Because it's in a gossip column?'

'If you like.'

'Gossip is trivial and pointless?'

Jamie found his temper growing. There were wood pigeons in the trees of the rectory opposite; every quarter of an hour the church clocks chimed, and they flew off, only to settle again moments later. The traffic rumbled a comfortable distance away. It seemed to him quite pointless to wonder what sold newspapers, and why anyone should remember anything they read about the doings of the rich. He had begun to hate the pretence that even this inoffensive family made, that the things that mattered and the people that were in the papers were part and parcel of the same thing.

'I think I would prefer a life without gossip,' he said.

'I'm quite sure,' Lydia Harper said. 'But that doesn't render it pointless.'

Dibs wandered in from the garden through the rather drunken French windows. She wore a sundress that made her feel fat and foolish, and her arms had picked up a bright red burn. Jamie glanced at her too briefly. In a swing of mood he was getting used to,

Dibs took this as rejection, utter repudiation. She lived in fear of such a thing. She flinched from his too-casual glance as if he had struck her.

'I'm hot,' she said.

'Make some lemonade,' Lydia suggested.

'What are you talking about?'

'Go and make some lemonade, Dibs. I am talking to Jamie.'

'Yes, but what about?'

'Oh for goodness sake,' Lydia said in such a weary tone of voice that Jamie felt bound to say something himself.

'Nothing special,' he promised.

Dibs walked out of the room.

Lydia threw the remaining sections of the paper on to the floor and sighed. He tried to come to the point.

'I suppose you want to know what Dibs and I are up to.'

'Oh, Jamie . . .'

'We're very close.'

She lit a thin brown cigarette and waved the smoke about in front of her face.

'I know that. I like you Jamie: I admire you. But I'm pretty much an expert on being wounded – we all are in this family. We're not very tough.'

'Maybe you have a prepared speech, Mrs Harper. Perhaps you ought to make it. Is it that I'm a viscount, or that I'm bisexual?'

Lydia smiled.

'I don't know. As to your being the son of an earl, the things you'll inherit come into it, yes. It seems an awful responsibility to me. Dibs is hardly more than a child. I want you to give each other time.'

She rubbed her brow with her thin fingers. Her pale-blue eyes searched his out.

'I never expected to be making a speech like this – I always thought life would be completely different from my generation onward. I suppose everybody believes that when they're young. But now I sound like my own mother.'

'Could we get to the heart of what you're saying?'

'What Dibs knows about is school, here, this house, playing the piano and the organ, and Chelworth. It isn't enough.'

'Suppose I said simply that I want to marry her? Can I talk to your husband about it?'

'He has deputed me to say all this, and I do not enjoy it. Don't make it any more difficult than it is already, Jamie.'

'You haven't said anything yet!'

'She's too young, and too innocent. And too vulnerable.'

'You make her sound retarded.'

'I'm trying to make her sound – oh, I don't know. I know you love her.'

'Then what is it? Aren't I good enough for your family?'

'He doesn't think so,' Lydia said with unanswerable simplicity. Jamie left shortly after, driving away fast at first, and then very fast. He drove straight past his own house – *his* house! – and headed for the motorway and London. He left behind a wordless Dibs, standing at the gate to their drive, tears running down her cheeks as if she would never see him again.

Bill Toller was staying at Chelworth. Virginia had fetched her father down from London after her weekly telephone call had picked up a note, a tone, that she had been dreading for years. It was as if he were drifting away. His own explanation was laconic: he had been under the weather, as he put it. When she went to fetch him, she found him in the same imperturbable good humour, but with a faint warning in his eyes. He permitted himself to be driven to the country, where for three days he played the invalid. He sat in the gardens with a rug over his knees, talking to Dorothy and Hodnett, and reading up much more recent history than was his usual passion.

'What happened to Jack Cade's Rebellion?' Virginia asked.

'Still there,' Bill said in his dry way. 'Won't go away, just because I do. But I was asked to read this book on Auchinleck. The Auk.'

'You knew him.'

'I worked for him, and yes, I knew him. Rather better than this young man.'

He smiled as Virginia kissed him, her hand in his.

'I would like to ask you a favour. If you can spare the time, I would rather like one of you to drive me over to our old house. The place where I was born.'

Virginia frowned for a moment, and then laughed.

'My goodness,' she said, trying to keep the wobble out of her voice, 'what a very dramatic thing to ask. Are you saying goodbye?'

'D'you remember the game of consequences, and having to write at the bottom "what the world said"? Well, the world says, "never mind," just as nanny always said it did. It would please me to see the old place.'

'Would you like Michael to take you? You could go tomorrow.'

'Don't be afraid, Ginny. I'm not exactly hale and hearty, but I'm not dead either. Or not as far as I know.'

She snorted another laugh, the tears bursting from her eyes.

'Oh, Daddy! What am I going to do without you?'

'Remember me with affection,' he suggested.

He looked up, and she followed his glance. Walking across the lawns towards them was a very forlorn Dibs, and Michael, holding her hand. Bill Toller held out both his arms, and Dibs ran to him, sobbing. He patted her back.

'Good Lord,' he said. 'Oh Dibsy, Dibsy, this won't do at all.'

'I had no idea you knew each other that well,' Michael said.

'Whenever Dibs feels in need of a macaroon in London, she comes to me. Don't you, pudding?'

She began to boo-hoo in earnest. Virginia touched her on the arm.

'Come here,' she said. 'Let's leave my father alone.'

Dibs turned and collapsed into her arms. While she hugged the girl, it crossed Virginia's mind almost as a piece of absent-mindedness that such a round, warm, bulky thing as this was Jamie's chosen alternative to sex with men. Her arms could hardly join behind Dibs's back. She kissed her cheek and neck.

'Hush, hush,' she soothed.

They left Bill out on the lawn and walked back to the house. Michael poured three enormous gin and tonics. They sat listening to a plane drift across the sky. Somewhere in the woods, Thornton had a chainsaw going. In the room it was quiet enough to hear the ice crack in the glasses. Michael raised eyebrows at his wife, who shook her head, and they waited out the awful, hopeless silence.

'I'm very sorry,' Dibs said at last, in the tiniest of voices.

'It's your father,' Michael guessed.

'Yes.'

'It very often is.'

'Jamie and I want to marry.'

'This is the official announcement, is it?'

Virginia took her hand and bounced it lightly in her lap.

'Never mind him, what does your father say?'

'I hate myself for breaking down like this, but my mother spoke to Jamie about it and he just flew out of the house. He left in such a rage, without saying goodbye.'

'He'll turn up.'

'You can imagine what my father says he wants.'

'Or doesn't want,' Michael said into his glass.

He ruffled Dibs's hair gently.

'I believe you love each other, Dibs. I know you do. And when that is so, things often resolve themselves in a pretty obvious way, don't they?'

'I love him for what he is. Whatever he is.'

'Of course,' Michael said. He and Virginia exchanged glances.

Dibs set down her drink.

'I'm not completely stupid. We are sleeping together, and it does work. It works. I can make him happy.'

'I think you do,' Virginia said swiftly. 'I know you do. But your father may be thinking of whether *he* can make *you* happy.'

'Of course he can. He does.'

Jamie came home that night around midnight. He was startled to find Dibs's 2CV in the courtyard. When he went into the house, Michael was reading with a whisky at his elbow. He smiled and took off his glasses.

'She's asleep,' he said. 'Where the hell have you been?'

'In London. I've been caught for speeding, incidentally. Pretty much the cliché, wouldn't you say? Upper-class twit in motorway madness chase.'

'I'll read about it in the papers when your case comes up. Do you want to talk, or merely feel sorry for yourself?'

Jamie sat down opposite his father.

'There has been some fairly obvious trouble with Harper. He

won't see me, or talk to me. I'm just part of the gay plague to him. Perhaps he thinks I'm going to steal her make-up, or ask to borrow one of her mother's frocks.'

'Perhaps he worries about her future.'

Jamie glowered.

'Look, I need to marry, right?'

'I haven't said so.'

'You haven't said so, but it's all a bit pointless otherwise, isn't it? I need to carry the great struggle on into the next century, to provide an heir.'

'You make me say this, Jamie: I am rather more selfish than you imagine, but not as selfish as that. I am living here, and doing all this, for myself, principally. I have tried not to ask anything of you. The girl worships you, that much is obvious. I think she needs you. Not quite the same thing, and *that* ought to be a perception in my favour. Harper is quite right to ask whether you need her in the same way. It doesn't have to be a slur on your sexuality. You could see it as a common anxiety fathers have concerning their daughters.'

'I am going to marry her.'

'So she says,' Michael said dryly.

'Doesn't that count in *my* favour?'

'Not if you want to pretend you're doing it to please me. Nor if you're doing it to prove something.'

Jamie hesitated, jingling his car-keys.

'This is more or less repeating the conversation I had in London.'

'Oh yes? With whom?'

'Nobody you know.'

At Roman Arches the lights were also burning late. Barbara had been drinking fairly steadily since seven, and was in a mean, confused mood. Ewan matched her drink for drink, although he watered his whisky down so that it was hardly more than a tint. For a time she had played records, and for a short while they played dice together; but the evening was a sullen and acrimonious one.

'I hate this house,' she said, to fill what had been a long silence. Ewan shrugged.

'That's why we're buying Barlow Court.'

'To please me, is it? Or so that you can hang out on the fringes of the posh set, nibbling all the little crumbs of gossip? This bloody Harper character. What in hell's name are we doing with him?'

'Nothing,' Ewan said.

'What use can we find for him, as if I didn't already know? The only classy bloke you've ever met is Michael and you're sick with jealousy. What are we going to do at Barlow Court, have intimate little supper parties with Dullington and his cow of a wife? Are we going to *be* somebody at last, Ewan?'

'That's for you to decide,' he said coldly.

'You mean I should learn how to behave?'

'Since you put it in the form of a question, yes, you should.'

'And you'll give me lessons?'

'If necessary.'

Barbara was drinking from a crystal goblet. She smashed it down hard enough for it to shatter, and stumbled from the room. Ewan brushed a little sliver of crystal from his sleeve and followed.

In the bathroom Barbara had a long glass shelf on which she kept her scents and bottles of shampoo and conditioner, her bath milk and cleansing lotions, her entire armoury of cosmetics and beauty aids. She swept the lot to the floor with a sickening crash and sat down on the edge of the bath, sobbing. Ewan watched her carefully, alert to anything else that might happen.

'I'm scared,' she said.

'There's nothing to be afraid of Barbara. What happened to Russell – to Eileen – was unforgivable. Michael made that happen. He destroyed a friend of ours. What do you expect me to feel about that?'

'Russell stole from him!'

'That isn't it, and you know that isn't it. The man is a vindictive bastard. He's dangerous.'

She shook her head, tore a piece of toilet paper from the roll and blew her nose loudly.

'I don't like who we are any longer, Ewan. I wish that we had kids, or friends. Real friends. That at least.'

'We do have friends.'

'Russell was never my friend. Eileen Fairless isn't a friend. I don't want to load myself up with jewellery and hang my tits out for people you know, just to prove to them that you're happy.'

'Then don't,' he said sharply.

'I don't want to pretend we've got all we ever wanted from life.'

'Let's clean this lot up,' he said.

'If we had had children, Ewan, it would be different.'

'Not that,' he said in a voice of ice. 'Not now.'

She stood up and turned her back on him, bending over the bath to turn on the taps. After he had left the room he heard the lock turn. He went and sat in the deep leather sofa, staring at the pool outside the windows, lit from underwater. By a trick of the light, his reflected image hung suspended over the mirror calm. There he sat, out on the surface of the water, his head in his hands, a coffee table at his knees, and the treacherous night kept him suspended there, neither rising nor sinking.

Barbara was still in the bath when he clawed his way upstairs to bed. He did not hear her join him.

Nineteen

The road to Bill Toller's birthplace was away to the west, across countryside that on this particular morning lay in an idyllic, windless haze of watery sunshine. Michael drove. Bill sat beside him in wonderfully ancient tweeds, his frail and freckled hands clasped on his lap. Not until after eleven did the sun finally burn off the mist; they had stopped for coffee at a little place by the river near Sturminster Newton, and no sooner were they on the road again than the sky became blue from horizon to horizon.

Michael found great pleasure in the journey, all the more so because of the many detours he took. The last of them led to a halt on the old Somerset and Dorset line that had once been at the very heart of Bill's childhood. It was a little surprise Michael had planned, for the halt figured in many of Bill's most entertaining stories, and especially in recollections of his eccentric father, Gifford. They bowled down country lanes arched over by magnificent trees until they came to a scrubby little rectangle of ground, with unmistakable railway architecture in ruins round about. Michael was somehow reminded of the train set that had been in the library at Chelworth when he first inherited the house. He helped Bill from the car. The old man was enraptured. He stared about him with unashamed tears of pleasure in his eyes.

'This was my father's pride and joy,' he said. 'He thought it very grand to have what amounted to your own railway station – which it never really was, but we treated it as such all the same. How wonderful to see it again.'

The track had long since vanished. There were allotments where once the permanent way had been. The buildings were derelict, and the platform was now no more than its brick piles, the timbers having vanished. Sand martins huddled against the walls of a nearby cutting, where bees from a row of hives buzzed around the clover and nettles. Bill walked about slowly. He pointed out features that were hardly visible any longer, like the steps his father had cut illegally into railway property, the better to reach the road and the chauffeured car that would complete his journey from London. Michael felt huge affection for the old man.

'Do you feel all right?' he asked.

'I feel ripped up and overgrown. But then, Isaiah 38:6 – "The voice said cry, and he said what shall I cry? All flesh is grass, and all the goodliness thereof is as the flowers of the field . . ." Rather grand, that, Michael.'

'Grandly spoken.'

'I suppose one can't say one rests one's hopes on it, exactly – I resign my life to it with pleasure at the thought. Virginia's mother taught me the text. Very hot on the Old Testament, Dorothy. As literature, that is.'

They were interrupted by a shout. An old man in a baggy grey cardigan had emerged from a nearby cottage and was advancing on them with every sign of recognition. He waved his hands above his head.

'Now then, my lord,' he cried.

Bill peered.

'Good God, Prentice! The station master!'

'No, no, sir. I'm not Dad, I'm his son!'

Bill poked with his stick in delight.

'But you have the look of him. You are what is called a chip off the old block, Prentice. How very lovely to see you still here.'

Prentice nodded impatiently.

'Yes, yes. Now I know it's you because we see you in the House of Lords – yes, on television – never miss it, though you're not always there, we realize that, you'll be busy elsewhere. But when you drove up just now, I looked out of the window and I said to Amy, that's Lord Toller, and she said it never is, is it? And I said yes, it is. And I have this for you, milord.'

He passed Bill a cyclostyled pamphlet with a card cover showing the halt in its heyday. The artwork on the cover was hand-drawn, and showed Prentice Senior in a billycock hat, looking at what appeared to be a Dali watch. Bill handled it with fond attention.

'Did you write this?'

'Wrote it, my pictures, my drawings, published it meself. The whole history of our little halt.'

His wife peered from the doorway of the cottage uncertainly. When Prentice waved her to come out, she retreated hastily, but the author hardly missed a stride. He poked a bony finger at Bill.

'Now there's copies of that in Canada – we had two Canadians here last year – in Holland, in Australia . . . Oh yes! It has a world-wide circulation, you might say. I've sold more than seventy. The BBC has a copy for their consideration, and every fact in that little book has been verified.'

'I am very honoured and grateful to receive it,' Bill said.

Prentice blinked.

'One pound sixty,' he said.

'Let me treat you to it,' Michael said, laughing.

'It's a bargain,' Prentice said. 'You're not in it, milord, but you'll find it a mine of information.'

'Is my father in it?'

'Your father?'

'Is the story about the kippers there?'

'The kippers?' Prentice asked, crestfallen.

'The Sheringham kippers. That were more or less phosphorescent when they arrived.'

'Ah. Well that would not have been the responsibility of the Somerset and Dorset. That would have been a Great Western matter. My father would have made that clear to his lordship. He would have cited the appropriate timetables, do you see?'

'That is more or less the story,' Bill said. 'Give or take my father threatening your father with a blackthorn stick.'

'Those times have gone for good, I trust,' Prentice observed.

'We are going on up to the house,' Bill said; and something in the look Prentice gave them both might have forewarned Michael of what was to come.

They had discussed in the car how they might present themselves to the administrators of the college of education that Bill's home had become. When they finally arrived there, it was to discover that the college had been closed. In its place was a mesh fence eight feet high surrounding the property, with little triangular plaques wired to it at intervals saying that guard dogs were on permanent patrol. There was a padlocked gate in the fence, but no means of raising attention within the house. It was caged inside the wire, silent and to all appearances dead. Many of the ground-floor windows were covered in dull orange plywood screens. Bill stood looking at all this for quite a time.

'During the First War, you know,' he said quite conversationally, 'my father let it be used as a military hospital. I can remember that quite well. We seemed to have more than our fair share of blinded soldiers, or at least that was always his complaint. He felt we had been singled out by Lloyd George.'

'Bill, I am so sorry to have you see it like this.'

The old man smiled his famous puckish smile.

'When my brother inherited, I used to hope against hope he would live for ever, as he had every intention of doing, so that I could enjoy my marriage, and Ginny. Then, when it came to my turn . . .'

He laughed aloud suddenly and, turning his back on the house, began walking slowly away up the asphalt drive, already beginning to green over with grass and alder.

'Doesn't it sometimes strike you as funny that we all had such wonderful houses and in some absurd way that lends strength to metaphor, the roof came down on our heads?'

'You never lived here?'

'After I inherited? For a year, yes. World War Two had made me a bit of a crock myself. The winter of 1947 did me in. The cellars flooded to a depth of four feet, you know. The wallpaper fell off the wall. Then the county bought it as a college of education. To start with I was on the Board of Governors. I believe they named a wing after us, a hostel for the students.'

'And now this.'

'I suppose it was all in the papers, as they say. But it has been a shock.'

Michael had a silver flask with brandy in it that some premonition had told him might be needed. Bill took the little silver cup with slightly shaking fingers.

'Would you like to please me, Michael? This is a funny time to ask, but a good one, too, perhaps. I would like you to take your seat in the House of Lords.'

'It's something you often ask.'

Bill sipped his brandy, leaning against the car and looking very tired all of a sudden.

'We're very unlucky in one respect, the English. We have no immediate national stereotype, unlike the Scots or the Welsh. We're a pretty sorry mess. All the more so now, perhaps. But we do have an invaluable sense of place, and some idea of history. That poor Prentice with his book about the railway is an instance of it. And we have some idea of injustice, and what to do to right it.'

'Can you still say so, after all these years?'

'I can,' Bill said.

He passed Michael the drinking cup.

'I'm dying,' he said simply. 'Rather more quickly than I intended. Ginny has been pestering to find out from my doctor, of course, but I am telling you. For many years you caused me great grief, Michael. But I admired you at the same time. I am delighted you came home. I want you to prosper, as I know you will.'

'Bill, don't talk like this.'

'I want to, do you see? Dorothy really was rather good on Isaiah. He takes account of most human ambition, at least to my satisfaction. But it is too early for you to study him. Work. Trust in yourself, and work.'

'I will come into the Lords in your memory,' Michael said.

Bill clasped his hand.

'I may have mentioned,' he said, in one of the last drolleries he ever made to Michael, 'that the lunch there is really quite respectable.'

They drove home more quickly and directly than they had come. It seemed as though they were coming from the past to a more ugly present.

'Ah well,' Bill murmured. 'That's Dorset for you.'

Charles Harper was standing a hundred miles away in the yards belonging to Dudley Wolverton. The owner had kept him waiting for five minutes while he conferred with the head lad. When he came down the yard to meet him, he was in a combative mood.

'What do you know about horses, Harper? That's Hebdomad in the box there, an unraced three-year-old. He'll go up to Ripon in a fortnight. You can safely put your shirt on him.'

'I came to ask you what you know about Jamie Anstey.'

Wolverton grinned slyly.

'Upset you, didn't I? Know Marchness at all? Big gambler. Pretty awful man, but never wrong about gossip. Bets on favourites, never makes a mistake.'

'Is that the other man?'

Wolverton goggled.

'You bloody fool. Know what I like least in the world? A loser. Life is very hard, Harper, and there's no such thing as a gracious defeat. No, Marchness isn't interested in your bum-boy. But he knows who is. That place Chelworth is worth a bit, and your girl wouldn't lack for a few bob if she took him on. Evens the family can't keep it, but then they don't deserve it in the first place.'

'Money doesn't come into this,' Harper snapped.

'That makes it a very novel circumstance.'

'We are talking about my child.'

'What the bloody hell is that to me? If you came for an apology you can have it. No intention of upsetting you. But if you think I'm going to hold your hand and tell you who you're looking for, think again. Any *man* would get the boy by the balls and squeeze the answer out of him. Now be a good chap and bugger off out of my yard.'

He turned away without a farewell and caught one of his stable-girls round the waist. His hands went up inside her sweater and grabbed her breasts.

'Now, Fiona,' he bellowed. 'Where's my bloody coffee?'

Michael drove his father-in-law all the way to London. He left it until they passed the Chelsea Hospital to broach what was on his mind.

'Bill, I'm going to ask you to break a lifetime's habit. You can help me.'

'At the cost of what virtue?'

'Discretion. I need to know about Jamie.'

'What about him?'

'I need to know for Dibs's sake. You know what I'm asking.'

'Pull up in Tite Street if you can find a space,' Bill said.

In the end they parked outside the Arts Club.

'In a way, I have been expecting this. What matters most to me is Virginia, Michael. I'm not half as wise or good as you are kind enough to believe. And of your children I like Tish the better, because I greatly prefer women to men. What makes you think I know what you ask?'

'I believe you do,' Michael said. 'The boy has asked Dibs to marry him, or maybe she has told him she wishes to marry. Even without what you told me in Dorset, I knew we could not have you for ever. Whatever Chelworth becomes, it must be something of which you can approve. Let's say, wherever you are.'

'The harp factory, I hope. What will you do with the information, if I give it?'

'I don't know. Jamie is my son. I love them all very dearly, Bill.'

Lord Toller looked out of the car window for quite a time, rubbing his thumbs together abstractedly.

'It's someone you know. His name is Rafe Hollingsworth.'

Hollingsworth lived in a studio flat in Camden Town, with a view of the canal. The place was neat and quiet, and not at all camp. Most of the walls were lined with books. There were a few excellent pieces of furniture and some stunning prints on the wall opposite the deep windows of the sitting room. He opened the door dressed in a dark blue shirt and white belted slacks. His smile was cautious. For his part, Michael was very uneasy. One glance at Rafe was enough to tell him that it was very unlikely anything physical had passed between him and Jamie – he thought he knew that by instinct, by some process by which men identify each other. As if reading the situation perfectly, the host's smile broadened.

'My, my,' he said. 'We're very tense.'

Michael studied him more carefully. He was perhaps sixty years old, and had once been fit. He had a square, intelligent face adorned with a broken nose; Michael remembered he had boxed at Cambridge for his half-blue. Although people who met him might divine that he was gay, most thinking people would be more impressed by his calm and a certain air of authority. In the City, where he worked, that was how he was described. Michael was a little bit flustered by him.

'The film cliché is that I was expecting you. How are you, Michael?'

'I'd almost completely forgotten you existed.'

'Of course.'

'You didn't get in touch when Richard died.'

Rafe's smile hardened a little.

'Get in touch to say what? I only drink red wine. Is that all right for you?'

'Yes, of course,' Michael said tetchily.

'Your brother and I were friends. I don't think it matters if we leave the description at that. You'll put your own construction on the word. He hated you, incidentally. He was very afraid of you – but then, Richard was afraid of almost everyone he ever met. We were friends, therefore, for a very long time.'

'Is Jamie also your friend?'

Rafe poured a glass of wine with a very steady hand.

'He came to see me. He sat there,' Rafe murmured, 'and I made him a cup of tea. He doesn't quite have your sense of black and white. Being your son doesn't completely exclude him from talking to me. In fact it rather occasioned it, I thought.'

'What about being Dibs's lover?'

The ex-friend of Richard and the current friend of Jamie looked perfectly calmly at Michael.

'That's what we talked about. Yes, of course he mentioned Dibs.'

'Does he have another man?'

Rafe studied him.

'Richard often talked of what would happen when you inherited. I'm an investment broker, Michael. Or am I not supposed to have a life outside being what I am in your eyes?'

'You might simply answer my question.'

'Did your son and I go in there? Did he confess to me about someone else? Is there yet another huge obstacle in your path?'

'In Dibs's path.'

'Dibs loves him,' Rafe reminded Michael. 'I have watched you over the past two years or so. I know you are more or less at the edge financially. We have, though I won't go into it, mutual friends in

Hong Kong, and I know the fall in the dollar more or less wiped you out. You represent just about everything I dislike in our class, Michael. I have spent my life making little go-away gestures to you and your kind. And then your son turns up here. He is lost, and he is anxious. It doesn't surprise me in the least.'

'But still you haven't answered my question.'

'You don't think so? You have made an entire family do your bidding. I can tell you – I very much want to tell you – that holding on to Chelworth is going to be an impossibility. I have told Jamie. Unfortunately, he does not believe me. You have a loyal son there. What you seem to want to hear is, will he make Dibs a good husband?'

'What I want to hear is, will you leave him to find out for himself?'

'Will I?' Rafe asked slowly. 'I will spell it out. Your son doesn't set my pulses racing. Perhaps you always were better with money than with people, Michael. What kind of people do you really think we are? I loved your brother. And it was as well, because no one else did. Your son is an amiable prig. The girl sounds eminently sensible. As to what will happen, some things are a little beyond your reach – or mine. You might ponder that on your way home. I don't know what fool directed you here, but I would like you to leave. People of your sort disgust me.'

He had another call to make before he went home. That morning, before he took Bill down into Dorset, Barbara Chivers had rung him from a London hotel. Michael very nearly forgot, and had to double back at Baker Street to meet her. He found the hotel tucked away behind the Royal College of Music. He found Barbara in her room, stretched out on the bed, watching television and drinking. When he went to kiss her cheek, she moved her head so that he kissed her on the lips. She was very drunk indeed.

'I thought you'd stood me up,' she said.

'It's been a long day. What made you come here? You have a flat, I seem to remember.'

Now she was leaning against him. Her breasts flattened themselves against his ribs, and she clung round his waist with surprisingly strong arms.

'I like hotels. You don't mind this?'

'Not a bit. Is that why I'm here?'

'If only,' Barbara said. She pushed him away and staggered to the dressing table to pour them both a drink.

'I'm driving down to Wiltshire,' Michael said gently.

'Good luck to you! I wish you weren't. I shall go out tonight, to a show or somewhere, and wait to get picked up. Believe me?'

'If you say so.'

'A night of flirtation. Ewan thinks it's good for me, like jogging, or working out.'

She laughed.

'My God, Michael, I really fancy you. I like all of you, you upper-crust Chelworth bastards, but you I really fancy. I've been watching something about the dollar. It dropped below one-fifty this afternoon. That's bad for you, right?'

'Yes,' he said.

She took his hand and kissed it.

'Ewan is with Cissie Hollar-Wilson, helping her to house-hunt. She fancies something by the sea. Cap Ferrat, probably.'

'You'll really move into Barlow Court?'

'It's our destiny. We move up, you fall down. I didn't know what the exchange rate was until I met you. Ewan might have planned this bloody slump personally, for all the pleasure he's taken in it. Kiss me again. Properly.'

Her lips were hot and moist. In spite of himself, Michael felt himself wondering about the bulk of her, the strangeness of holding someone a completely different weight to the woman he knew, who was waiting in Hincham. Barbara's eyes were closed. Tears glistened between the lashes.

'What a coward I am,' she said thickly.

'Not in my book.'

She kissed him again and broke free. On the table, next to the vodka bottle, was a scuffed leather ring-box in maroon leather. She undid the clasp with a bright red finger-nail. Before she could take the ring from the box, Michael had gently snatched it away.

'Recognize it?'

'Oh, Barbara . . .'

'It's your mother's, presumably.'

'From her family, yes. She wore it at the Coronation. We have a portrait of her done at the time. A forebear of hers was given it by the Empress Eugénie. We assumed it had been taken by Firbank.'

'Ewan's one big mistake in life. It would make a lovely story if I had begged him not to do it, not to buy it from that bastard Bob Firbank. But the exact opposite was the truth. I *made* him buy it for me. I screamed and ranted until he did.'

'Even knowing where it came from?'

'Just because of that. It's been my one hold over him. It's insurance, Michael, against being dumped. I crawled on my knees to get it, and the fool didn't realize what he was doing.'

Michael tossed the ring gently in his palm.

'Why have I got it now?'

'Because it's yours.'

His face must have shown scepticism.

'Because I like you,' Barbara said.

She staggered to the bathroom, and Michael sat down on the rumpled bed, the ring clenched in his fist. There had been enough excitements for one day: with this ring I thee destroy. He tried to picture the circumstances under which Ewan would have done such a foolish thing, the calculation of risk he had made. Barbara came back into the room, her mouth smelling of toothpaste. She immediately poured them both another vodka.

'Did you ever wonder why we don't have children, Michael? It's something huge and missing in my life. When Ewan found me, I was nineteen and had already been everybody's in the romantic town of Swindon. I got him into bed on the second date and I thought, well, this is it. You're going to pay for your pleasures, Ba. With babies, I mean. Marry the guy, watch him make money, look after your kids, and learn to read in your spare time. Like who the hell was the Empress Eugénie and stuff like that.'

She threw the pillows against the bed-head and crashed past him, making the mattress bounce.

'How it ended up was with your mother's ring in a safe deposit box in Knightsbridge, no kids, and enough fat to make little shopgirls snigger. I'm the most notorious size fourteen in South-west England.'

'He decided not to have any?'

'After ten years, I persuaded him to have tests. He had just bought a hill of yours and was turning it into money. He was excited, and it was my last chance. Poor Ewan. He can't make children. The ring was a surrogate baby. He gave me something I really wanted, in place of a child. And you have to believe me, he did it out of love. You love Virginia, don't you?'

'Yes.'

'Ewan loves me. He doesn't know how to say it, but he does. It's terrible, isn't it? He's ninety-per-cent unlovable, but we're stuck with each other. See what I'm trying to say?'

'That you love him.'

'He's all I've got,' Barbara said simply. 'If I were a modern woman, la-di-dah, I'd have myself. Don't hurt him, Michael.'

He took her hand and kissed it affectionately.

'Suppose I were to say you have delivered him to me trussed and bound, Barbara?'

'Oh, if he had the same power over you, he would die of pleasure. I gather you're used to not being liked, but Ewan loathes your guts. What's that play, the Shakespeare play?'

'Which one?'

'*Othello*. There's this big, gormless black man, and every time he looks round there's this nippy little white bugger just messing up his life. And we never really know why. Or at least, I couldn't ever work it out. Except that Ewan would make a great Iago. That's what I got from it.'

'And Desdemona?'

Barbara shook her head.

'Don't hurt him. He deserves it, but don't destroy him. Use the ring, but leave him intact. Leave me intact.'

Michael rose from the bed, where he had been sitting, the warmth of her hip against the warmth of his. He felt tired, and utterly dispirited. Barbara lolled against the pillows, her vodka balanced on the bare flesh of her chest. Her hands were surprisingly strong.

'I must go.'

'You won't stay for an hour, just for an hour?'

'No.'

She closed her eyes.

At the door, he turned and said:

'There's quite a lot to like in you, Barbara.'

She threw the glass of vodka aimlessly away.

'You mean all the terrific luck I've had in my life? Go and fuck yourself, my noble lord.'

Virginia could not sleep, and went down to the silent kitchens to make herself a cup of hot chocolate. She read Hodnett's paper, the local weekly, and engrossed herself for a while in the small ads. She tried to scale down her imagination to the man who wished to dispose of a wooden greenhouse, or the woman who had been given a complete set of golf clubs as an unwanted gift. In the personal columns a serious non-smoking bachelor whose interests were walking and dinners out was seeking someone twenty years his junior for what he had called, in some desperate kitchen of his own, a full relationship.

She was walking back to her bedroom when she noticed Michael's car in the drive. She found him staring at the computer screens in the office. He was slumped in a chair, drinking vodka.

'I didn't hear the car,' she said.

'The house seemed to be asleep. Where've you come from?'

'Chocolate, in the kitchen.'

'Did Bill ring you?'

'Yes, he's safely ensconced.' She hesitated. 'The dollar broke one-fifty.'

'I heard it on the car radio.'

'And that's bad.'

'Not good.'

He swivelled the chair and she reached and took his hands. She was going to tell him about the man and his greenhouse in the local paper, when his grip tightened. She looked at him in alarm. His face had slipped its mask.

'What is it?'

'How much more do I have to give, Ginny?'

'Let me put on more lights.'

He would not let her hands go.

'What do people want of me?'

They stayed in that way for a while, he sitting, she standing with her hands being clenched so that the bone showed white through the skin. He was drunk, of course, but not so drunk that she could dismiss it. At last he kissed her knuckles and let her go. Virginia sat beside him, perched on the computer desk.

'Do you want to give up?' she asked practically. 'We could sell. I should imagine there'll be a land rush after this business in the shares market. We could go away somewhere new.'

'Mention somewhere new.'

She smiled sadly.

'I want to fight,' Michael said. 'I want to triumph, actually, and I know that can't happen. Has Jamie gone?'

'Gone? He's not here tonight, but he's not gone away. Or at least I don't think so. Is it Jamie that's bothering you?

'No,' he said, after a pause.

'Tell me something. What is the point and purpose of Chelworth? What is its first and last imperative, in your eyes?'

'To exist.'

'Good,' Virginia said. 'Then answer me this. Here, tonight, what is the next cab on the rank?'

'Virginia –'

'Don't hedge,' she said. 'You can't change the whole world, Michael. You can't even change a hundredth of your tiny part in it. For me, here, tonight, the next cab on the rank is you.'

He looked at her with such longing that she was secretly and desperately afraid, for all her assumed levity.

'You mean it?'

'Come to bed,' she said.

Bill Toller's call to his daughter had been cheerful and almost robust. After he had spoken to Virginia, he rang Mrs Wilson to let her know he was back in town, and she arranged to come and stock up the larder for him next morning.

When she found him, he was sitting at the desk in his study, utterly peaceful, as if asleep. The brass swan-neck lamp by which he wrote was lit, and on the blotter in front of him was a note. He had got no further than the first line, 'My dear Jamie'. And then, perhaps, he had sat back for reflection; maybe to confess a breach of confidence, maybe for some other purpose. The pen with which he wrote was on the carpet by his feet. Otherwise, there was very little to suggest that he was not still alive, and would not in a moment or two raise his head to greet a new day with his customary sardonic expression.

Twenty

Only a little over a month later, Michael was on the front page of every paper. As overture, he appeared on late-night television with an incensed Secretary of State for Social Services. The issue was perfectly simple and made what was called good television. For a day or so, he was news.

He had taken his place in the Lords on the day after Bill Toller's funeral. He made his maiden speech from Bill's seat on the crossbenches almost at once, to the consternation of the party managers. He spoke more to honour his father-in-law's memory than anything else; but what he had to say greatly assisted a vote against the government's proposed social services legislation. It was a rare defeat for the government and a politically sensitive one. Downing Street was outraged. He seemed, that afternoon, to have come from nowhere, breathing fire and destruction. Bill's old friends in the Lords were greatly entertained.

Lewis, the Secretary of State, was not. He was one of those young, smooth-haired and cheerfully plump figures that surrounded the Prime Minister, and whose principal cosmetic attraction was an urbane and fluting good humour. Unfortunately, the Bill he had introduced in the summer had already been savaged in the Commons. Michael's intervention in the Lords was being presented, on television, as virtually a one-man stand. Lewis was no intellectual, but he was no fool either. He knew just how much he was despised by journalists. Meeting Michael for the first time on television was potentially very bad public relations. The problem was, he had been despatched to the studios by an infuriated Prime Minister and told to hammer Michael into the ground like a tent-peg.

'The Bill,' he said, trying to keep his voice pitched to the same drawled note sounded by his chief Cabinet colleagues, whom he admired and feared in about equal measure, 'has had the very great merit of having passed through an intensive period of debate – and amendment . . .'

The anchor for the discussion was a woman he loathed. She interrupted him without effort, but as if the life of the nation were at stake, as if the time for flim-flam had passed and what mattered now, more than breath itself, was the facts.

'– after which, to the consternation of the Government, it meets this quite extraordinary attack in the Lords from a source –'

'– all of which is complete nonsense –' Lewis said.

'– from a source that creates a new personality overnight. Lord Hincham, perhaps the most surprising thing about this setback for the Government is the passion with which you spoke today.'

Michael shrugged.

'This legislation, if enacted, would increase rather than lessen the plight of homeless people in this country. That is the widely held opinion of people concerned with the problem. It is also the general position of the Upper House.'

'What complete poppycock!' Lewis crowed. Unfortunately for him, the camera stayed with Michael, who thus regarded an invisible somebody to his right unsmilingly, and with grave attention, as if registering a call from a querulous invalid in the next room.

'Nobody lightly takes on a subject of this importance in a Lords maiden speech, you are right. Nor would I have made my intervention without the strongest belief in the justice of what I am saying. This is a bad Bill, not through being hasty, but through being mean.'

'Secretary of State?'

Lewis looked away from her a milli-second too quickly, making himself look shifty and petulant. He knew what he had done, and frowned. He tried to recover by looking up again, as if bored. But it wasn't working. The bitch who was interviewing them was poised for his throat. Christ, the bastards were killing him!

'What?' he asked, momentarily thrown completely. 'That Lord Hincham has a conscience? I don't dispute it.'

'Is this a mean Bill?' the presenter asked.

Lewis had come to the studios from Downing Street, after a taut little conversation with the Prime Minister and a glum press secretary. There he had given an undertaking not to lose his temper, by which the Prime Minister meant, not to muff things. He gathered up his most ministerial manner.

'This is not a mean Bill, because this is not a mean government. In the past year alone, we have spent an additional nine and a half million –'

And now the bloody man Hincham himself was interrupting! Lewis waved his hand.

' – No, you hear me out,' he said. His Kent vowels pinged the microphone. 'I believe, when you have had time to reflect a little more, you will accept, as most people watching this programme already do, that the keynote to this government, its electoral appeal, has been its compassion.'

'I was going to say,' Michael said, with infuriating calm, 'that when I walk the streets of London and see people sleeping rough who are not tramps, or winos, or in any other way acceptably touching figures of our compassion, who do not come from the pages of literary history, are not Dickensian figures, but young people and even families, who a short while ago had, through assisted rents and the like, a place to lay their head, then I know that something somewhere is wrong. This Bill will make it worse.'

'Oh really!' Lewis scorned.

'Without a roof over your head, no chance of a job. Without a job, no chance of a home. The poorest of the poor cannot stay passive for ever.'

'The government will consider what you have to say,' Lewis said, with an attempt at good-humoured negligence.

'It has just been defeated in a vote of the Upper Chamber,' Michael pointed out. 'It doesn't have a choice.'

'Yes, yes! I've said, we'll consider things in that light!'

'The Bill will be further amended?' the presenter asked swiftly.

Lewis wanted more than anything else to jump up and slap her, tear her blouse, wipe the smile off her face. Instead, he put his hands together in what could be construed – was construed by the Prime Minister – as a *pranam*, a little Indian gesture of deference.

'The Government will consider what Lord Hincham and his

noble peers have to say. As they always do. With great good will.'

'What has good will to do with ineptitude?' Michael asked.

'Whose ineptitude are we talking about?' Lewis demanded.

'Because someone mishandles your affairs, do you excuse it for the good will he says he's exercising on your behalf?'

It was the last item on the programme, and there was some football match or other on ITV; after the wrap-up and signature tune, Lewis took off his microphone in the faint hope that he had just about broken even. He felt a sinking feeling, however. He smiled at the cameraman covering his shot, a bearded giant. The cameraman looked clean through him. The Secretary of State brushed past the presenter without speaking to her and walked off into the dark of the studio, his eyes aching.

A researcher caught up with him. She was a young girl with her shirt-tails outside her knitted trousers and what looked like a leather bootlace round her neck. The varnish on her fingernails appeared to be jet-black.

'Would you like a drink?' she asked.

'I would not like a drink, and I very much hope you have a car to take me back to the Commons.'

He looked round as Michael joined him.

'We can more or less predict the headlines,' Lewis said bitterly.

'That's completely irrelevant, of course.'

'I don't suppose you will be short of press coverage, all the same. Congratulations on a telling political début.'

The girl researcher tried once more.

'I know our producer will be down from the gallery in a moment.'

'You can tell your producer from me he's a shit.'

Lewis blundered out. When she turned back to Michael he was smiling.

'Is he?' he asked.

'Peter? Yes, of course. But I'm not going to tell him.'

'No,' Michael said, grave. 'I hope not.'

Next morning, Virginia found Peter Thornton waiting for her. The topic they were to discuss was his idea of a trout farm at the Bonnington end of the estate: it cheered Virginia a little to see the good-natured Yorkshireman, crisp in a clean white shirt, his arms brown from the sun.

'Can we walk as we talk?'

'For sure,' Thornton smiled. 'Better'n sitting inside, a morning like this.'

The trout farm idea was one of a steady stream of suggestions coming from the estate office these days. There had been a minor sensation in the pubs recently when, under intense pressure from Thornton, Michael had managed to untangle the agreement between himself and six retired workers and sell their cottages to young London commuters. He mentioned this now. The estate was to the better by three hundred and fifty thousand pounds.

'Dollar seems to have done someone some good,' Thornton observed.

'I don't know. I hated doing that to the tied cottages.'

'His lordship no less. You can say the symbols of your forefathers' greed and niggardliness have been removed, maybe.'

'You know damn well I don't think that way.'

They took Virginia's favourite route, down the sloping meadows towards the river. The field flowers fascinated her. It was Thornton who first pointed out to her the three kinds of cranesbill to be found in this mile or so of pasture and light woodland. He was a very curious mixture of delicacy and brutal realism.

'When I was a child,' Virginia said, 'I used to think living in the country was like being on holiday for ever.'

'You always lived in London?'

'We had a flat in Bayswater. Rather a grand one, but not the best address, as I never tired of pointing out to my parents.'

Thornton hesitated and then took from his lips the stem of grass he was chewing.

'I wanted to say: your father was a very great man.'

'He was. He thought extremely well of you, too.'

'See his lordship last night on television?'

'Oh goodness,' Virginia sighed. 'Hodnett asked me the same question. Is there anyone who didn't see it in this valley? Yes, I saw him. He was pretty good, I thought.'

'Put the cat among the pigeons all right. Needed saying.'

Virginia laughed.

'Thank you.'

'You look exhausted, my lady.'

'We're not going to get much trout talk in today, I'm afraid, Peter. Things are stalled, a little, until my husband gets back. You want to know if we're broke or not, don't you? That's the big issue. Why do you smile?'

'I don't care whether you're broke or not. None of my business. But the smile is saying I know damn well you're not.'

'You don't think so?'

'Can I talk freely?'

'Yes, of course.'

'It's not whether you're broke, but whether you want to go on. This place is worth four million or more, we all know that. That's a lot of holidays in Benidorm, like. So, the question is a bit different.'

'Do you think we want to go on?'

'I wouldn't presume, my lady.'

He bent and retrieved a handful of soil from a scrape of new-turned earth. He held it out as proudly as any cranesbill he had found her in the past.

'I hate money. Afraid of it, baffled by it. But in the end, after all the money's been vaporized, along with all the rest, this'll be all that's left. Nothing matters but this. I'm your agent. I have to see it with your fences and hedges round it. But I count it ours — everybody's. In the end, it's all we have. That, and a few seeds and the muscles in our back.'

'One day, perhaps.'

'Oh, it's not a forecast. That's where it all comes from now. Always has done.'

'You'd never make an economist.'

'I never "lost everything" neither, as they're saying in the City now. I hope his lordship comes out of the crash all right. But more than that, I hope you never sell this place. It has a chance.'

He smiled his sudden, dazzling smile.

'Said too much again. Learned nothing from me father. Never spoke at all, old Fred. Never harmed him.'

He pointed. In the lane coming towards them was the familiar BMW of Barbara Chivers.

'What does she want?'

'Someone to talk to, I should think,' Thornton said with his staggering impudence.

He was right. Barbara drove them both to a very strange Roman Arches, from which all the furniture had been removed. The rooms were boxy with echoes. But out in the pool there swam a young blonde, with a long back and long legs, her hair tied in a chiffon bow.

'What on earth is she doing here?'

'The contracts are exchanged the day after tomorrow. We're putting up at the Dolphin until we move into Barlow Court. Meanwhile, I said she could use the pool. What a cheek! All of twenty-two, my dear. He's thirty. If Action Man ever went into the Stock Market, he would look just like Caspar.'

'Caspar!'

'Isn't it wonderful?' Barbara asked. 'He told me his family was thirteenth century. So was mine. The one in the pool's called Tressida. She was definitely run up in some designer workshop. She doesn't come from the thirteenth century, she's a totally now person.'

'I shall miss you, Barbara,' Virginia said.

'We're not going very far. You could come over to tea. I know Ewan and Michael will never speak to each other again, unless they absolutely have to, but . . .'

Virginia laid her hand on her neighbour's plump arm.

'Keep your chin up,' she said.

Barbara's smile was a bit unfocused.

'I'm bloody miserable as a matter of fact.'

Dorothy Wild watched Jamie mooching towards the house with his hands stuffed in his pockets. She was not especially surprised when he came into the office and sat silently in Michael's chair, his chin on his chest.

'Well?' Dorothy asked at length.

'Well nothing.'

'Want me to say what I feel about things? I married in a church when I was nineteen, with four bridesmaids and a dress from London. Two hundred guests and a marquee. My father's wedding present was a gift-wrapped car.'

'Jolly good.'

'And so said all of us. Four years later, I started having an affair with an airline pilot.'

Jamie shifted in his chair.

'I'm sure you're trying to be helpful.'

'I'm saying grow up. One of the things you can't do, if you're going to run off and scandalize everybody, is to hang around at the door. Go. Or stay.'

He got up and left with such abruptness that Dorothy was forced to run after him down the corridor. There was a large mahogany door nearly always left open. It slammed in her face. Dorothy cursed under her breath and walked back to the office. The phone was ringing.

Jamie went to the library, his usual refuge, and found his mother there, to his surprise. She was skimming the index of a book and had clearly just come in. Jamie smiled shortly and began a retreat. Virginia waved at him.

'Oh, don't be so stuffy. Come in. Close the door behind you.'

She studied him.

'What's up, Jamie?'

'Don't ask me anything.'

'Of course not. But tell me what's up.'

He straightened a pile of books on the library desk. Virginia sat down in the armchair he had provided for himself. The light was wonderful, and it crossed her mind absently that she could read all day, lose herself in a book. She had been very anxious to bring her father's books to Chelworth and shelve them separately. Jamie had promised to look into it, but had done nothing.

'Look, I'm going away for a bit.'

She remained calm, at least on the surface.

'Have you cleared your diary with Dorothy?'

'Yes.'

Virginia looked out of the window. At the wire boundary to the Home Farm, some Friesians had come to look in at the mown grass and lavender scent of the gardens.

'A break,' she suggested.

'Something like that.'

She gave him a long look.

222

'I see.'

He heaved up a better mood from somewhere.

'What are you reading?'

'Does it matter?' Virginia asked. 'But, as it happens, Phipps on the Armies of the First French Republic. It was your grandfather's.'

'Volume Three is missing.'

In a flash she saw him as Dibs must see him, tall, good-looking, spoiled a little, uncertain. He was beginning to lose that peach-like innocence she had associated with him since childhood.

'You don't want to talk about it?' she suggested.

'I really can't say more than I have,' he muttered. Virginia felt a sharp stab of impatience.

'Very well. Have a nice break.'

In London, Michael was taking coffee at his club with Lord Stanedge, the Government whip in the Lords. That is to say they were sitting down together and coffee had been sent for. Stanedge was the urbane and patrician man the unfortunate Lewis had tried to be on television the night before. He wore his fifteen stone with a lightness that Michael found impressive. His face was no more lined than a nun's, and his eyes were clear and sharp.

'Good of you to see me. A very kind piece about you in the *Guardian*.'

'Thank you.'

'I'll come straight to the point. What the bloody hell do you think you are doing?'

'I was told last night you were upset.'

'More astonished than anything else. But you accept the Government is entitled to be upset?'

'I accept that you must say so, yes.'

Stanedge leaned back as the waiter brought coffee in a silver pot. He had the knack of patience. He gave the appearance of a man pleasantly diverted by the ceremony of being fetched his coffee by an old man in a monkey jacket. Michael poured.

'First of all,' Stanedge said, without the slightest increase in the temperature of his voice, 'we have a very good constituency MP down there who is forced to resign. The PM was less than enchanted with that one, I can tell you. You refused an invitation to Downing Street when the Foreign Office had Li Po T'ien over here. That was considered churlish.'

'I can't see why. You got what you wanted without my help.'

Stanedge pushed a faint air of disbelief into his smile.

'I think the invitation was a courtesy extended to you.'

'Or a chance to browbeat me about Fairless.'

'You flatter yourself a little. You then take up your seat in the Lords, and without a by-your-leave, you make your maiden speech an attack on the Secretary of State for Social Services.'

'I had an excellent brief prepared by my father-in-law before he died. It was an attack on a shoddy and disreputable Bill of Lewis's, and I know that privately you share that opinion yourself.'

Stanedge now found an openly incredulous smile from his armoury of facial expressions.

'They said you were like this. Look, if you want to make a nuisance of yourself, would you please find something more in your line.'

'You mean the baiting of badgers, or the trade in live horses to the Continent – that sort of thing?'

'That sort of thing,' Stanedge agreed, with ice in his voice. 'Not complicated pieces of social legislation about which you know next to nothing at first hand. What is it, Hincham? Are you bored? Some people are saying you're bored and looking for a fight.'

'I must tell you,' Michael said, 'I don't give a damn about the difficulties this vote presents to the Government. I'm not a member of any party, and I don't give a damn about that either. I'm a private citizen exercising my freedoms.'

'You've been seduced by a good review,' Stanedge scoffed. 'Do you really think we're going to let you crash about in the Lords making a fool of yourself? They are quite right about you, Hincham. You don't know us.'

'That sounds faintly ominous.'

'Oh please!' Stanedge begged. 'Not heroics. Not the "tribune of the people" stuff. You don't know us, and yet you want to judge us. There's no threat in that remark, just disappointment.'

He looked round the room with an amiable scrutiny.

'I'm seeing the Downing Street Press Office in half an hour. We shall see. I'm afraid you may have some choppy water to contend with. In the meantime' – his smile was dazzling and to anyone who might have been watching in the dusty sunshine of the club rooms, affectionate – 'in the meantime I should tell you I'm on the Committee here. I think you'll find there are a growing number of people who would prefer not to speak to you.'

Dorothy found an opportunity to waylay Jamie and make her apologies. He was coming in from his second walk in the grounds that day. His lips were set in a straight line, and his gait was brisk. She intercepted him crossing the huge front hall.

'Jamie! Look, I'm sorry. I spoke completely out of turn this morning. Forget what I said. I hope you can.'

She spoke in a low whisper, and to her astonishment, he replied at the same pitch. He sat on the arm of the brocade settee and looked at his hands for a moment.

'What you said was quite right. Needed saying. What happened to your airline pilot?'

For a moment he confused her. She looked distracted.

'What? Oh, what does happen? I just meant to say that nobody can plan the rest of their life. Things happen. Talk to your mother and father.'

Jamie looked up. He caught her gaze and smiled wanly.

'Dorothy, listen. I am marrying Dibs by special licence tomorrow. I want you to tell my mother.'

'Me!'

'Please. I have tried to tell her, but I can't.'

'You can't ask me to do it.'

'I'm leaving to join Dibs in half an hour.'

'Getting married where?' Dorothy asked, very alarmed.

'Getting married. I'm taking her abroad for a few weeks, a month maybe. Then . . . well, we'd both like to come back here. You must help me.'

'Won't you let them come to the wedding?'

'The Harpers would stop it. It's the only way.'

He stood up and kissed Dorothy gently on the cheek.

'You can do it,' he said. 'For me.'

Twenty-one

Michael stood listening to the soughing of the wind in the magnificent yew that overshadowed Bill's grave. The soft yellow stone of the church, with its crust of oxidized salts, gleamed in the late evening sunshine. Across the boundary wall of the graveyard, the wind ran in catspaws across the head of corn that would be cut any day now. Virginia watched him with a cautious fondness. He had arrived at Salisbury station from London with a copy of every daily paper folded into a huge wodge. It was there that she told him about Jamie. Right there on the station he had dumped his papers in a waste-bin. It was an unforced gesture for which she loved him. On an impulse, they had driven straight from the train down to the churchyard where Bill was buried.

Virginia smiled as he stood attentively in the graveyard, honouring the moment with his capacity to be serious, the ability to give himself completely to an event, even one as small as the wind in the yew and the susurrating field of wheat that lay just beyond Bill's last resting place. She knew he was thinking about Jamie and Dibs.

'It's quite an aristocratic tradition,' she said. Michael turned, a wry grin on his face.

'Elopement? Yes, I remember similar circumstances . . . All the same, I would like to kick his shins until they bleed. Have we told the Harpers?'

'Not yet, no. This evening, perhaps. We could go and see them.'

'God, no,' Michael said. 'Ask them to come to us tomorrow. We'll try to make amends. I suppose there's no point in looking for the couple meanwhile?'

'They could be anywhere. And what would anyone say? He loves her, she loves him. End of story. You're not angry, are you?'

The place where Bill had been interred was still covered with raw earth, on to which had been piled the flowers from the funeral, now dead and wind-blown. The path was strewn with petals. Michael took her hand.

'No, I'm not angry.'

He looked down at the grave.

'They loved your father, you know, all his charities. It is just amazing how well he was known – on the street, all his bag ladies and so on. Will you believe me if I say I did what I did in the Lords for Bill?'

'Of course. You're not a political person, Michael. The TV made a fool of Lewis last night, and you looked quite wonderful as a consequence . . . But you're not a politician. I take it things are pretty bloody, are they?'

'Things could not be worse, financially.'

'We're still afloat, we haven't sunk.'

'The Government Chief Whip is a fellow called Stanedge; I think you know him slightly. He asked me if I was bored. He meant restless.'

Virginia stooped to her father's grave and gathered up an armful of withered flowers.

'We ought to find someone and get them to chuck all this away,' she said, biting her lip, the stems clutched to her. She chose not to look him in the eye.

'When aren't you restless?' she said. 'You come back to England in a towering rage to set things right. But on a single wonderful canvas – Chelworth. And it responded. You've made it from a house into a home, a place of permanence, and I love it there. I don't give a fig for anything else.'

'You're angry,' he said, surprised.

'I am, rather. I don't need the Government Chief Whip to tell me you're restless. I'm your wife, damn it. What are you going to do, plunge into politics, take all that on board too? Change the entire world? Are we going to pretend, even, that you have it in you?'

He moved to her and embraced her gently.

'Hush,' he said. 'Bill was right. Chelworth has changed me. He, the wise old bird, foresaw it. Enough is enough. But . . .'

'Go on,' she said, still stiff in his arms.

'Well, I do envy him his life. I wouldn't be human if I didn't.'

Virginia laid her head against his beating heart. The sun was still very warm, and the nap of his coat smelled vaguely of London, and business, and (to be fanciful) ambition. Except that the word would not quite go away. He patted her back, while the yew whispered, and up above the corn there was a dance of skylarks.

Through the open hotel window came the sounds of music from an amusement arcade, and from time to time raucous shouting, sometimes with screams of laughter, sometimes with children's tears. The sea was calm and ended in a horizon of smoky greys and blues, for the tide was on the turn and would bring in with it the fret that had been in the offing all day. Dibs stood at the window with the top sheet of the bed round her shoulders as a shawl, naked beneath. Her feet tingled with sand that had not been properly cleaned from the carpet. She wiped her nose on the sheet, crying uncontrollably.

Jamie lay in bed, likewise naked.

'Tomorrow,' he said.

'Yes, tomorrow.'

'Dibs, don't cry. Everything is going to be fine. We'll marry, we'll catch the ferry to Cherbourg and just drive somewhere – Arcachon, maybe.'

'Have you been there before?'

'Not for a long time.'

She came back to sit on the bed, trying not to sob.

'I wish you had told them.'

'I couldn't. How could I? They would be bound to tell your parents, and then . . . I did tell them, indirectly. That wasn't easy, either.'

'God, I'm so fat,' Dibs wailed.

He stroked her back.

'Oh, Dibs, come on. Everything will work out fine.'

She rolled on to her hip, and the glorious weight of her spilled towards him. He kissed her breast, his hands stroking her rounded flank. His face pushed into her chest, and she fondled his hair gently.

'Tell me you love me.'

228

'I would rather do this, with you, than with anyone else on earth,' Jamie said.

'Then tell me we'll be happy.'

He paused before answering, long enough for her to flop on to her back, the sweat glistening in the creases made by her breasts, the rolls of flesh below them. Where she had cried, her make-up was ruined, and she looked at him from panda eyes. But the effect was very unfunny. The hair was matted to her cheek. Jamie brushed it free.

'We can try,' he said at last, unsmiling. 'Tomorrow. We can start tomorrow.'

'Eleven-thirty,' Dibs sobbed uncontrollably. 'And it is forbidden to throw confetti.'

He drew her to him and hugged her for a long while, listening to the eerie sounds of Weymouth enjoying itself on a late summer's day. Inside the hotel itself the stairs thundered and doors slammed. From all over the building came the thunder of running bath water. Jamie and Dibs stayed stuck together with their mingled perspiration, dozing and kissing. For a time he slept quite deeply, snoring gently into the crook of her neck. When at last they rose, the sea-fret had rolled in with the tide and the whole beach was in an opalescent fog. They huddled together in the shower like babes in the wood.

There was a wine bar close to Ewan's London accountants where he would occasionally go to drink and watch the world go by for half an hour before catching the train home. He was walking towards it that evening when, to his astonishment, he saw Tish getting down from a taxi. She looked lean and brown, and her hair was bleached a much lighter colour by sun and salt. Ewan was delighted to see her. He crept up on her with a joke, of sorts.

'Hello, sailor.'

'You!' Tish said, uncertain.

'Me, yes. What are you doing in London? I thought you were in Antigua. That's what we heard.'

'I was.'

'Good boat? Good skipper?'

'Very,' Tish said, with her old defensiveness. Ewan laughed.

'I'm just going in here. Come and have a drink.'

She accepted, and they found a table. It was very noisy with people Tish's age and younger: he noted with a faint smile that she looked round carefully before relaxing her guard a little.

'You look absolutely gorgeous on it,' Ewan said. 'Wonderful tan, much thinner, if I may say so . . .'

'And wiser. Tougher, anyway. There was a piece about Daddy on the news.'

'You didn't see him on television? We haven't seen his like since Shaftesbury and the chimney boys. It was wonderful! The Government, I may say, will go after his throat. It used to be Sleepy Hollow down there before he came back home.'

'Is it a joke, what he's done?'

'Piping up in the House of Lords about the homeless when you have a sixteen-bedroom house of your own is the beginnings of a joke, surely?'

Tish shrugged her shoulders and sipped her wine.

'How is Roman Arches?'

'No longer ours. We move into Cecily Hollar-Wilson's place the day after tomorrow. We're camping at the Dolphin in Salisbury, meanwhile. Where are you?'

'Just round the corner, with friends of friends. I'd rather my parents didn't know I was here just for the moment. How is Jamie?'

'The rumour is –'

'– Yes, I know what the rumour is,' Tish said, with some of her new toughness. 'He wrote telling me he wanted to marry Dibs. But how is he? How are they?'

Ewan found, with a thrill of pleasure, that for the first time in a long time he could experience desire. He laid his hand on quite a lot of bronzed flesh exposed above her knee. It made his own skin jump with excitement.

'I can't tell you how pleased I am to see you home,' he said.

He took away his hand almost immediately. For as long as he talked to her, he was thinking of her in bed. The sheer surprise of it carried him home to Salisbury in the best of tempers. Some minute shift, some slip or fall within her, had made Tish . . . he searched for the word . . . necessary.

This feeling was reinforced when he got to the Dolphin. Barbara had drunk too much at lunchtime, grown abusive in the restaurant and slapped a girl's face. He was told all this by a shocked young boy who identified himself as the under-manager. When he went up to the room, Barbara was asleep on her stomach, sprawled across the bed in her underwear. The best part of a bottle of vodka had helped while away the long hours of his absence. Ewan picked up her clothes and threw them on to a chair. He walked into the bathroom with the remains of the vodka and emptied it down the sink.

They were due that evening at a drinks and barbecue party given by the Ryans. Barbara was in fighting mood, storming around the lawns in an outrageous off-the-shoulder dress, towing Caspar and Tressida in her wake. The Ryans' son, who fancied himself as a disco expert, had provided the music, which belted out from speakers wired up into trees. Strings of Chinese lanterns swayed in the breeze. Caspar was entranced.

'Do you have these things regularly?' he asked.

'*Me?* Christ, no. This is Maureen Ryan's speciality, open-air gossip and woodsmoke. You get blinded by Gerry Ryan and deafened by the gormless Craig. This is a barbecue.'

'I think it's all super.'

'What isn't in life?' Barbara wanted to know.

Ewan came out of the house and sauntered towards them.

'Tress here was saying what super fun this all is.'

'Oh, it's sweet,' Tressida said.

'They're good sports, the Ryans.' He turned to Barbara. 'I've just been watching the ITV news with Gerry. Your pal Lord Hincham has been given the most tremendous roasting in the House of Commons.'

'My pal?' Barbara asked dangerously.

'Do you know him?' Tressida asked.

'Barbara has a bit of a thing about him.'

She tossed her wine full in his face and stumbled off, her heels sinking in the turf of the lawn. Ewan laughed. He dabbed at his cheeks with a spotless white handkerchief and seized Tressida by the elbow.

'Now then,' he said. 'Who haven't you met?'

Caspar smiled and let him take the girl off. He set out to find

Barbara. She had been absolutely right: the smoke from the barbecue was quite ridiculous. He found her by a long table, mixing herself a drink.

'Have you been sent to be polite?'

'By whom? I thought you were a terrific shot. He got it right between the eyes.'

'Michael Hincham, my dear Caspar, is worth ten of anyone here tonight.'

'For sure. Except –'

'Except nothing!'

'It is a bit off, claiming to have such a huge social conscience and living off an inherited income at the same time.'

'You've worked hard for your pot of gold,' Barbara suggested.

'Absolutely right! No question.'

'Doing what?'

'Investment broking.'

Barbara put her arms round his neck, and she was not too drunk to notice that it gave him pleasure. (But then, she could not tell whether her dress had popped open in doing so.)

'Shall I tell you something about all this? If you saw it from the road, if you were my old mum passing humbly by on your bicycle, you'd think it was disgusting luxury, while the poor starve.'

'Nonsense,' Caspar said. 'It's just people having a nice time. And as a matter of fact, I do think this Hincham bloke is a bit of a fraud. I don't like smart-alecs.'

'Oh Caspar!' Barbara cried in mock alarm. 'Then whatever do you do for chums?'

The Harpers arrived at Chelworth next morning at almost exactly the time their daughter was marrying Jamie in a Weymouth registry office. Virginia immediately and unselfconsciously took Mrs Harper arm-in-arm into the sunshine. Michael poured Charles Harper a large whisky. The two men watched their wives appearing to find the whole thing very funny.

'Cheers,' Michael said.

Harper nodded and looked into his glass. He sipped.

'Knock it back, I would,' Michael encouraged. 'I'm really very sorry they've done this, but of course from our point of view we are delighted to welcome Dibs as part of the family. She's a lovely girl.'

'You've no idea where this wedding will take place?'

'None at all. It's just possible they are already married.'

Harper glanced at his watch.

'What will your son do?'

'Eventually? Come back here.'

'Can you be sure of that?'

Michael suggested they sit down. Accordingly, they seated themselves on sofas yards apart from each other, very much like characters in a *New Yorker* cartoon. Michael lit a cigarette while Harper watched him glumly.

'I know you haven't met Jamie. He has worked extremely hard here. In some ways the place is very much his, in point of atmosphere, and I'm very proud of what he's done.'

'I'm sure you are,' Harper said faintly. 'I'm told he's very clever.'

'He's loving, and he's very loyal,' Michael said evenly.

There was a long silence that Michael was content to let linger. He knew exactly what the other father was thinking, and Harper surprised him when he did at last speak.

'I understand you've taken a hammering financially.'

Michael raised an eyebrow.

'Is this mere conversation?'

'You must forgive me . . .'

'I would have to point you to what this room looked like only a couple of years ago to understand why. I have sunk everything I had into Chelworth, Mr Harper. I'm not about to quit.'

'Will your son want to continue here?'

'Do you know, I've never asked him. I can't say. He has no money of his own, of course. He loves it here – and Dibs loves it too, I think. We have been exploring ways to increase the revenue from the estate, but that isn't exactly Jamie's line. It is in the house itself that we shall see the next phase of development. There is no question but that we'll have to open it, in some way or another. That's quite a job. I want him to do it, to decide how to do it.'

Harper looked thoughtful.

'Alone?'

'With Dibs, if she wishes.'

Harper drained his glass in one gigantic swallow. He stood and extended his hand to Michael.

'I have been very churlish to you and your family, I believe.'

'There have been reasons. But there is a lot here to envy, perhaps. When you and I were younger, the way may have been harder.'

Michael looked out of the window and smiled.

'Well I'm damned,' he said.

Tish was running across the lawn.

He sat very contentedly in the Yellow Room, his arm round Tish, the effects of a good lunch and a great deal more to drink making his face glow. He was proud of her. She had transformed Charles Harper into something resembling a cheerful man. It helped that he could sail. Tish made him tramp up and downstairs looking at the pictures, about which she had only the sketchiest ideas herself; all the while flattering him with questions about himself when young and part-owner of a Finn Class boat.

'You have acquired some wonderful social skills,' Michael murmured, now they were alone, Virginia having taken the Harpers to the river for consultation about fly-fishing.

'Most of the charters we got were American,' Tish said. 'You learn to bullshit with champions.'

'Don't spoil it,' he protested weakly.

'Do you think Jamie will come back?'

'Of course. How about you? Will you?'

Tish wriggled free of his enfolding arm.

'One day. I think it took you thirty years . . .'

'What will you do next? Are you going back to deep-water sailing?'

She looked down at the carpet.

'One day.'

Michael took her hand. It was hot and dry. The back was scarred with rope burns and the knuckles were scarred. A very fine gold chain was around her wrist.

'Tish, you are wanted here, you know. You are needed.'

'I know,' she said. 'That makes it more difficult sometimes, don't you think?'

He was very shocked to see her eyes filled with tears, caused, he could guess, by something not yet spoken between them. He reached out for her, but she jumped up and walked from the room on stiff legs.

'I'm going to see this famous library of his,' she said, her throat thickened by the tears that now ran down her cheek and fell from her jaw and chin.

Michael listened to her wooden sandals clatter from a walk to a run and dwindle down the corridors. He rubbed his own eyes and closed them painfully against the light, against the things he would rather not see, and the things he would rather not think.

That day there had been racing at Salisbury. The town was unusually full, and the shops and streets were busy. Outside every chemist there was a knot of youngsters examining newly printed holiday photographs. Sales continued in most stores and in the boutiques there were fifty-per-cent reductions. The market square was jammed solid with cars, and hundreds of sightseers lallygagged round the Cathedral. It was a summer's day with the faintest hint of autumn, a new school term, evening classes – all those things that seem to reach back into summer from the future. To live a year in England, in one place, is a lengthy and sometimes arduous business. On this particular day in Salisbury, it was as though the year had commenced in May and would end with the last returning holidaymaker in September. The year, in short, had been the few muddled months of summer.

Ewan went into the Dolphin expecting to find Barbara at least awake. But she was sleeping, with the radio and television on full blast, the curtains drawn. The room was strewn with clothes and newspapers. On television some Australians shouted at each other beside a beach of towering surf. Someone fired a pistol. Another ran away.

'Put that back on,' Barbara said from the pillow. 'I was listening.'

'For God's sake, Barbara. It's nearly five in the afternoon. What the hell's got into you?'

'I've been thinking.'

She rolled on to her back, her arm above her head.

'What's the matter, Ewan? Don't you like what you see? Neither do I. Fat cow in hotel bedroom.'

'You've been drinking, I take it.'

'Not much surprise there, I shouldn't have thought. Yes, I've had a tipple or two.'

'Now listen to me. We can play these games, or we can do the things we need to do before the move.'

'Or we can stop talking like Nanny.'

'I don't know what you'd know about that,' Ewan said grimly. 'Get off the bed, and try to act like a grown woman.'

'You don't fancy a bit?' she suggested.

'Get up, Barbara. You're not clever enough to play the whore.'

She jumped out of the bed and went into the bathroom to splash water over her face. Ewan turned off the television, which was still blasting away, and opened the windows. His eye caught a sheet of the hotel stationery, trapped beneath her bag. He extracted it and read the few lines written in Barbara's green ink. He folded the paper mechanically and put it in his jacket pocket.

'You disgust me when you're in this mood,' he said.

Barbara appeared in the doorway of the bathroom.

'I disgust you! That's very rich!'

'Look. At Barlow Court –'

'At Barlow Court, at Barlow Court! God, are we ever going to hear anything else from you from now on? What do you think is going to happen? You'll still be the same jumped-up nobody.'

'Take a shower,' he commanded. 'Sober yourself up.'

'Nobody likes us, Ewan. We haven't got any friends. Never mind about Barlow Court.'

'I want you to take your shower,' Ewan repeated, very still.

'You're disgusted, are you? Well, Ewie, I have grown to loathe you.'

He rushed her suddenly and unexpectedly. She was seized by the arms and, screaming, pushed back first into the bathroom and then into the bath. He held her with one hand while with the other he turned the shower on above their heads. It rained equally on them both, drenching down on their heads and shoulders.

'You stupid ignorant bitch! You gave him back the ring, didn't you?'

236

He struck her in the face.

'The ring, Barbara. You made me get it for you, you do your disgusting fan dance with it for ten years, and then you calmly give it back.'

'No,' Barbara shrieked.

He hit her again.

'Yes,' he screamed.

He let go of her and she slumped to the floor of the bath, the shower beating down on her. Ewan stepped back out of the bath himself and walked back into the room, where the sun came in cheerfully and beneath the window was the sound of a quite different conversation on the terrace below. His suit streamed water. He picked up her handbag and flung it at the wall.

'You drink too much and you leave your unfinished letters for me to find. Was that it, was I supposed to find what you'd written to Virginia? Is it my fault you haven't got what you want from life? Do you have to destroy me too?'

He seemed to discover for the first time that he was soaking wet. He picked up the hotel key.

'You have caused me a problem, Barbara.'

She heard him walk out and slam the door behind him. Painfully, she sat a little more upright on the floor of the bath and touched her cheeks and jaw to make sure that nothing was broken. Her ears were ringing, and blood drizzled from her nose to her chest, running in little lines thinned to a bright, sharp pink. When she tried to stand up, the clothes she wore weighed a ton. She pulled them off, ripping her dress down and dragging it over her hips, sobbing and coughing back water from the relentless shower. It was some time before it occurred to her to turn the water off.

When she looked in the mirror, one eye was almost closed.

Twenty-two

Stanley Kilbeck was making his way joyously through the derelict wing of Chelworth, exclaiming in delight at the holes in the floor through which you could see right down to the cellars, and patting the ramshackle timbers propping up a sagging ceiling. Michael followed after him, smiling.

'I really had no idea! It's a bit of a thing with me, actually –'

He found a huge panelled door and pushed on it eagerly.

'Have a care, Kilbeck!'

The door swung open and the accountant recoiled just in time. On the far side was a complete void, where two floors of the wing had collapsed into the basement. A terrified sparrow flew about in the dusty sunshine.

'My God!'

'A bit of a problem . . .'

'Absolutely! But it's all so very exciting!'

'An excited accountant is a first in my experience,' Michael observed dryly. Kilbeck, who was nearly sixty, giggled like a schoolboy.

'I do think you have the most terrific place here. I'm terribly envious. I think I told you about this place we bought in the Camargue, just a shell really –'

He smiled sheepishly.

'Parts of the main house were like this when first we came here,' Michael explained.

'Then you have done wonders. No doubt about it.'

He brushed cobwebs and dust from his suit.

'Tell me what I can do. May we sit down on the ledge there?'

'We can go into the house proper, if you like.'

'No,' Kilbeck said. He smiled shyly. 'That is, I'm quite happy here if it suits you.'

Michael stood at a window and watched the magpies walking about at the far end of the lawn. There was a spellbinding quality in this wing, as he knew from his early-morning vigils on the attic floor. He turned to face Kilbeck.

'Very well. Your place in France, in the Camargue – what is it for?'

'Holidays, obviously. Retirement – things may work out that way. My children . . . their children . . .'

'For you,' Michael pressed. 'What does it mean for you?'

Kilbeck nodded. He refused a cigarette, holding up instead a pipe that he filled from a fifty-gram tin newly opened that morning.

'I get your drift, I think. It has to a large extent become me, or an expression of one aspect of me. Before that we had boats, you know. I taught myself to glide. I did furniture for a long time – I enjoy making things with my hands . . . The farmhouse fills up that side of me.'

Michael smiled.

'Forgive me, but aren't you tempering your enthusiasm just a little? When we talked earlier, and you said then the place had absorbed you, become you, taken you over completely –'

'It can never be completely, of course.'

Michael shrugged and drew on his cigarette.

'Exactly. I want to give this wing to my son – to Jamie. He'll live here, with his new wife, and I want him to put our stuff in here.'

'Your . . . stuff . . . ?'

'Anything we have that he considers worthy of display or permanent exhibition. He can run it any way he likes. If necessary he can fund the capital cost, or some of it, from selling a picture or so.'

'You're putting the house to some use,' Kilbeck decided.

'It has a use. It's my home.'

'Then . . . ? I don't quite understand.'

'I have made Chelworth my home. If you like, I have satisfied myself with it. End of story. It is completely mine, and at the same time, if it doesn't sound too fanciful, it has made me its own. We are a perfect fit.'

239

Kilbeck nodded vigorously.

'That I do see, yes. But then . . . this place, the wing here . . . it's hardly a loft conversion or a granny room over the garage, is it? Who will make that happen? It's a difficult job.'

'Jamie,' Michael said.

'You think?' Kilbeck asked cautiously. 'Isn't he very young?'

'Yes. It's a wedding present to him, perhaps one he'll very soon come to regret. I can find him enough to make a head start; say a flat for the two of them.'

Kilbeck was about to open his mouth to speak when Michael stopped him.

'Indeed,' he grinned. 'Flat may be the wrong word. An apartment. But the point is, Kilbeck, from now on I want him to have a free hand. It won't happen overnight; it may never happen. We shall have to see. It isn't my problem, that's the point.'

Kilbeck paced a few yards across the dusty and littered floor. He ran his hand lovingly down the mouldings to a door. He did seem a man genuinely in love with craftsmanship. It was easy enough to picture him taking on the derelict wing.

'You're not bowing out altogether, I hope?'

'The place won't let me, but he's your client from now on. I want you to help him. Let me ask you a question. How far have you got with your farmhouse in the Camargue?'

'Pof!' Kilbeck threw up his hands. 'If he lacks patience, I can certainly teach him that. Is he starting from absolute scratch?'

'No.'

'There are some funds?'

'There will be,' Michael promised.

'Of what sort of order?'

'You'll see.'

Tish had gone to the Dolphin looking for Barbara, but also to find a convenient place to park in town. When she phoned to the room from reception, she was really quite surprised to get an answer.

'Stay there,' Barbara said in a faintly thickened voice. 'I'll be right down.'

Tish gasped when she saw her. One eye was blackened, and her lip had puffed enormously.

'You wouldn't have a voddie and tonic for an old mate, would you?'

Tish was appalled.

'My God! What have you done to your face?'

'I was offered a drive in the German Grand Prix,' Barbara said. 'You know me, never turn down a challenge.'

'God, everyone's looking at you, Barbara.'

'I bloody well hope so,' Barbara said grimly. 'In this hotel they know only too well I haven't been to Hockenheimer.'

Tish could more or less reconstruct the true story from the expression on the face of the barman when they went into the cocktail bar for a drink. She ordered doubles.

'And spare ice,' she said.

Barbara took her hand when she returned with the drinks. Tish was surprised to find it hot and moist. The fingers trembled slightly in hers. She squeezed back, fighting off tears of her own.

'You look marvellous,' Barbara mumbled. 'You must have lost a stone at least. You look like a real woman, my dear old shipmate.'

'Ewan did it,' Tish guessed.

'I walked into a cupboard door. Look, I'm going away in a couple of days.'

'But Mummy said you were moving into Barlow Court.'

'Ewan's handling that. Try not to do a bunk before I get back.'

'Going away where?'

'Nowhere special. Well, the Seychelles, actually.'

'Who do you know in the Seychelles?'

'Give me a chance,' Barbara protested. 'I only got the tickets this morning. But I'll find some lucky old bastard, don't you worry. Perhaps I'll meet Jamie and Dibs.'

'You've heard?'

'News gets around.'

'They eloped, more or less. Want to put some of this spare ice on your lip?'

'Certainly not. Good old Jamie.'

'Good old Dibs.'

'I'll drink to that,' Barbara said.

She raised her glass to Tish, and then in a separate toast to the barman and a frowning young man beside him.

'The under-manager of this rat-hole. They can't wait to get rid of us here. Anyway, I've packed, and I've taken both sheets and all the towels. I had the room-girl in tucks of bloody laughter. I wanted to take the table lamp and the pictures of the cockatoo over the bed.'

'Where's Ewan?' Tish demanded.

'Not at confession.'

Laughing, Tish took up Barbara's plump hands and kissed them.

'Don't *you* bunk off,' she said. 'You come back from the Seychelles, you hear?'

'You bet,' Barbara said. 'I ought to know my place, etcetera etcetera, by now. Don't wince. I mean it. I like you, Tish. You're okay. I shall want to come back to see how it all turns out. Told your parents?'

Tish frowned, mystified.

'Told my parents what?'

'Okay. Forget I said anything,' Barbara said, smiling. 'Wish me luck in the Hotel Swanko de Posh.'

'Take care.'

'You're talking to a natural-born survivor, darling. And as for this, I did ask for it.'

Ewan was just where Tish expected to find him, at Barlow Court. The front door to the house was open, as if he expected her. She tracked him down to the former sitting room. He looked quite small and forlorn in a space denuded of all furniture except the carpet. If he was surprised to see her, he concealed it very well. Instead, he gave her his schoolboy grin.

'We're having this room done out in a sort of soft mulberry. What do you think?'

'How is Barbara?'

'Mmm? Terrific.'

'You bastard, Ewan.'

'Ah. You've been to the Dolphin. I don't know how she is: how is she?'

'Somebody ought to do the same to you.'

'I never give the same provocation. Have you come here to deliver a little sermon?'

'You don't like us, do you, Ewan? There's something about us – our family I mean – that you can't stomach.'

'Let's settle for the realization – the late realization – that I don't need you. Desirable though you are, some of you.'

He ran his hand over the wall.

'Paint, I think, not paper. White woodwork, and to please you, dear Tish, a touch of gilt . . .'

'You're a pretty bloody frightening man, Ewan.'

He crossed to her and took her by both hands high up on the arms. He pushed her back against the wall and stepped inside her spread feet. For a second she felt her skin crawl with genuine panic.

'And you are very soft,' he murmured. His breath was brushing her cheek. Tish tried to stay calm and impassive.

'Let go of me.'

His hip touched hers for a moment; and then he did release her. He laughed, and stroked back his hair with the palm of his hand. He knew the moment had been a shared one.

'So Barbara showed you her black eye? Good. It should have happened years ago. I should have married someone like you, Tish. The unexploded bomb, that's how I always picture you. Barbara has turned out to be rather predictable. But you . . . ticking away . . .'

'Isn't this the "my wife doesn't understand me" speech?'

He laughed.

'Maybe. I very seldom make it.'

'Barbara told me about the ring you stole from us.'

'From *you*? I didn't know you then. I stole it from that weakling, your uncle, and gave it to an overweight woman who drinks too much. I shall have to do something about that. But I'm serious about you. Want to look round? Things might have been very different . . . Come and look round with me, Tish. I won't bite you.'

'Why did you do it?'

'Steal the ring? Pure, plain stupidity. Let me kiss you.'

'Barbara's gone. She's left you.'

His uproarious laughter boomed in the empty room. He took her hand and wagged it.

'Now that would be the day!'

'You think not?'

'I can live in hope, I suppose. You realize you can all destroy me, if you wish? Your father can ruin me.'

'I hope he does.'

He reached and kissed her very gently. Although she turned her face, she did not flinch. His lips touched her temple briefly.

'No you don't, Tish,' he said softly. 'You've already found out: it's people like me who make the world go round. Isn't that so?'

He kissed her again on the corner of her mouth.

Tish broke free and wiped her lips on her sleeve.

'I hope he kills you.'

'Not very likely. I am going to see him, but violence isn't in his line.'

'More's the pity.'

Just before Ewan arrived at the house to make his confession, Michael had a word with Thornton. The big Yorkshireman always showed a disinclination to go anywhere in the Hall except the office: Michael was in a teasing mood and made him sit down in the Yellow Room.

'Wanted to say, first off, it's good to see Lady Patricia back.'

'Tell her yourself,' Michael suggested.

'Oh, I shall, but I'm no good at it. She thinks I'm common as muck.'

'I thought that was your proudest boast,' Michael murmured.

Thornton glowered.

'Cricket match. Charity job. It's all been put up by Jack Wilson. Tomorrow, up at All Saints. Forty overs. They're two light.'

'You play.'

'I am playing,' Thornton said indignantly. 'I'm the captain of our side. Charity. You can't refuse.'

'Oh God, *must* I? I'm pretty preoccupied, one way and another.'

'You'd be filling in for Mr Jamie, who's given back-word, if we can put it that way. So I've already said yes for you.'

'Well, you've got a bloody cheek.'

'Checked it in your diary with Dorothy. And anyway, you'll want to do it, for a reason.'

'Amaze me.'

'Your lot has Chivers in it.'

Michael gawped.

'You're sure?'

'Fancies himself.'

'Not our captain by any chance?'

'He is.'

'So I could run him out!'

'That's the way to look at it from a gentleman's point of view,' Thornton said with a grim smile. 'Course, I shall be bowling to knock his head off. I've got Jack Hodnett to make up your numbers. He reckons to have played a bit.'

'Hodnett! He couldn't hit a skin off a pudding.'

'Says the same about you. Has a bet he'll make more runs.'

'What sort of a bet?'

'Tenner.'

Michael drummed his fingers briskly.

'That clinches it. I'll play,' he said.

The circumstance of the cricket match made a strange difference to Michael's interview with Ewan. He already knew what he would say, and how much he would exact from the afternoon, but pouring tea for his rival was a specially charged affair. Ewan was extremely nervous. He chose Earl Grey and peered into his cup, seeing his own eyes reflected in the smoky surface.

'It may have been thought we had nothing left to say to each other,' he observed wryly.

'The ring was a great surprise. My mother's family were related to the Lyons. Lord Lyons was ambassador in Paris at the time of the last Tuileries ball in 1869. Eugénie gave Tildy – my great-grandmother – the ring a year later, when the war with Prussia broke out. It's quite a famous jewel, or anyway, a well documented one. Had you not taken it, it would have gone to Olivia, and then I suppose to Tish.'

'Would you like to know why I took it?'

'I can tell you why,' Michael said with a glance. 'Nobody is as stupid as you have been, except for love.'

Ewan looked at his hands. When he looked up, Michael was surprised to see a completely frank expression in his eyes.

'You believe that?'

'Yes.'

'This is pretty heavy emotional slaughter. It isn't a sexual thing: she's the only friend I've got in the world.'

'That's why she has a black eye.'

Ewan looked at him bleakly. Michael waited out the silence, knowing he would put two and two together.

'Tish,' he guessed.

'Yes. Didn't you hit her because you'd been found out, because of the power it suddenly gave me over you?'

'You're not like that, of course,' Ewan muttered.

This annoyed Michael. He scowled. He put down his bone china teacup with a gesture of impatience.

'I destroyed Fairless.'

'But then, Fairless didn't have Barbara.'

Michael considered this. Snatching up a sandwich, he walked away from the table. He munched it hungrily, wanting to find a way to hurt Ewan, but stung by the half-truth in what he had just said.

'You think I'll spare you, out of regard for Barbara?'

'It's possible.'

'You're as slippery as a snake. What do you think should happen, then?'

'Give me a chance to make amends.'

'This is what I expected to hear. Go on.'

'Clearly, I would much rather this never came out. I would prefer that we settled something amicably. And privately. I realize you can set the terms. Whatever you wish.'

'I might wish you to clear off out of this valley altogether and find somewhere else to live.'

'Yes,' Ewan admitted. 'That would be the worst case.'

'Then what are you offering? Money?'

Ewan bit his lip.

'Of course, money.'

'So I thought. Come with me.'

He took him the same tour he had taken Kilbeck. Ewan followed along in silence behind Michael as (practised by the morning session with the exuberant accountant) he pointed out the failings of the West Wing, and its extraordinary potential as a home for the fine arts of Chelworth.

'We shall have to secure grants, perhaps some help from the government; private investment, even. But I think we have the bones of a very good idea. We have a lot of glass, for example. We have some rather good pottery and plate. Jamie wants to display it all.'

'How much?' Ewan asked bleakly.

Michael let him sweat for a few seconds, before smiling in what he hoped was his most civilized manner.

'I think you can afford a hundred thousand pounds.'

'A hundred –! I certainly can't.'

'You can't?' Michael asked, making it a sympathetic enquiry. 'Then that's a pity. That's the sum I had in mind. I mustn't keep you. We meet again tomorrow by the way. The charity cricket match.'

'What are you saying? What's the alternative to this?'

'Let the law take its course.'

'That's a bluff.'

Michael's smile returned, but this time coated in ice.

'Try me.'

'You cold bastard! This is out of all proportion to the offence.'

'I think I must be the judge of that, not you.'

Ewan kicked at a loose plank and sent it scampering. Dust flew up in their faces. Up above their heads, there was a sympathetic scuttle of noise.

'Let me tell you,' Ewan said vehemently, 'a hundred thousand pounds is very much more than a gesture of good intent.'

'Your good intent?' Michael snapped back. 'What is that? I have had protestations of your good intent since almost the first day we met. We seem to have no more to say, so perhaps you'll leave.'

He led the way back out into the open and rubbed his arms briskly in the sudden warmth and humidity of the light of day. It was several degrees warmer than inside the wing. Though he had asked Ewan to leave, he was waiting for the final turn of the merry-go-round. He walked ahead towards the BMW sunning itself on the gravel.

'You're serious, about the sum of money?' Ewan called.

Michael turned and faced him.

'Money is serious. I made a very careful calculation in your case. You're almost the vainest man I ever met. You'll pay, and I can tell you why. You'll pay because in the end, your vanity will enable you to reassure yourself that you got me out of a hole . . .'

He waved back towards the slumbering West Wing.

'And I will give you a leg over the stile, with pleasure. Apart from the income from the estate in rents, and certain sales, though not, alas for you, Chivers, of land – apart from that revenue, I am broke. I don't have a halfpenny of my own to put into the scheme. That is why I am extorting it from you. The problem from your point of view is that you won't be able to tell anyone.'

'I think I would prefer to call your bluff.'

'In hope that I won't go to the police on Barbara's account? Then you're an even bigger bloody fool than I imagined. I'll give you half an hour before I phone. Now get out of my drive, there's a good chap.'

'If I made a public donation,' Ewan suggested.

'You can make an anonymous gift,' Michael said. 'But the moment it becomes public, you're finished, my friend.'

Ewan cursed. He picked up a stone and winged it over the balustrade. They heard it fizz in the air.

'I don't think you need to turn up tomorrow,' he snarled.

'For the cricket? Wouldn't miss it for the world . . .'

'It would have to be cricket,' Virginia complained. She, Hodnett and Tish were crashing around in the biggest glory-hole of the West Wing, turning over chests and chests of lumber.

'Somewhere in this hell-hole, which has furnished so much pleasure over the centuries, there has to be a cricket bat. I need practice.'

'Can't you just shoot him?' Virginia demanded.

'Ginny, he is the captain of our side. I am not looking for a bat the better to brain him. I don't want to let the side down.'

'There's a lacrosse stick here, my lord,' Hodnett called.

'Very amusing, Hodnett. I understand from Tish you played for Wiltshire Colts.'

'I may have given that impression,' Hodnett said after a moment.

'You didn't?' Tish called.

'If he told you that, he's an even bigger liar than I am.'

'A serious charge, my lord.'

'Here you are,' Virginia said, dragging a bat free from a chest stuffed with foils, golf clubs, umbrellas, curtain rods.

They all gathered. Michael weighed the bat in the palm of his hand.

'It was Richard's,' he said softly.

There was an evening of fatuous pleasure, holding nets in a corridor of the Hall and getting Daisy Hodnett to bowl her husband off-breaks. The glass in several pictures was smashed and Michael spent too long hugging Tish too often and laughing. They sat up in the kitchen singing shanties, all of them, and drinking mulled wine of Virginia's recipe. It was all very silly and – as Daisy kept saying – quite out of the ordinary.

Going upstairs to bed, Michael had his arm round Virginia, though she in fact was half carrying him.

'Angry?' he asked.

'Are you really going to open the West Wing?'

'With a little help from my friends.'

'And us?'

'What about us?'

'When do we do our living?'

'Isn't this it?'

The moon flooded in at the top of the stairs. Some of those who would otherwise have attended the charity cricket match had looked at the sky before going to bed and decided instead to cut the fields. Virginia thought about his question for a moment or two.

'Yes,' she said, 'this sort of thing would do, I suppose.'

The plan was for Dorothy to work in the morning and then come up to the ground at All Saints after lunch. Michael and Virginia had gone into Hincham to buy some whites and have a very necessary hair of the dog. Tish stayed behind with Dorothy, and Daisy made them a small picnic to eat on the terrace.

'I heard you all let your hair down last night.'

'It was fun.'

Dorothy looked at Michael's daughter with her dark intelligent eyes and smiled slightly.

'Better get it off your chest, Tish.'

'You must be sick of us. First Jamie, now me.'

'And others, from time to time,' Dorothy observed diplomatically. 'But before you say anything, I should tell you that your being here has made an incredible difference. They've missed you terribly. I don't know how you do it, but whatever it is you have, it's potent stuff. Now, tell me. What is it you want to say?'

Tish put down her plate and went to lean on the terrace, her dress back-lit by the sun. She gazed out over the gardens, listening to the harvesters rumbling away on the far side of the valley.

'I'm pregnant,' she said.

She turned and stared down Dorothy with some of her old defiance. The secretary did not flinch, did not even blink. A few paces separated them, and many seconds of silence. Slowly, unconsciously, Tish's teeth tugged at her lower lip. Dorothy pushed back her chair and stood.

'Whose is it?'

'A man. Nobody.' Tish paused. 'It's why I've come home.'

Only then did Dorothy cross to her.

'Come here,' she commanded.

They embraced with a gentle politeness to begin with, but then Dorothy hugged the girl harder.

'Good,' she said.

'Good?'

'You must realize what a wonderful thing that will be to them. You must tell them straight away.'

'At the cricket?'

'Yes, at the cricket! May I give you another hug? I'm green with envy.'

'It's easy enough,' Tish said wryly.

'Belonging in a family and a place like this,' Dorothy observed.

250

The remark, which was spontaneous and without spite, entered Tish's heart like an arrow.

The two women, the secretary and the pregnant girl, drove to the village green at All Saints through lanes dappled with shadow. At the top of the ridge, where Thornton had found the flint he had once given to Virginia, the trees thinned out and you could see for miles, to a horizon that melted somehow into the sky, mixed with it and merged, so that beyond was somewhere vague and indefinite, a different story altogether. Beyond (yet not so far after all) was another landscape, unknowable to the people of this one, similar in a hundred points, yet different in close and particular ways because of the people who lived there, and what they wanted from life, and what life had afforded them.

No doubt over there, Tish thought, there were other cricket matches in progress, and beyond that horizon others still. The one she was journeying to revealed itself at the end of a straight stretch of road. A large and not wonderfully kempt field was occupied by thirteen men in white, a pony, and some disobliging little boys for whom summer was over, a wholly finished business, and football the next and necessary passion.

Cat Chaser Elmore Leonard

'*Cat Chaser* really moves' – *The New York Times Book Review* 'Elmore Leonard gets so much mileage out of his plot that just when you think one is cruising to a stop, it picks up speed for a few more twists and turns' – *Washington Post*

The Mosquito Coast Paul Theroux

Detesting twentieth century America, Allie Fox takes his family to live in the Honduran jungle. 'Imagine the Swiss Family Robinson gone mad, and you will have some idea of what is in store . . . Theroux's best novel yet' – *Sunday Times*

Skallagrigg William Horwood

This new book from the author of *Duncton Wood* unites Arthur, a little boy abandoned many years ago in a grim hospital in northern England, with Esther, a radiantly intelligent young girl who is suffering from cerebral palsy, and with Daniel, an American computer-games genius. 'Some of the passages would wring tears of recognition, not pity' – Yvonne Nolan in the *Observer*

The Second Rumpole Omnibus John Mortimer

'Rumpole is worthy to join the great gallery of English oddballs ranging from Pickwick to Sherlock Holmes, Jeeves and Bertie Wooster' – *Sunday Times* 'Rumpole has been an inspired stroke of good fortune for us all' – Lynda Lee-Potter in the *Daily Mail*

The Lion's Cage John Clive

As the Allies advance across Europe, the likes of Joe Porter are making a killing of another kind. His destiny becomes woven with that of Lissette, whose passionate love for a German officer spells peril for Porter and herself – and the battle for survival begins.

FOR THE BEST IN PAPERBACKS, LOOK FOR THE

PENGUIN BESTSELLERS

Illusions Charlotte Vale Allen

Leigh and Daniel have been drawn together by their urgent needs, finding a brief respite from their pain in each other's arms. Then romantic love turns to savage obsession. 'She is a truly important writer' – Bette Davis

Snakes and Ladders Dirk Bogarde

The second volume of Dirk Bogarde's outstanding biography, *Snakes and Ladders* is rich in detail, incident and character by an actor whose many talents include a rare gift for writing. 'Vivid, acute, sensitive, intelligent and amusing' – *Sunday Express*

Wideacre Philippa Gregory

Beatrice Lacey is one of the most passionate and compelling heroines ever created. There burns in Beatrice one overwhelming obsession – to possess Wideacre, her family's ancestral home, and to achieve her aim she will risk everything: reputation, incest, even murder.

A Dark and Distant Shore Reay Tannahill

'An absorbing saga spanning a century of love affairs, hatred and high points of Victorian history' – *Daily Express* 'Enthralling . . . a marvellous blend of *Gone with the Wind* and *The Thorn Birds*. You will enjoy every page' – *Daily Mirror*

Runaway Lucy Irvine

Not a sequel, but the story of Lucy Irvine's life *before* she became a castaway. Witty, courageous and sensational, it is a story you won't forget. 'A searing account . . . raw and unflinching honesty' – *Daily Express* 'A genuine and courageous work of autobiography' – *Today*